"I'll tell you what," h̲... give you a kiss. And if afterward you ca̲... walk away, then you should."

She blinked. "I don't want to walk away."

"See how you feel after the kiss."

He already knew.

He already knew that he was going to have a hard time getting his hands off her once they'd been on her.

She took a step toward him, those ridiculous high heels somehow skimming over the top of the dirt and rocks. She was soft and elegant, and he was half-dressed and sweaty from chopping wood, his breath a cloud in the cold air.

She reached out and put her hand on his chest. And it took every last ounce of his willpower not to grab her wrist and pin her palm to him. To hold her against him, make her feel the way his heart was beginning to rage out of control.

He couldn't remember the last time he'd wanted a woman like this.

* * *

Rancher's Wild Secret by *New York Times* bestselling author Maisey Yates is part of the Gold Valley Vineyards series.

NEW YORK TIMES and *USA TODAY*
BESTSELLING AUTHOR

MAISEY YATES

Rancher's Wild Secret & Hold Me, Cowboy

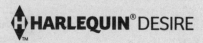

HARLEQUIN® DESIRE

ISBN-13: 978-1-335-14716-5

Rancher's Wild Secret & Hold Me, Cowboy

Copyright © 2019 by Harlequin Books S.A.

Rancher's Wild Secret
Copyright © 2019 by Maisey Yates

Hold Me, Cowboy
Copyright © 2016 by Maisey Yates

Recycling programs
for this product may
not exist in your area.

This edition published by arrangement with Harlequin Books S.A.

For questions and comments about the quality of this book, please contact us at CustomerService@Harlequin.com.

Printed in U.S.A.

CONTENTS

RANCHER'S WILD SECRET

One

The launch party for Maxfield Vineyards' brand-new select label was going off without a hitch, and Emerson Maxfield was bored.

Not the right feeling for the brand ambassador of Maxfield Vineyards, but definitely the feeling she was battling now.

She imagined many people in attendance would pin the look of disinterest on her face on the fact that her fiancé wasn't present.

She looked down at her hand, currently wrapped around a glass of blush wine, her fourth finger glittering with the large, pear-shaped diamond that she was wearing.

She wasn't bored because Donovan wasn't here.

Frankly, *Donovan* was starting to bore her, and that reality caused her no small amount of concern.

But what else could she do?

Her father had arranged the relationship, the engagement, two years earlier, and she had agreed. She'd been sure that things would progress, that she and Donovan could make it work because on paper they *should* work.

But their relationship wasn't…changing.

They worked and lived in different states and they didn't have enough heat between them to light a campfire.

All things considered, the party was much less boring than her engagement.

But all of it—the party and the engagement—was linked. Linked to the fact that her father's empire was the most important thing in his world.

And Emerson was a part of that empire.

In fairness, she cared about her father. And she cared about his empire, deeply. The winery was her life's work. Helping build it, grow it, was something she excelled at.

She had managed to get Maxfield wines into Hollywood awards' baskets. She'd gotten them recommended on prominent websites by former talk show hosts.

She had made their vineyard label something *better* than local.

Maxfield Vineyards was the leading reason parts of Oregon were beginning to be known as the new Napa.

And her work, and her siblings' work, was the reason Maxfield Vineyards had grown as much as it had.

She should be feeling triumphant about this party.

But instead she felt nothing but malaise.

The same malaise that had infected so much of what she had done recently.

This used to be enough.

Standing in the middle of a beautiful party, wearing a dress that had been hand tailored to conform perfectly to her body—it used to be a thrill. Wearing lipstick like this—the perfect shade of red to go with her scarlet dress—it used to make her feel…

Important.

Like she mattered.

Like everything was put together and polished. Like she was a success. Whatever her mother thought.

Maybe Emerson's problem was the impending wedding.

Because the closer that got, the more doubts she had.

If she could possibly dedicate herself to her job *so much* that she would marry the son of one of the world's most premier advertising executives.

That she would go along with what her father asked, even in this.

But Emerson loved her father. And she loved the winery.

And as for romantic love…

Well, she'd never been in love. It was a hypothetical. But all these other loves were not. And as far as sex and passion went…

She hadn't slept with Donovan yet. But she'd been with two other men. One boyfriend in college, one out of college. And it just hadn't been anything worth upending her life over.

She and Donovan shared goals and values. Surely they could mesh those things together and create a life.

Why not marry for the sake of the vineyard? To make her father happy?

Why not?

Emerson sighed and surveyed the room.

Everything was beautiful. Of course it was. The party was set in her family's gorgeous mountaintop tasting room, the view of the vineyards stretching out below, illuminated by the full moon.

Emerson walked out onto the balcony. There were a few people out there, on the far end, but they didn't approach her. Keeping people at a distance was one of her gifts. With one smile she could attract everyone in the room if she chose. But she could also affect a blank face that invited no conversation at all.

She looked out over the vineyards and sighed yet again.

"What are you doing out here?"

A smile tugged at the corner of Emerson's mouth. Because of course, she could keep everyone but her baby sister Cricket from speaking to her when she didn't want to be spoken to. Cricket basically did what she wanted.

"I just needed some fresh air. What are *you* doing here? Weren't you carded at the door?"

"I'm twenty-one, thank you," Cricket sniffed, looking...well, not twenty-one, at least not to Emerson.

Emerson smirked. "Oh. How could I forget?"

Truly, she *couldn't* forget, as she had thrown an absolutely spectacular party for Cricket, which had made Cricket look wide-eyed and uncomfortable, particularly in the fitted dress Emerson had chosen for her. Cricket did not enjoy being the center of attention.

Emerson *did* like it. But only on her terms.

Cricket looked mildly incensed in the moonlight. "I didn't come out here to be teased."

"I'm sorry," Emerson responded, sincere because she

didn't want to hurt her sister. She only wanted to mildly goad her, because Cricket was incredibly goadable.

Emerson looked out across the vast expanse of fields and frowned when she saw a figure moving among the vines.

It was a man. She could tell even from the balcony that he had a lean, rangy body, and the long strides of a man who was quite tall.

"Who's that?" she asked.

"I don't know," Cricket said, peering down below. "Should I get Dad?"

"No," Emerson said. "I can go down."

She knew exactly who was supposed to be at the party, and who wasn't.

And if this man was one of the Coopers from Cowboy Wines, then she would have reason to feel concerned that he was down there sniffing around to get trade secrets.

Not that their top rival had ever stooped to that kind of espionage before, but she didn't trust anyone. Not really.

Wine-making was a competitive industry, and it was only becoming more so.

Emerson's sister Wren always became livid at the mere mention of the Cooper name, and was constantly muttering about all manner of dirty tricks they would employ to get ahead. So really, anything was possible.

"I'll just run down and check it out."

"You're going to go down and investigate by yourself?"

"I'm fine." Emerson waved a hand. "I have a cell phone, and the place is heavily populated right now. I don't think I'm going to have any issues."

"Emerson…"

Emerson slipped back inside, and out a side door, moving quickly down the stairs, not listening to her sister at all. She didn't know why, but she felt compelled to see who the man was for herself.

Maybe because his arrival was the first truly interesting thing to happen all evening. She went in the direction where she'd last seen the figure, stepping out of the golden pool of light spilling from the party and into the grapevines. The moonlight illuminated her steps, though it was pale and left her hands looking waxen.

She rounded one row of grapevines into the next, then stopped, frozen.

She had known he was tall, even from a distance. But he was…very tall. And broad.

Broad shoulders, broad chest. He was wearing a cowboy hat, which seemed ridiculous at night, because it wasn't keeping the sun off him. He had on a tight black T-shirt and a pair of jeans.

And he was not a Cooper.

She had never seen the man before in her life. He saw her and stopped walking. He lifted his head up, and the moonlight caught his features. His face was sculpted, beautiful. So much so that it immobilized her. That square jaw was visible in even this dim light.

"I… Have you lost your way?" she asked. "The party is that way. Though… I'm fairly certain you're not on the guest list."

"I wasn't invited to any party," he said, his voice rough and raspy, made for sin.

Made for sin?

She didn't know where such a thought had come from.

Except, it was easy to imagine that voice saying all kinds of sinful things, and she couldn't credit why.

"Then... Forgive me, but what are you doing here?"

"I work here," he said. "I'm the new ranch hand."

Damn if she wasn't Little Red Riding Hood delivered right to the Big Bad Wolf.

Except, she wasn't wearing a scarlet cloak. It was a scarlet dress that clung to her generous curves like wrapping paper around a tempting present.

Her dark hair was lined silver by the moonbeams and tumbling around naked shoulders.

He could picture her in his bed, just like that. Naked and rumpled in the sheets, that hair spread everywhere.

It was a shame he wasn't here for pleasure.

He was here for revenge.

And if he had guessed correctly based on what he knew about the Maxfield family, this was Emerson Maxfield. Who often had her beautiful face splashed across magazine covers for food and wine features, and who had become something of an It Girl for clothing brands as well. She was gorgeous, recognizable... and engaged.

But none of that would have deterred him, if he really wanted her.

What the hell did he care if a man had put a ring on a woman's finger? In his opinion, if an engaged or married woman was looking elsewhere, then the man who'd put the ring on her finger should've done a better job of keeping her satisfied.

If Holden could seduce a woman, then the bastard he seduced her away from deserved it.

Indiscretion didn't cause him any concern.

But there were a whole lot of women and a whole lot of ways for him to get laid, and he wasn't about to sully himself inside a Maxfield.

No matter how gorgeous.

"I didn't realize my father had hired someone new," she said.

It was funny, given what he knew about her family, the way that she talked like a little private school princess. But he knew she'd gone to elite schools on the East Coast, coming back home to Oregon for summer vacations, at least when her family wasn't jet-setting off somewhere else.

They were the wealthiest family in Logan County, with a wine label that competed on the world stage.

Her father, James Maxfield, was a world-class visionary, a world-class winemaker…and a world-class bastard.

Holden had few morals, but there were some scruples he held dear. At the very top of that list was that when he was with a woman, there was no coercion involved. And he would never leave one hopeless, blackmailed and depressed. No.

But James Maxfield had no such moral code.

And, sadly for James, when it came to dealing out justice to men who had harmed someone Holden cared about very much, he didn't have a limit on how far he was willing to go. He wondered what Emerson would think if she knew what her father had done to a woman who was barely her age.

What he'd done to Holden's younger sister.

But then, Emerson probably wouldn't care at all.

He couldn't see how she would *not* know the way her

father behaved, given that the whole family seemed to run the enterprise together.

He had a feeling the Maxfield children looked the other way, as did James's wife. All of them ignoring his bad behavior so they could continue to have access to his bank account.

"I just got here today," he said. "Staying in one of the cabins on the property."

There was staff lodging, which he had found quaint as hell.

Holden had worked his way up from nothing, though his success in real estate development was not anywhere near as splashed over the media as the Maxfield's success was. Which, in the end, was what allowed him to engage in this revenge mission, this quest to destroy the life and reputation of James Maxfield.

And the really wonderful thing was, James wouldn't even see it coming.

Because he wouldn't believe a man of such low status could possibly bring him down. He would overlook Holden. Because James would believe that Holden was nothing more than a hired hand, a lackey.

James would have no idea that Holden was a man with a massive spread of land in the eastern part of the state, in Jackson Creek.

Because James Maxfield thought of no one but himself. He didn't think anyone was as smart as he was, didn't think anyone was anywhere near as important.

And that pride would be his downfall in the end.

Holden would make sure of it.

"Oh," she said. She met his eyes and bit her lip.

The little vixen was flirting with him.

"Aren't you meant to be in there hosting the party?"

She lifted a shoulder. "I guess so." She didn't seem at all surprised that he recognized who she was. But then, he imagined Emerson was used to being recognized.

"People will probably be noticing that you're gone."

"I suppose they might be," she said. She wrinkled her nose. "Between you and me, I'm getting a little tired of these things."

"Parties with free food and drinks? How could you get tired of that?"

She lifted one elegant shoulder. "I suppose when the drinks are always free, you lose track of why they're special."

"I wouldn't know anything about that."

He'd worked for every damn thing he had.

"Oh. Of course. Sorry. That's an incredibly privileged thing to say."

"Well, if you're who I think you are, you're incredibly privileged. Why wouldn't you feel that way?"

"Just because it's true in my life doesn't mean it's not a tacky thing to say."

"Well, I can think of several tacky things to say right back that might make you feel a little bit better."

She laughed. "Try me."

"If you're not careful, Little Red, wandering through the wilderness like this, a Big Bad Wolf might gobble you up."

It was an incredibly obvious and overtly sexual thing to say. And the little princess, with her engagement ring glittering on her left hand, should have drawn up in full umbrage.

But she didn't. Instead, her body seemed to melt slightly, and she looked away. "Was that supposed to be tacky?"

"It was," he said.

"I guess it didn't feel that way to me."

"You should head back to that party," he said.

"Why? Am I in danger out here?"

"Depends on what you consider danger."

There was nothing wrong—he told himself—with building a rapport with her. In fact, it would be a damned useful thing in many ways.

"Possibly talking to strange men in vineyards."

"Depends on whether or not you consider me strange."

"I don't know you well enough to have that figured out yet." A crackle of interest moved over his skin, and he didn't know what the hell was wrong with him that the first time he'd felt anything remotely like interest in a hell of a long time was happening now.

With Emerson Maxfield.

But she was the one who took a step back. She was the one whose eyes widened in fear, and he had to wonder if his hatred for the blood that ran through her veins was as evident to her as it was to him.

"I have to go," she said. "I'm... The party."

"Yes, ma'am," he said.

He took a step toward her, almost without thinking.

And then she retreated, as quickly as she could on those impractical stiletto heels.

"You better run, Little Red," he said under his breath.

And then he rocked back on his heels, surveying the grapevines and the house up on the hill. "The Big Bad Wolf is going to gobble all of this up."

Two

"Emerson," her dad said. "I have a job for you."

Emerson was tired and feeling off balance after last night. She had done something that was so out of character she still couldn't figure out what she'd been thinking.

She had left the party, left her post. She had chased after a strange man out in the grapevines. And then...

He had reminded her of a wolf. She'd gone to a wolf sanctuary once when she was in high school, and she'd been mesmerized by the powerful pack alpha. So beautiful. So much leashed strength.

She'd been afraid. But utterly fascinated all at once. Unable to look away...

He worked on the property.

And that should have been a red light to her all the way down. An absolute *stop, don't go any further.* If the diamond on her finger couldn't serve as that warning, then his status as an employee should have.

But she had felt drawn to him. And then he'd taken a step toward her. And it was like suddenly the correct instincts had woken up inside of her and she had run away.

But she didn't know why it had taken that long for her to run. What was wrong with her?

"A job," she said blankly, in response to her father.

"I've been watching the profits of Grassroots Winery down in town," he said. "They're really building a name for themselves as a destination. Not just a brand that people drink when they're out, but a place people want to visit. We've proved this is an incredibly successful location for weddings and other large events. The party you threw last night was superb."

Emerson basked in the praise. But only for a moment. Because if there was praise, then a request couldn't be far behind.

"One of the things they're offering is rides through the vineyard on horseback. They're also doing sort of a rustic partnership with the neighboring dude ranch, which sounds more like the bastion of Cowboy Wines. Nothing I want to get involved with. We don't want to lower the value of our brand by associating with anything down-market. But horse rides through the vineyards, picnics, things like that—I think those could be profitable."

Emerson had met the owner of Grassroots Winery, Lindy Dodge, on a couple of occasions, and she liked the other woman quite a lot. Emerson had a moment of compunction about stepping on what had clearly been Lindy's idea, but then dismissed it.

It wasn't uncommon at all for similar companies to

try comparable ventures. They often borrowed from each other, and given the number of wineries beginning to crop up in the area, it was inevitable there would be crossover.

Plus, to the best of her ability Emerson tried not to look at the others as competition. They were creating a robust wine trail that was a draw in and of itself.

Tourists could visit several wineries when they came to Logan County, traveling from Copper Ridge through Gold Valley and up into the surrounding mountains. That the area was a destination for wine enthusiasts was good for everyone.

The only vineyard that Maxfield Vineyards really viewed as competition was Cowboy Wines. Which Emerson thought was funny in a way, since their brand could not be more disparate from Maxfield's if they tried.

And she suspected they *did* try.

She also suspected there was something darker at the root of the rivalry, but if so, James never said.

And neither had Wren, the middle sister. Wren's role in the company often saw her clashing with Creed Cooper, who worked in the same capacity for his family winery, and Wren hated him with every fiber of her being. Loudly and often.

"So what is the new venture exactly?" Emerson asked.

"I just told you. Trail rides and picnics, but we need a way to make it feel like a Maxfield endeavor. And that, I give over to you."

"That sounds like it would be more Wren's thing." Wren was responsible for events at the winery, while Emerson dealt more globally with brand representation.

"I think ultimately this will be about the way you

influence people. I want you to find the best routes, the prime views for the trips, take some photos, put it up on your social media. Use the appropriate pound signs."

"It's a… It's a hashtag."

"I'm not interested in learning what it is, Emerson. That's why I have you."

"Okay. I can do that."

She did have a massive online reach, and she could see how she might position some photos, which would garner media interest, and possibly generate a story in *Sip and Savor* magazine. And really, it would benefit the entire area. The more that Maxfield Vineyards—with its vast reach in the world of wine—brought people into the area, the more the other vineyards benefited too.

"That sounds good to me," she said.

"That's why I hired a manager for the ranching portion of the facility. I need him to oversee some new construction, because if we're going to have guests in the stables, everything needs to be updated, I need for him to oversee the acquisition of a few horses. Plus, the rides, etc."

"Oh," she said. "This…person. This man you hired. He's…tall?"

James shrugged. "I don't know. I didn't consider his height. Did you?"

"No," she said, her face flaming. She felt like a child with her hand caught in the cookie jar. "I just… I think I saw him last night. Down in the vineyard. I left the party to check and see what was happening." Total honesty with her father came as second nature to her.

She tried to be good. She tried to be the daughter he had raised her to be, always.

"You left the party?"

"Everything was well in hand. I left Cricket in charge."

That might be a stretch. But while she was as honest with her father as possible, she tended to leave out some things like…her feelings. And this would be one of those times.

"I met him briefly, then I went back to the house. That's all. He told me he worked on the property."

"You have to be careful," her father said. "You don't want any photographs taken of you alone with a man who's not Donovan. You don't need anything to compromise your engagement."

Sometimes she wondered if her father realized they didn't live in the Victorian era.

"Nothing is going to compromise my engagement to Donovan."

"I'm glad you're certain about it."

She was, in spite of her occasional doubts. Her father might not understand that times had changed, but she did. She felt certain Donovan was carrying on with other women in the absence of a physical relationship with her. Why would she assume anything else? He was a man, after all.

She knew why her father was so invested in her marriage to Donovan. As part of his planned retirement, her father was giving ownership stakes in the winery to each of his daughters' husbands.

He felt Donovan would be an asset to the winery, and Emerson agreed. But she wasn't sure how that fit into a marriage.

Clearly, Donovan didn't much care about how that fit into a marriage either.

And she doubted he would be able to muster up any jealousy over her behavior.

"Image," her father said, bringing her back to the moment. "It isn't what you do that matters, Emerson, it's what the world *thinks* you're doing."

There was something about the way her father said it, so smooth and cold, that made her feel chilled. It shouldn't chill her, because she agreed that image was important in their business.

Still, it *did* chill her.

Emerson shifted. "Right. Well, no worries there. Image is my expertise."

"It's all about the brand," he said.

"I tell you that," she said.

"And you've done it well."

"Thank you," she said, nearly flushed with pleasure. Compliments from James Maxfield were rare, and she clung to them when she got them.

"You should head down to the stables. He'll be waiting for you."

And if that made her stomach tighten, she ignored the sensation. She had a job to do. And that job had nothing to do with how tall the new ranch manager was.

She was as pretty in the ridiculously trendy outfit she was wearing now as she'd been in that red dress.

She was wearing high-cut black pants that went up past her belly button, loose fitted through the leg, with a cuff around the ankle, paired with a matching black top that was cropped to just beneath her breasts and showed a wedge of stomach. Her dark hair was in a high bun, and she was wearing the same red lipstick she'd had on the night before, along with round sunglasses that covered her eyes.

He wished he could see her eyes. And as she approached, she pushed the glasses up to the top of her head.

He hadn't been prepared for how beautiful she was.

He thought he'd seen her beauty in the moonlight, thought he'd seen it in photographs, but they didn't do her justice. He'd been convinced that the blue of her eyes was accomplished with some kind of a filter. But it was clear to him now, out in the bright sun with the green mountains surrounding them, and her eyes reflecting that particular blue from the center of the sky, that if anything, her eyes had been downplayed in those photographs.

"Good morning," she said.

"Good morning to you too. I take it you spoke with your father?"

It took all of his self-control for that word to come out smoothly.

"Yes," she said. "I did."

"And what do you think of his proposition?"

In Holden's opinion, it was a good one. And when he was through ruining James and sinking his brand, Holden might well buy the entire property and continue making wine himself. He was good at selling things, making money. He could make more money here.

"It's good. I think a few well-placed selfies will drum up interest."

"You're probably right. Though, I can't say I'm real up on selfies."

That was a lie. His younger sister was a pretty powerful influencer. A model, who had met James Maxfield at one of the parties that had brought their type together. He was angry at himself for the part his own money had played in all of this.

Because Soraya had been innocent. A sweet girl from a small town who had been catapulted into a lifestyle she hadn't been prepared to handle.

Holden could relate well enough.

He certainly hadn't known how to handle money in the beginning.

But he'd been helping his family dig out of the hole they'd found themselves in. The first thing he'd done was buy his mother a house. Up on a hill, fancy and safe from the men who had used her all throughout Holden's childhood.

And his sweet, younger half sister… She'd tumbled headfirst into fame. She was beautiful, that much had always been apparent, but she had that lean, hungry kind of beauty, honed by years of poverty, her backstory lending even more interest to her sharp cheekbones and unerring sense of style.

She had millions of people following her, waiting to see her next picture. Waiting to see which party she would attend.

And she attended the wrong one when she met James Maxfield.

He'd pounced on her before Holden could say "daddy issues." And James had left her devastated. Holden would never forget having to admit his sister for a psychiatric hold. Soraya's suicide attempt, the miscarriage… The devastation.

It was burned in him.

Along with the reality that his money hadn't protected her. His money had opened her up to this.

Now all that was left was revenge, because he couldn't make it right. He couldn't take her pain away.

But he could take everything away from the Maxfield family.

And that was what he intended to do.

"I don't think we've officially met," she said. She stuck her hand out—the one that didn't have the ring on it. That one angled at her side, the gem sparkling in the sunlight. "I'm Emerson Maxfield."

"Holden Brown," he said, extending his own hand.

If James Maxfield weren't a raging narcissist, Holden might have worried about using his real first name.

But he doubted the older man would ever connect the younger model he'd used for a couple of months and then discarded with Holden. Why would he? James probably barely remembered Soraya's first name, much less any of her family connections. Holden himself wasn't famous. And that was how he liked it. He'd always thought it would be handy to have anonymity. He hadn't imagined it would be for reasons of revenge.

He closed his hand around hers. It was soft, desperately so. The hand of a woman who had never done hard labor in her life, and something in him suddenly felt desperate to make this little princess do some down and dirty work.

Preferably on his body.

He pulled his hand away.

"It's nice to meet you, Holden," she said.

"Nice to meet you too." He bit the pleasantry off at the end, because anything more and he might make a mistake.

"I have some routes in mind for this new venture. Let's go for a ride."

Three

Let's go for a ride was not sexual.

Not in the context of the ranch. Not to a woman who was so used to being exposed to horses. As she was.

Except, she kept replaying that line over and over in her head. Kept imagining herself saying it to him.

Let's go for a ride.

And then she would imagine herself saying it to him in bed.

She had never, ever felt like this in her entire life.

Her first time had been fine. Painless, which was nice, she supposed, but not exactly exciting.

It had been with her boyfriend at the time, who she'd known very well, and who had been extraordinarily careful and considerate.

Though, he'd cared more about keeping her comfortable than keeping her impassioned. But they had been young. So that seemed fair enough.

Her boyfriend after that had been smooth, urbane and fascinating to her. A world traveler before she had done any traveling of her own. She had enjoyed conversations with him, but she hadn't been consumed by passion or lust or anything like that.

She had just sort of thought she was that way. And she was fine with it. She had a lot of excitement in her life. She wasn't hurting for lack of passion.

But Holden made her feel like she might actually be missing something.

Like there was a part of herself that had been dormant for a very long time.

Right. You've been in the man's presence for...a combined total of forty minutes.

Well, that made an even stronger case for the idea of exploring the thing between them. Because in that combined forty minutes, she had imagined him naked at least six times.

Had thought about closing the distance between them and kissing him on the mouth no less than seven times.

And that was insane.

He was working on the ranch, working for her father. Working for her, in essence, as she was part of the winery and had a stake in the business.

And somehow, that aroused her even more.

A man like her fiancé, Donovan, knew a whole lot about the world.

He knew advertising, and there was a heck of a lot of human psychology involved in that. And it was interesting.

But she had a feeling that a man like Holden could teach her about her own body, and that was more than interesting. It was a strange and intoxicating thought.

Also, totally unrealistic and nothing you're going to act on.

No, she thought as she mounted her horse, and the two of them began riding along a trail that she wanted to investigate as a route for the new venture. She would never give in to this just for the sake of exploring her sensuality. For a whole list of reasons.

So you're just going to marry Donovan and wonder what this could have been like?

Sink into the mediocre sex life that the lack of attraction between you promises. Never know what you're missing.

Well, the thing about fantasies was they were only fantasies.

And the thing about sex with a stranger—per a great many of her friends who'd had sex with strangers—was that the men involved rarely lived up to the fantasy. Because they had no reason to make anything good for a woman they didn't really know.

They were too focused on making it good for themselves. And men always won in those games. Emerson knew her way around her own body, knew how to find release when she needed it. But she'd yet to find a man who could please her in the same way, and when she was intimate with someone, she couldn't ever quite let go… There were just too many things to think about, and her brain was always consumed.

It wouldn't be different with Holden. No matter how hot he was.

And blowing up all her inhibitions over an experience that was bound to be a letdown was something Emerson simply wasn't going to risk.

So there.

She turned her thoughts away from the illicit and forced them onto the beauty around her.

Her family's estate had been her favorite place in the world since she was a child. But of course, when she was younger, that preference had been a hollow kind of favoritism, because she didn't have a wide array of experiences or places to compare it to.

She did now. She'd been all over the world, had stayed in some of the most amazing hotels, had enjoyed food in the most glamorous locales. And while she loved to travel, she couldn't imagine a time when she wouldn't call Maxfield Vineyards home.

From the elegant spirals of the vines around the wooden trellises, all in neat rows spreading over vast acres, to the manicured green lawns, to the farther reaches where it grew wild, the majestic beauty of the wilderness so big and awe-inspiring, making her feel appropriately small and insignificant when the occasion required.

"Can I ask you a question?" His voice was deep and thick, like honey, and it made Emerson feel like she was on the verge of a sugar high.

She'd never felt anything like this before.

This, she supposed, was chemistry. And she couldn't for the life of her figure out why it would suddenly be *this* man who inspired it. She had met so many men who weren't so far outside the sphere of what she should find attractive. She'd met them at parties all around the world. None of those men—including the one her father wanted her to be engaged to—had managed to elicit this kind of response in her.

And yet… Holden did it effortlessly.

"Ask away," she said, resolutely fixing her focus on

the scene around them. Anything to keep from fixating on him.

"Why the hell did you wear *that* knowing we were going out riding?"

She blinked. Then she turned and looked at him. "What's wrong with my outfit?"

"I have never seen anyone get on a horse in something so impractical."

"Oh, come now. Surely you've seen period pieces where the woman is in a giant dress riding sidesaddle."

"Yes," he said. "But you have other options."

"It has to be photographable," she said.

"And you couldn't do some sexy cowgirl thing?"

Considering he was playing the part of sexy cowboy—in his tight black T-shirt and black cowboy hat—she suddenly wished she were playing the part of sexy cowgirl. Maybe with a plaid top knotted just beneath her breasts, some short shorts and cowgirl boots. Maybe, if she were in an outfit like that, she would feel suitably bold enough to ask him for a literal roll in the hay.

You've lost your mind.

"That isn't exactly my aesthetic."

"Your aesthetic is… *I Dream of Jeannie* in Mourning?"

She laughed. "I hadn't thought about it that way. But sure. *I Dream of Jeannie* in Mourning sounds about right. In fact, I think I might go ahead and label the outfit that when I post pics."

"Whatever works," he said.

His comment was funny. And okay, maybe the fact that he'd been clever a couple of times in her presence was bestowing the label of *funny* on him too early. But it made her feel a little bit better about her wayward hormones that he wasn't just beautiful, that he was fascinating as well.

"So today's ride isn't just a scouting mission for you," he said. "If you're worried about your aesthetic."

"No," she said. "I want to start generating interest in this idea. You know, pictures of me on the horse. In fact, hang on a second." She stopped, maneuvering her mount, turning so she was facing Holden, with the brilliant backdrop of the trail and the mountains behind them. Then she flipped her phone front facing and raised it up in the air, tilting it downward and grinning as she hit the button. She looked at the result, frowned, and then did it again. The second one would be fine once she put some filters on it.

"What was that?"

She maneuvered her horse back around in the other direction, stuffed her phone in her pocket and carried on.

"It was me getting a photograph," she said. "One that I can post. 'Something new and exciting is coming to the Maxfield label.'"

"Are you really going to put it like that?"

"Yes. I mean, eventually we'll do official press releases and other forms of media, but the way you use social media advertisements is a little different. I personally am part of that online brand. And my lifestyle—including my clothes—is part of what makes people interested in the vineyard."

"Right," he said.

"People want to be jealous," she said. "If they didn't, they wouldn't spend hours scrolling through photos of other people's lives. Or of houses they'll never be able to live in. Exotic locations they'll never be able to go. A little envy, that bit of aspiration, it drives some people."

"Do you really believe that?"

"Yes. I think the success of my portion of the family empire suggests I know what I'm talking about."

He didn't say anything for a long moment. "You know, I suppose you're right. People choose to indulge in that feeling, but when you really don't have anything, it's not fun to see all that stuff you'll never have. It cuts deep. It creates a hunger, rather than enjoyment. It can drive some people to the edge of destruction."

There was something about the way he said it that sent a ripple of disquiet through her. Because his words didn't sound hypothetical.

"That's never my goal," she said. "And I can't control who consumes the media I put out there. At a certain point, people have to know themselves, don't they?"

"True enough," he said. "But some people don't. And it's worse when there's another person involved who sees weakness in them even when they don't see it themselves. Someone who exploits that weakness. Plenty of sad, hungry girls have been lost along that envious road, when they took the wrong hand desperate for a hand up into satisfaction."

"Well, I'm not selling wild parties," she said. "I'm selling an afternoon ride at a family winery, and a trip here is not that out of reach for most people. That's the thing. There's all this wild aspirational stuff out there online, and the vineyard is just a little more accessible. That's what makes it advertising and not luxury porn."

"I see. Create a desire so big it can never be filled, and then offer a winery as the consolation prize."

"If the rest of our culture supports that, it's hardly my fault."

"Have you ever had to want for anything in your entire life, Emerson?" The question was asked innocuously enough, but the way he asked it, in that dark, rough voice, made it buzz over her skin, crackling like electricity as it moved through her. "Or have you always been given everything you could ever desire?"

"I've wanted things," she said, maybe too quickly. Too defensively.

"What?" he pressed.

She desperately went through the catalog of her life, trying to come up with a moment when she had been denied something that she had wanted in a material sense. And there was only one word that burned in her brain.

You.

Yes, that was what she would say. *I want you, and I can't have you. Because I'm engaged to a man who's not interested in kissing me, much less getting into bed with me. And I'm no more interested in doing that with him.*

But I can't break off the engagement no matter how much I want to because I so desperately need...

"Approval," she said. "That's...that's something I want."

Her stomach twisted, and she kept her eyes fixed ahead, because she didn't know why she had let the word escape out loud. She should have said nothing.

He wasn't interested in hearing about her emotional issues.

"From your father?" he asked.

"No," she said. "I have his approval. My mother, on the other hand..."

"You're famous, successful, beautiful. And you don't have your mother's approval?"

"Yeah, shockingly, my mother's goal for me wasn't to take pictures of myself and put them up on the internet."

"Unless you have a secret stash of pictures, I don't see how your mother could disapprove of these sorts of photographs. Unless, of course, it's your pants. Which I do think are questionable."

"These are *wonderful* pants. And actually deceptively practical. Because they allow me to sit on the horse comfortably. Whatever you might think."

"What doesn't your mother approve of?"

"She wanted me to do something more. Something that was my own. She doesn't want me just running publicity for the family business. But I like it. I enjoy what I do, I enjoy this brand. Representing it is easy for me, because I care about it. I went to school for marketing, close to home. She felt like it was…limiting my potential."

He chuckled. "I'm sorry. Your mother felt like you limited your potential by going to get a degree in marketing and then going on to be an ambassador for a successful brand."

"Yes," she said.

She could still remember the brittle irritation in her mother's voice when she had told her about the engagement to Donovan.

"So you're marrying a man more successful in advertising in the broader world even though you could have done that."

"You're married to a successful man."

"I was never given the opportunities that you were

given. *You don't have to hide behind a husband's shadow. You could've done more."*

"Yeah, that's about the size of it," she said. "Look, my mother is brilliant. And scrappy. And I respect her. But she's never going to be overly impressed with me. As far as she's concerned, I haven't worked a day in my life for anything, and I took the path of least resistance into this version of success."

"What does she think of your sisters?"

"Well, Wren works for the winery too, but the only thing that annoys my mother more than her daughters taking a free pass is the Cooper family, and since Wren makes it her life's work to go toe-to-toe with them, my mother isn't quite as irritated with everything Wren does. And Cricket… I don't know that anyone knows what Cricket wants."

Poor Cricket was a later addition to the family. Eight years younger than Emerson, and six years younger than Wren. Their parents hadn't planned on having another child, and they especially hadn't planned on one like Cricket, who didn't seem to have inherited the need to please…well, anyone.

Cricket had run wild over the winery, raised more by the staff than by their mother or father.

Sometimes Emerson envied Cricket and the independence she seemed to have found before turning twenty-one, when Emerson couldn't quite capture independence even at twenty-nine.

"Sounds to me like your mother is pretty difficult to please."

"Impossible," she agreed.

But her father wasn't. He was proud of her. She was

doing exactly what he wanted her to do. And she would keep on doing it.

The trail ended in a grassy clearing on the side of the mountain, overlooking the valley below. The wineries rolled on for miles, and the little redbrick town of Gold Valley was all the way at the bottom.

"Yes," she said. "This is perfect." She got down off the horse, snapped another few pictures with herself in them and the view in the background. And then a sudden inspiration took hold, and she whipped around quickly, capturing the blurred outline of Holden, on his horse with his cowboy hat, behind her.

He frowned, dismounting the horse, and she looked into the phone screen, keeping her eyes on him, and took another shot. He was mostly a silhouette, but it was clear that he was a good-looking, well-built man in a cowboy hat.

"Now, *there's* an ad," she said.

"What're you doing?"

He sounded angry. Not amused at all.

"I just thought it would be good to get you in the background. A full-on Western fantasy."

"You said that wasn't the aesthetic."

"It's not mine. Just because a girl doesn't want to wear cutoff shorts doesn't mean she's not interested in looking at a cowboy."

"You can't post that," he said, his voice hard like granite.

She turned to face him. "Why not?"

"Because I don't want to be on your bullshit website."

"It's not a website. It's… Never mind. Are you… You're not, like, fleeing from the law or something, are you?"

"No," he said. "I'm not."

"Then why won't you let me post your picture? It's not like you can really see you."

"I'm not interested in that stuff."

"Well, that stuff is my entire life's work." She turned her focus to the scenery around them and pretended to be interested in taking a few random pictures that were not of him.

"Some website that isn't going to exist in a couple of years is not your life's work. Your life's work might be figuring out how to sell things to people, advertising, marketing. Whatever you want to call it. But the *how* of it is going to change, and it's going to keep on changing. What you've done is figure out how to understand the way people discover things right now. But it will change. And you'll figure that out too. These pictures are not your life's work."

It was an impassioned speech, and one she almost felt certain he'd given before, though she couldn't quite figure out why he would have, or to who.

"That's nice," she said. "But I don't need a pep talk. I wasn't belittling myself. I won't post the pictures. Though, I think they would have caused a lot of excitement."

"I'm not going to be anyone's trail guide. So there's no point using me."

"You're not even *my* trail guide, not really." She turned to face him, and found he was much closer than she had thought. All the breath was sucked from her body. He was so big and broad, imposing.

There was an intensity about him that should repel her, but instead it fascinated her.

The air was warm, and she was a little bit sweaty,

and that made her wonder if *he* was sweaty, and something about that thought made her want to press her face against his chest and smell his skin.

"Have you ever gone without something?"

She didn't know why she'd asked him that, except that maybe it was the only thing keeping her from actually giving in to her fantasy and pressing her face against his body.

"I don't really think that's any of your business."

"Why not? I just downloaded all of my family issues onto you, and I'm not even sure why. Except that you asked. And I don't think anyone else has ever asked. So… It's just you and me out here."

"And your phone. Which is your link to the outside world on a scale that I can barely understand."

Somehow, that rang false.

"I don't have service," she said. "And anyway, my phone is going back in my pocket." She slipped it into the silky pocket of her black pants.

He looked at her, his dark eyes moving over her body, and she knew he was deliberately taking his time examining her curves. Knew that his gaze was deliberately sexual.

And she didn't feel like she could be trusted with that kind of knowledge, because something deep inside her was dancing around the edge of being bold. That one little piece of her that felt repressed, that had felt bored at the party last night…

That one little piece of her wanted this.

"A few things," he said slowly. And his words were deliberate too.

Without thinking, she sucked her lip between her

teeth and bit down on it, then swiped her tongue over the stinging surface to soothe it.

And the intensity in his eyes leaped higher.

She couldn't pretend she didn't know what she'd done. She'd deliberately drawn his focus to her mouth.

Now, she might have done it deliberately, but she didn't know what she wanted out of it.

Well, she did. But she couldn't want *that*. She couldn't. Not when…

Suddenly, he reached out, grabbing her chin between his thumb and forefinger. "I don't know how the boys who run around in your world play, Emerson. But I'm not a man who scrolls through photos and wishes he could touch something. If I want something, I take it. So if I were you… I wouldn't go around teasing."

She stuttered, "I… I… I…" and stumbled backward. She nearly tripped down onto the grass, onto her butt, but he reached out, looping his strong arm around her waist and pulling her upright. The breath whooshed from her lungs, and she found herself pressed hard against his solid body. She put her hand gingerly on his chest. Yeah. He was a little bit sweaty.

And damned if it wasn't sexy.

She racked her brain, trying to come up with something witty to say, something to defuse the situation, but she couldn't think. Her heart was thundering fast, and there was an echoing pulse down in the center of her thighs making it impossible for her to breathe. Impossible for her to think. She felt like she was having an out-of-body experience, or a wild fantasy that was surely happening in her head only, and not in reality.

But his body was hot and hard underneath her hand,

and there was a point at which she really couldn't pretend she wasn't touching an actual man.

Because her fingers burned. Because her body burned. Because everything burned.

And she couldn't think of a single word to say, which wasn't like her, but usually she wasn't affected by men.

They liked her. They liked to flirt and talk with her, and since becoming engaged, they'd only liked it even more. Seeing her as a bit of a challenge, and it didn't cost her anything to play into that a little bit. Because she was never tempted to do anything. Because she was never affected. Because it was only ever a conversation and nothing more.

But this felt like more.

The air was thick with *more*, and she couldn't figure out why him, why now.

His lips curved up into a half smile, and suddenly, in a brief flash, she saw it.

Sure, his sculpted face and body were part of it. But he was...an outlaw.

Everything she wasn't.

He was a man who didn't care at all what anyone thought. It was visible in every part of him. In the laconic grace with which he moved, the easy way he smiled, the slow honeyed timbre of his voice.

Yes.

He was a man without a cell phone.

A man who wasn't tied or tethered to anything. Who didn't have comments to respond to at two in the morning that kept him up at night, as he worried about not doing it fast enough, about doing something to damage the very public image she had cultivated—not just for herself—but for her father's entire industry.

A man who didn't care if he fell short of the expectations of a parent, at least he didn't seem like he would.

Looking at him in all his rough glory, the way that he blended into the terrain, she felt like a smooth shiny shell with nothing but a sad, listless urchin curled up inside, who was nothing like the facade that she presented.

He was the real deal.

He was like that mountain behind him. Strong and firm and steady. Unmovable.

It made her want a taste.

A taste of him.

A taste of freedom.

She found herself moving forward, but he took a step back.

"Come on now, princess," he said, grabbing hold of her left hand and raising it up, so that her ring caught the sunlight. "You don't want to be doing that."

Horror rolled over her and she stepped away.

"I don't… Nothing."

He chuckled. "Something."

"I… My fiancé and I have an understanding," she said. And she made a mental note to actually check with Donovan to see if they did. Because she suspected they might, given that they had never touched each other. And she could hardly imagine that Donovan had been celibate for the past two years.

You have been.

Yeah, she needed to check on the Donovan thing.

"Do you now?"

"Yes," she lied.

"Well, I have an understanding with your father that I'm in his employment. And I would sure hate to take advantage of that."

"I'm a grown woman," she said.

"Yeah, what do you suppose your daddy would think if he found that you were fucking the help?"

Heat washed over her, her scalp prickling.

"I don't keep my father much informed about my sex life," she said.

"The problem is, you and me would be his business. I try to make my sex life no one's business but mine and the lady I'm naked with."

"Me nearly kissing you is not the same as me offering you sex. Your ego betrays you."

"And your blush betrays you, darlin'."

The entire interaction felt fraught and spiky, and Emerson didn't know how to proceed, which was as rare as her feeling at a loss for words. He was right. He worked for her father, and by extension, for the family, for her. But she didn't feel like she had the power here. Didn't feel like she had the control. She was the one with money, with the Maxfield family name, and he was just…a *ranch hand*.

So why did she feel so decidedly at a disadvantage?

"We'd better carry on," she said. "I have things to do."

"Pictures to post."

"But not of you," she said.

He shook his head once. "Not of me."

She got back on her horse, and he did the same. And this time he led the way back down the trail, and she was somewhat relieved. Because she didn't know what she would do if she had to bear the burden of knowing he was watching the back of her the whole way.

She would drive herself crazy thinking about how to

hold her shoulders so that she didn't look like she knew that he was staring at her.

But then, maybe he wouldn't stare at her, and that was the thing. She would wonder either way. And she didn't particularly want to wonder.

And when she got back to her office, she tapped her fingers on the desk next to her phone, and did her very best to stop herself from texting Donovan.

Tap. *Don't*. Tap. *Don't*.

And then suddenly she picked up the phone and started a new message.

Are we exclusive?

There were no dots, no movement. She set the phone down and tried to look away. It pinged a few minutes later.

We are engaged.

That's not an answer.

We don't live in the same city.

She took a breath.

Have you slept with someone else?

She wasn't going to wait around with his back-and-forth nonsense. She wasn't interested in him sparing himself repercussions.

We don't live in the same city. So yes, I have.

And if I did?

Whatever you do before the wedding is your business.

She didn't respond, and his next text came in on the heels of the last.

Did you want to talk on the phone?

No.

K.

And that was it. Because they didn't love each other. She hadn't needed to text him, because nothing was going to happen with her and Holden.

And how do you feel about the fact that Donovan had slept with other people?

She wasn't sure.

Except she didn't feel much of anything.

Except now she had a get-out-of-jail-free card, and that was about the only way she could see it. That wasn't normal, was it? It wasn't normal for him to be okay with the fact that she had asked those questions. That she had made it clear she'd thought about sleeping with someone else.

And it wasn't normal for her to not be jealous when Donovan said he *had* slept with someone else.

But she wasn't jealous.

And his admission didn't dredge any deep feelings up to the surface either.

No, her reaction just underlined the fact that something was missing from their arrangement. Which she had known. Neither of them was under the impression they were in a real relationship. They had allowed themselves to be matched, but before this moment she had been sure feelings would grow in time, but they hadn't, and she and Donovan had ignored that.

But she couldn't...

Her father didn't ask much of her. And he gave her endless support. If she disappointed him...

Well, then she would be a failure all around, wouldn't she?

He's not choosing Wren's husband. He isn't choosing Cricket's.

Well, Wren would likely refuse. Emerson couldn't imagine her strong-headed sister giving in to that. And Cricket... Well, nobody could tame Cricket.

Her father hadn't asked them. He'd asked her. And she'd agreed, because that was who she was. She was the one who could be counted on for anything, and it was too late to stop being who she was now.

Texting Donovan had been insane, leaning in toward Holden had been even more insane. And she didn't have time for any of that behavior. She had a campaign to launch and she was going to do it. Because she knew who she was. She was not the kind of person who kissed men she barely knew, not the kind of person who engaged in physical-only flings, not the kind of person who crossed professional boundaries.

The problem was, Holden made her feel very, very *not* like herself. And that was the most concerning thing of all.

Four

Emerson was proving to be deeply problematic.

What he should do was go down to the local bar and find himself a woman to pick up. Because God knew he didn't need to be running around getting hard over his enemy's daughter. He had expected to be disgusted by everything the Maxfield family was. And indeed, when he had stood across from James Maxfield in the man's office while interviewing for this position, it had taken every ounce of Holden's willpower not to fly across the desk and strangle the man to death.

The thing was, death would be too easy an out for a man like him. Holden would rather give James the full experience of degradation in life before he consigned him to burning in hell for all eternity. Holden wanted to maximize the punishment.

Hell could wait.

And hell was no less than he deserved.

Holden had finally gotten what he'd come for.

It had come in the form of nondisclosure agreements he'd found in James's office. He'd paid attention to the code on the door when James had let him in for the interview, and all he'd had to do was wait for a time when the man was out and get back in there.

It fascinated Holden that everything was left unguarded, but it wasn't really a mystery.

This was James's office in his family home. Not a corporate environment. He trusted his family, and why wouldn't he? It was clear that Emerson had nothing but good feelings about her father. And Holden suspected everyone else in the household felt the same.

Except the women James had coerced into bed. Employees. All young. All dependent on him for a paycheck. But he'd sent them off with gag orders and payoffs.

And once Holden figured out exactly how to approach this, James would be finished.

But now there was the matter of Emerson.

Holden hadn't expected the attraction that had flared up immediately the first time he'd seen her not to let up.

And she was always…around. The problem with taking on a job as an opportunity to commit corporate espionage, and to find proof either of monetary malfeasance or of the relationship between James and Holden's sister, was that he had to actually *work* during the day.

That ate up a hell of a lot of his time. It also meant he was in close proximity to Emerson.

And speak of the devil, right as he finished mucking out a stall, she walked in wearing skintight tan breaches that molded to every dimple of her body.

"That's a different sort of riding getup," he said.

"I'm not taking selfies today," she said, a teasing gleam in her blue eyes that made his gut tight.

"Just going on a ride?"

"I needed to clear my head," she said.

She looked at him, seeming vaguely edgy.

"What is it?"

But he knew what it was. It was that attraction that he felt every time she was near. She felt it too, and that made it a damn sight worse.

"Nothing. I just… What is it that you normally do? Are you always a ranch hand? I mean, you must specialize in something, or my father wouldn't have hired you to help with the horses."

"I'm good with horses."

Most everything he'd said about himself since coming to the winery was a lie. But this, at least, was true. He had grown up working other people's ranches.

Now he happened to own one of his own, a good-sized spread, but he still did a portion of the labor. He liked working his own land. It was a gift, after so many years of working other people's.

If there was work to be given over to others, he pre ferred to farm out his office work, not the ranch work.

He'd found an affinity with animals early on, and that had continued. It had given him something to do, given him something to *be*.

He had been nothing but a poor boy from a poor family. He'd been a cowboy from birth. That connection with animals had gotten him his first job at a ranch, and that line of work had gotten him where he was today.

When one of his employers had died, he'd gifted Holden with a large plot of land. It wasn't his ranch, but totally dilapidated fields a few miles from the ranch he now owned.

He hadn't known what the hell to do with land so undeveloped at first, until he'd gone down to the county offices and found it could be divided. From there, he'd started working with a developer.

Building a subdivision had been an interesting project, because a part of him had hated the idea of turning a perfectly good stretch of land into houses. But then, another part of him had enjoyed the fact that new houses meant more people would experience the land he loved and the town he called home.

Making homes for families felt satisfying.

As a kid who had grown up without one at times, he didn't take for granted the effect four walls could have on someone's life.

And that had been a bargain he'd struck with the developer. That a couple of the homes were his to do with as he chose. They'd been gifted to homeless families going on ten years ago now. And each of the children had been given college scholarships, funded by his corporation now that he was more successful.

He'd done the same ever since, with every development he'd created. It wouldn't save the whole world, but it changed the lives of the individuals involved. And he knew well enough what kind of effect that change could have on a person.

He'd experienced it himself.

Cataloging everything good you've done in the past won't erase what you're doing now.

Maybe not. But he didn't much care. Yes, destroying the Maxfield empire would sweep Emerson right up in his revenge, which was another reason he'd thought it might be more convenient to hate everyone connected with James Maxfield.

He'd managed to steer clear of the youngest daughter, Cricket, who always seemed to be flitting in and out of the place, and he'd seen Wren on many occasions, marching around purposefully, but he hadn't quite figured out exactly what her purpose was. Nor did he want to.

But Emerson... Emerson he couldn't seem to stay away from. Or maybe she couldn't stay away from him. At the end of it all, he didn't know if it mattered which it was.

They kept colliding either way.

"You must be very good with horses," she said.

"I don't know about that. But I was here, available to do the job, so your father gave it to me."

She tilted her head to the side, appraising him like he was a confusing piece of modern art. "Are you married?"

"Hell no," he said. "No desire for that kind of nonsense."

"You think love is nonsense?" she pressed.

"You didn't ask me about love. You asked me about marriage."

"Don't they usually go together?"

"Does it for you? Because you nearly kissed me yesterday, and you're wearing another man's ring."

Great. He'd gone and brought that up. Not a good idea, all things considered. Though, it might make her angry, and if he could get her good and angry, that might be for the best.

Maybe then she would stay away.

"I told you, we're not living near each other right now, so we…have an arrangement."

"So you said. But what does that mean?"

"We are not exclusive."

"Then what the hell is the point of being engaged? As I understand it, the only reason to put a ring on a woman's finger is to make her yours. Sure and certain. If you were my woman, I certainly wouldn't let another man touch you."

Her cheeks flushed red. "Well, you certainly have a lot of opinions for someone who doesn't see a point to the institution of marriage."

"Isn't the point *possession*?"

"Women aren't seen as cattle anymore. So no."

"I didn't mean a woman being a possession. The husband and wife possess each other. Isn't that the point?"

She snorted. "I think that often the point is dynasty and connections, don't you?"

"Damn, that's cynical, even for me."

She ignored that. "So, you're good with horses, and you don't believe in marriage," she said. "Anything else?"

"Not a thing."

"If you don't believe in marriage, then what do you believe in?"

"Passion," he said. "For as long as it burns hot. But that's it."

She nodded slowly, and then she turned away from him.

"Aren't you going to ride?"

"I… Not right now. I need to… I need to go think."

And then without another word, Emerson Maxfield ran away from him.

* * *

The cabin was a shit hole. He really wasn't enjoying staying there. He had worked himself out of places like this. Marginal dwellings that had only woodstoves for heat. But this was the situation. Revenge was a dish best served cold, and apparently his ass had to be kind of cold right along with it.

Not that he didn't know how to build a fire. It seemed tonight he'd have to.

He went outside, into the failing light, wearing nothing but his jeans and a pair of boots, and searched around for an ax.

There was no preprepared firewood. That would've been way too convenient, and Holden had the notion that James Maxfield was an asshole in just about every way. It wasn't just Soraya that James didn't care about. It was everyone. Right down to the people who lived and worked on his property. He didn't much care about the convenience of his employees. It was a good reminder. Of why Holden was here.

Though, Emerson seemed to be under the impression that James cared for *her*. An interesting thing. Because when she had spoken about trying to earn the approval of one of her parents, he had been convinced, of course, that she had meant James's.

But apparently, James was proud of his daughter, and supported her.

Maybe James had used up every ounce of his humanity in his parenting. Though, Holden still had questions about that.

And it was also entirely possible that Emerson knew the truth about how her father behaved. And that she was complicit in covering up his actions in order to protect the brand.

Holden didn't know, and he didn't care. He couldn't concern himself with the fate of anyone involved with James Maxfield.

If you drink water from a poison well, whatever happened, happened.

As far as Holden was concerned, each and every grapevine on this property was soaked through with James Maxfield's poison.

He found an ax and swung it up in the air, splitting the log in front of him with ease. That, at least, did something to get his body warmed up, and quell some of the murder in his blood. He chuckled, positioned another log on top of the large stone sitting before him and swung the ax down.

"Well," came the sound of a soft, feminine voice. "I didn't expect to find you out here. Undressed."

He paused, and turned to see Emerson standing there, wearing a belted black coat, her dark hair loose.

She was wearing high heels.

Nothing covered her legs.

It was cold, and she was standing out in the middle of the muddy ground in front of his cabin, and none of it made much sense.

"What the hell are you doing here?" He looked her up and down. "Dressed like that."

"I could ask you the same question. Why didn't you put a shirt on? It's freezing out here."

"Why didn't *you* put pants on?"

She hesitated, but only for a moment, and then her expression went regal, which he was beginning to recognize meant she was digging deep to find all her stubbornness.

"Because I would be burdened by having to take them off again soon. At least, that's what I hope." Only the faint pink color in her cheeks betrayed the fact that she'd embarrassed herself. Otherwise he'd have thought she was nothing more than an ice queen, throwing out the suggestion of a seduction so cold it might give his dick frostbite.

But that wasn't the truth. No, he could see it in that blush. Underneath all that coolness, Emerson was burning.

And damned if he wasn't on fire himself.

But it made no damn sense to him, that this woman, the princess of Maxfield Vineyards, would come all the way out here, dragging her designer heels in the mud, to seduce him.

He looked behind his shoulder at the tiny cabin, then back at her.

"Really," he said.

The color in her cheeks deepened.

Lust and interest fired through him, and damned if he'd do anything to stop it. Dark, tempting images of taking Emerson into that rough cabin and sullying her on the rock-hard mattress... It was satisfying on so many levels, he couldn't even begin to sort through them all.

His enemy's daughter. Naked and begging for him, in a cabin reserved for workers, people James clearly thought so far beneath his own family that he'd not even given a thought to their basic needs.

Knowing Holden could have her in there, in a hundred different ways, fired his blood in a way nothing but rage had for ages.

Damn, he was hungry for her. In this twisted, intense way he had told himself he wasn't going to indulge.

But she was here.

Maybe with nothing on under that coat. Which meant they were both already half undressed, and it begged the question whether or not they should go ahead and get naked the rest of the way.

A look at her hand. He noticed she didn't have her engagement ring on.

"What the hell kind of game are you playing?" he asked.

"You said that whatever happened between you and a woman in bed was between you and that woman. Well, I'm of the same mind. It's nobody's business but ours what happens here." She bit her lip. "I'm going to be really, really honest with you."

There was something about that statement that burned, because if there was one thing he was never going to be with her, it was honest.

"I don't love my fiancé. I haven't slept with him. Why? Because I'm not that interested in sleeping with him. It's the strangest thing. We've been together for a couple of years, but we don't live near each other. And every time we could have, we just didn't. And the fact that we're not even tempted... Well, that tells you something about the chemistry between us. But this...you. I want to do this with you. It's all I can think about, and trust me when I say that's not me. I don't understand it, I didn't ask for it, or want it, but I can't fight it."

"I'm supposed to be flattered that you're deigning to

come down from your shining tower because you can't stop thinking about me?"

"I want you," she said, lifting her chin up. "You asked me earlier if there was anything I had ever wanted that I couldn't have. It's you. I shouldn't have you. But I want you. And if my father found out that I was doing this, he would kill us both. Because my engagement to Donovan matters to him."

"You said you had an arrangement," he stated.

"Oh, Donovan wouldn't care. Donovan knows. I mean, in a vague sense. I texted him to make sure I wasn't just making assumptions. And I found out he already has. Been with someone else, I mean. So, it's not a big deal. But my father… He would never want it being made public. Image is everything to him, and my engagement to Donovan is part of the image right now."

And just like that, he sensed that her relationship with her father was a whole lot more complicated than she let on. But her relationship with James wasn't Holden's problem either way. And neither was whether or not Emerson was a good person, or one who covered up her father's transgressions. None of it mattered.

Nothing really mattered right here but the two of them.

The really fascinating thing was, Emerson didn't know who Holden was. And even if she did, she didn't need anything from him. Not monetarily. It had been a long damn time since he'd appealed to a woman in a strictly physical way. Not that women didn't enjoy him physically. But they also enjoyed what he had—a luxury hotel suite, connections, invitations to coveted parties.

He was standing here with none of that, nothing but a very dilapidated cabin that wasn't even his own.

And she wanted him.

And that, he found, was an incredibly compelling aphrodisiac, a turn-on he hadn't even been aware he'd been missing.

Emerson had *no idea* that he was Holden McCall, the wealthiest developer in the state. All she wanted was a roll in the hay, and why the hell not? Sure, he was supposed to hate her and everything she stood for.

But there was something to be said for a hate screw.

"So let me get this straight," he said. "You haven't even kissed me. You don't even know if I want to kiss you. But you were willing to come down here not even knowing what the payoff would be?"

Her face was frozen, its beauty profound even as she stared at him with blank blue eyes, her red lips pressed into a thin line. And he realized, this was not a woman who knew how to endure being questioned.

She was a woman used to getting what she wanted. A woman used to commanding the show, that much was clear. It was obvious that Emerson was accustomed to bulldozing down doors, a characteristic that seemed to stand in sharp contrast to the fact that she also held deep concerns over what her parents thought of her and her decisions.

"That should tell you, then," she said, the words stiff. "It should tell you how strong I think the connection is. If it's not as strong for you, that's fine. You're not the one on the verge of getting married, and you're just a man, after all. So you'll get yours either way. This might be *it* for me before I go to the land of boring, banal monogamous sex."

"So you intend to be fully faithful to this man you're marrying? The one you've never been naked with?"

"What's the point of marriage otherwise? You said that yourself. I believe in monogamy. It's just in my particular style of engagement I feel a little less...intense about it than I otherwise might."

He could take this moment to tell her that her father certainly didn't seem to look at marriage that way. But that would be stupid. He didn't have enough information yet to come at James, and when he did, he wasn't going to miss.

"So you just expect that I'll fuck you whether I feel a connection to you or not. Even if I don't feel like it."

She lifted her chin, her imperiousness seeming to intensify. "It's my understanding that men always feel like it."

"Fair enough," he said. "But that's an awfully low bar, don't you think?"

"I don't..."

"I'll tell you what," he said. "I'm going to give you a kiss. And if afterward you can walk away, then you should."

She blinked. "I don't want to."

"See how you feel after the kiss."

He dropped the ax, and it hit the frozen ground with a dull thump.

He already knew.

He already knew that he was going to have a hard time getting his hands off her once they'd been on her. The way that she appealed to him hit a primitive part of him he couldn't explain. A part of him that was something other than civilized.

She took a step toward him, those ridiculous high heels somehow skimming over the top of the dirt and rocks. She was soft and elegant, and he was half dressed and sweaty from chopping wood, his breath a cloud in the cold air.

She reached out and put her hand on his chest. And it took every last ounce of his willpower not to grab her wrist and pin her palm to him. To hold her against him, make her feel the way his heart was beginning to rage out of control.

He couldn't remember the last time he'd wanted a woman like this.

And he didn't know if it was the touch of the forbidden adding to the thrill, or if it was the fact that she wanted his body and nothing else. Because he could do nothing for Emerson Maxfield, not Holden Brown, the man he was pretending to be. The man who had to depend on the good graces of his employer and lived in a cabin on the property. There was nothing he could do for her.

Nothing he could do but make her scream his name, over and over again.

And that was all she wanted.

She was a woman set to marry another man. She didn't even want emotions from him.

She wanted nothing. Nothing but his body.

And he couldn't remember the last time that was the case, if ever. Everyone wanted something from him. Everyone wanted a piece of him.

Even his mother and sister, who he cared for dearly, needed him. They needed his money, they needed his support.

They needed him to engage in a battle to destroy the man who had devastated Soraya.

But this woman standing in front of him truly wanted

only this elemental thing, this spark of heat between them to become a blaze. And who was he to deny her?

He let her guide it. He let her be the one to make the next move. Here she was, all bold in that coat, with her hand on his chest, and yet there was a hesitancy to her as well. She didn't have a whole lot of experience seducing men, that much was obvious. And damned if he didn't enjoy the moment where she had to steel herself and find the courage to lean in.

There was something so very enjoyable about a woman playing the vixen when it was clear it wasn't her natural role. But she was doing it. For him. All for the desire she felt for him.

What man wouldn't respond to that?

She licked her lips, and then she pressed her mouth to his.

And that was the end of his control.

He wrapped his arm around her waist and pressed her against him, angling his head and consuming her.

Because the fire that erupted between them wasn't something that could be tamed. Wasn't something that could be controlled. Couldn't be tested or tasted. This was not a cocktail to be sipped. He wanted to drink it all down, and her right along with it.

Needed to. There was no other option.

He felt like a dying man making a last gasp for breath in the arms of this woman he should never have touched.

He didn't let his hands roam over her curves, no matter how much he wanted to. He simply held her, licking his way into the kiss, his tongue sliding against hers as he tasted the most luscious forbidden fruit that had ever been placed in front of him.

But it wasn't enough to have a bite. He wanted her

juices to run down his chin. And he was going to have just that.

"Want to walk away?" he asked, his voice rough, his body hard.

"No," she breathed.

And then he lifted her up and carried her into the cabin.

Five

If this moment were to be translated into a headline, it would read: Maxfield Heiress Sacrifices All for an Orgasm.

Assuming, of course, that she would have an orgasm. She'd never had one yet with a man. But if she were going to…it would be with him.

If it were possible, it would be now.

When she had come up to the cabin and seen him standing there chopping wood—of all things—his chest bare, his jeans slung low on his hips, she had known that all good sense and morality were lost. Utterly and completely lost. In a fog of lust that showed no sign of lifting.

There was nothing she could do but give in.

Because she knew, she absolutely *knew*, that whatever this was needed to be explored. That she could not marry Donovan wondering what this thing between herself and Holden was.

Not because she thought there might be something lasting between them—no—she was fairly certain this was one of those moments of insanity that had nothing to do with anything like real life or good sense.

But she needed to know what desire was. Needed to know what sex could be.

For all she knew, this was the key to unlocking it with the man she was going to marry. And that was somewhat important. Maybe Holden was her particular key.

The man who was destined to teach her about her own sexuality.

Whatever the excuse, she was in his arms now, being carried into a modest cabin that was a bit more run-down than she had imagined any building on the property might be.

She had never been in any of the workers' quarters before. She had never had occasion to.

She shivered, with cold or fear she didn't know.

This was like some strange, unexpected, delayed rebellion. Sneaking out of her room in the big house to come and fool around with one of the men who worked for her father. He would be furious if he knew.

And so he would never know.

No one would ever know about this. No one but the two of them.

It would be their dirty secret. And at the moment, she was hoping that it would be very, very dirty. Because she had never had these feelings in her life.

This desire to get naked as quickly as possible. To be as close to someone as possible.

She wanted to get this coat off and rub herself all over his body, and she had never, ever felt that before.

She was a woman who was used to being certain. She knew why she made the decisions she did, and she made them without overthinking.

She was *confident*.

But this was a part of herself she had never been terribly confident in.

Oh, it had nothing to do with her looks. Men liked her curves. She knew that. She didn't have insecurities when it came to her body.

It was what her body was capable of. What it could feel.

That gave her all kinds of insecurity. Enough that in her previous relationships she had decided to make her own pleasure a nonissue. If ever her college boyfriend had noticed that she hadn't climaxed, he had never said. But he had been young enough, inexperienced enough, that he might not have realized.

She was sure, however, that her last ex had realized.

Occasionally he'd asked her if she was all right. And she had gotten very good at soothing his ego.

It's nice to be close.

It was good for me.

And one night, when he had expressed frustration at her tepid response to his kisses, she had simply shrugged and said, *I'm not very sexual.*

And she had believed it. She had believed each and every one of those excuses. And had justified the times when she had faked it, because of course her inability to feel something wasn't his fault.

But just looking at Holden made a pulse pound between her thighs that was more powerful than any sensation she'd felt during intercourse with a man before.

And with his hands on her like they were right now, with her body cradled in his strong arms...

She could barely breathe. She could barely think.

All she felt was a blinding, white-hot shock of need, and she had never experienced anything like it before in her life.

He set her down on the uneven wood floor. It was cold.

"I was going to build a fire," he said. "Wait right here, I'll be back."

And then he went back outside, leaving her standing in the middle of the cabin, alone and not in his arms, which gave her a moment to pause.

Was she really about to do this?

She didn't have any experience with casual sex. She had experience with sex only in the context of a relationship. And she had never, ever felt anything this intense.

It was the intensity that scared her. Not so much the fact that it was physical only, but the fact that it was so incredibly physical.

She didn't know how this might change her.

Because she absolutely felt like she was on the cusp of being changed. And maybe that was dramatic, but she couldn't rid herself of the sensation. This was somehow significant. It would somehow alter the fabric of who she was. She felt brittle and thin, on the verge of being shattered. And she wasn't entirely sure what was going to put her back together.

It was frightening, that thought. But not frightening enough to make her leave.

He returned a moment later, a stack of wood in his arms.

And she watched as he knelt down before the wood-stove, his muscles shifting and bunching in his back as he began to work at lighting a fire.

"I didn't realize the cabins were so…rustic."

"They are a bit. Giving you second thoughts?"

"No," she said quickly.

If he changed his mind now, if he sent her away, she would die. She was sure of it.

He was kneeling down half naked, and he looked so damned hot that he chased away the cold.

"It'll take a bit for the fire to warm the place up," he said. "But I can keep you warm in the meantime."

He stood, brushing the dust off his jeans and making his way over to her.

She had meant to—at some point—take stock of the room. To look around and see what furniture it had, get a sense of the layout. But she found it too hard to look away from him. And when he fixed those eyes on her, she was held captive.

Utterly and completely

His chest was broad, sprinkled with just the right amount of hair, his muscles cut and well-defined. His pants were low, showing those lines that arrow downward, as if pointing toward the most masculine part of him.

She had never been with a man who had a body like this. It was like having only ever eaten store-bought pie, and suddenly being treated to a homemade extravaganza.

"You are… You're beautiful," she said.

He chuckled. "I think that's my line."

"No. It's definitely mine."

One side of his mouth quirked upward into a grin, and even though the man was a stranger to her, suddenly she felt like he might not be.

Because that smile touched her somewhere inside her chest and made her *feel* when she knew it ought not to. Because this should be about just her body. And not in any way about her heart. But it was far too easy to imagine a world where nothing existed beyond this cabin, beyond this man and the intensity in his eyes, the desire etched into every line of his face.

And that body. Hot *damn*, that body.

Yes, it was very easy to imagine she was a different girl who lived in a different world.

Who could slip away to a secluded cabin and find herself swept up in the arms of a rugged cowboy, and it didn't matter whether or not it was *on brand*. Right now, it didn't.

Right now, it didn't.

This was elemental, something deeper than reality. It was fantasy in all of its bright, brilliant glory. Except it was real. Brought to life with stunning visuals, and it didn't matter whether it should be or not.

It was.

It felt suddenly much bigger than her. And because of that, she felt more connected with her body than she ever had before.

Because this wasn't building inside of her, it surrounded her, encompassed her. She could never have contained so much sensation, so much need. And so it became the world around her.

Until she couldn't remember what it was like to draw breath in a space where his scent didn't fill her lungs, where her need didn't dictate the way she stood, the way she moved.

She put her hands on the tie around her waist.

And he watched.

His attention was rapt, his focus unwavering.

The need between her thighs escalated.

She unknotted the belt and then undid the buttons, let her coat fall to her feet.

She was wearing nothing but a red lace bra and panties and her black high heels.

"Oh, Little Red," he growled. "I do like that color on you."

The hunger in his eyes was so intense she could feel it echoing inside of herself. Could feel her own desire answering back.

No man had ever looked at her like this.

They had wanted her, sure. Had desired her.

But they hadn't wanted to consume her, and she had a feeling that her own personal Big Bad Wolf just might.

She expected him to move to her, but instead he moved away, walking over to the bed that sat in the corner of the humble room. He sat on the edge of the mattress, his thighs splayed, his eyes fixed on her.

"I want you to come on over here," he said.

She began to walk toward him, her heels clicking on the floor, and she didn't need to be given detailed instruction, because she somehow knew what he wanted.

It was strange, and it was impossible, that somehow this man she had barely spent any time with felt known to her in a way that men she'd dated for long periods of time never had.

But he did.

And maybe that was something she had overlooked in all of this.

What she wanted to happen between them might be physical, but there was a spiritual element that couldn't be denied. Something that went deeper than just attraction. Something that spoke to a more desperate need.

His body was both deliciously unknown, and somehow right and familiar all at the same time.

And so were his needs.

She crossed the room and draped an arm over his shoulder, lifting her knee to the edge of the mattress, rocking forward so that the center of her pressed against his hardness. "I'm here," she said.

He wrapped his arm around her waist, pushed his fingertips beneath the waistband of her panties and slid his hands down over her ass. Then he squeezed. Hard. And she gasped.

"I'm going to go out on a limb here and guess that part of the attraction you have to all of this is that it's a little bit rough."

She licked her lips, nodded when no words would come.

She hadn't realized that was what she'd wanted, but when he said it, it made sense. When he touched her like this—possessive and commanding—she knew it was what she needed.

"That suits me just fine, princess, because I'm a man who likes it that way. So you have to tell me right now if you can handle it."

"I can handle whatever you give me," she said, her voice coming out with much more certainty than she felt.

Rough.

The word skated over her skin, painted delicious

pictures in her mind and made that place between her legs throb with desire.

Rough. Uncivilized. Untamed.

Right then she wanted that, with a desperation that defied explanation.

She wanted to be marked by this. Changed by it. She wanted to have the evidence of it on her skin as well as on her soul.

Because somehow she felt that tonight, in this bed, it might be the only chance she'd have to find out what she was.

What she wanted.

What she desired apart from anything else, apart from family and social expectations. Tonight, this, had nothing to do with what anyone else might expect of her.

This was about her.

And on some level she felt like if she didn't have this, the rest of her life would be a slow descent into the madness of wondering.

"If anything goes too far for you, you just say it, you understand?"

"Yes," she said.

"I want to make you scream," he said. "But I want it to be the good kind."

She had never in her life screamed during sex.

The promise, the heat in his eyes, made her suspect she was about to.

That was when he tightened his grip on her and reversed their positions.

He pinned her down on her back, grabbing both wrists with one hand and stretching her arms up over her head. He had his thighs on either side of her hips, the denim rough against her skin. He was large and hard and glorious above her, his face filled with the kind of intensity that thrilled her down to her core.

She rocked her hips upward, desperate for fulfillment. Desperate to be touched by him.

He denied her.

He held her pinned down and began a leisurely tour of her body with his free hand.

He traced her collarbone, the edge of her bra, down the valley between her breasts and to her belly button. Before tracing the edge of her panties. But he didn't touch her anywhere that she burned for him. And she could feel the need for his touch, as if those parts of her were lit up bright with their demand for him. And still, he wouldn't do it.

"I thought you said this was going to be rough."

"Rough's not fun if you're not good and wet first," he said. And then he leaned in, his lips right next to her ear. "And I'm going to make sure you get really, really wet first."

Just those words alone did the job. An arrow of need pierced her center, and she could feel it, molten liquid there in her thighs. And that was when he captured her mouth with his, kissing her deep and long, cupping her breast with one hand and teasing her nipple with his thumb.

She whimpered, arching her hips upward, frustrated when there was nothing there for her to make contact with.

He touched her slowly, thoroughly, first through the lace of her bra, before pushing the flimsy fabric down and exposing her breasts. He touched her bare, his thumbs calloused as they moved over her body.

And then he replaced them with his mouth.

He sucked deep, and she worked her hips against nothing, desperate for some kind of relief that she couldn't find as he tormented her.

She would have said that her breasts weren't sensitive.

But he was proving otherwise.

He scraped his teeth across her sensitive skin. And then he bit down.

She cried out, her orgasm shocking her, filling her cheeks with embarrassed heat as wave after wave of desire pulsed through her core.

But she didn't feel satisfied, because he still hadn't touched her there.

She felt aching and raw, empty when she needed to be filled.

"There's a good girl," he said, and her internal muscles pulsed again.

He tugged her panties down her thighs, stopping at her ankles before pushing her knees wide, eyeing her hungrily as he did.

Then he leaned in, inhaling her scent, pressing a kiss to the tender skin on her leg. "The better to eat you with," he said, looking her in the eye as he lowered his head and dragged his tongue through her slick folds.

She gasped. This was the first time he had touched her there, and it was so... So impossibly dirty. So impossibly intimate.

Then he was done teasing. Done talking. He grabbed her hips and pulled her forward, his grip bruising as he set his full focus and attention on consuming her.

She dug her heels into the bed, tried to brace herself, but she couldn't. She had no control over this, over any of it.

He was driving her toward pleasure at his pace, and it was terrifying and exhilarating all at once.

She climaxed again. Impossibly.

It was then she realized he was no longer holding her in place, but she had left her own wrists up above her head, as if she were still pinned there.

She was panting, gasping for breath, when he moved up her body, his lips pressing against hers.

She could taste her own desire there, and it made her shiver.

"Now I want you to turn over," he said.

She didn't even think of disobeying that commanding voice. She did exactly as she was told.

"Up on your knees, princess," he said.

She obeyed, anticipation making the base of her spine tingle as she waited.

She could hear plastic tearing, knew that he must be getting naked. Getting a condom on.

And when he returned to her, he put one hand on her hip, and she felt the head of his arousal pressed against the entrance to her body.

She bit her lip as he pushed forward, filling her.

He was so big, and this was not a position she was used to.

It hurt a bit as he drove his hips forward, a short curse escaping his lips as he sank in to the hilt.

She lowered her head, and he placed his hand between her shoulder blades, drawing it down her spine, then back up. And she wanted to purr like a very contented cat. Then he grabbed hold of both her hips, pulling out slowly, and slamming back home.

She gasped, arching her back as she met him thrust for punishing thrust. She pressed her face down into the mattress as he entered her, over and over again, the only sounds in the room that of skin meeting skin, harsh breaths and the kinds of feral sounds she had never imagined could come from her.

He grabbed hold of her hair, and moved it to one side, and she felt a slight tug, and then with a pull that shocked her with its intensity, he lifted her head as he held her like that, the tug matching his thrust. She gasped, the pain on her scalp somehow adding to the pleasure she felt between her legs.

And he did it over and over again.

Until she was sobbing. Until she was begging for release.

Then he released his hold on her hair, grabbing both her hips again as he raced her to the end, his hold on her bruising, his thrusts pushing her to the point of pain. Then he leaned forward, growling low and biting her neck as he came hard. And she followed him right over the edge into oblivion.

Six

By the time Emerson went limp in front of him, draped over the mattress like a boneless cat, the fire had begun to warm the space.

Holden was a man who didn't have much in the way of regret in his life—it was impossible when he had been raised with absolutely nothing, and had gotten to a space where he didn't have to worry about his own basic needs, or those of his family. And even now, it was difficult to feel anything but the kind of bone-deep satisfaction that overtook him.

He went into the bathroom and took care of the practicalities, then went back to stoke the fire.

He heard the sound of shifting covers on the bed, and looked over his shoulder to see Emerson lying on her side now, her legs crossed just so, hiding that tempting shadow at the apex of her thighs, her arm draped coquettishly over her breast.

"Enjoying the show?" he asked.

"Yes," she responded, no shame in her voice at all.

"You might return the favor," he said.

She looked down at her own body, as if she only just realized that she was covering a good amount of the tempting bits.

"You're busy," she said. "Making a fire. I would hate to distract."

"You're distracting even as you are."

Maybe even especially as she was, looking timid when he knew how she really was. Wild and uninhibited and the best damn sex he'd ever had in his life.

Hard mattress notwithstanding.

She rolled onto her back then, stretching, raising her arms up above her head, pointing her toes.

He finished with the fire quickly, and returned to the bed.

"I couldn't do it again," she said, her eyes wide.

"Why not?"

"I've never come that many times in a row in my life. Surely it would kill you."

"I'm willing to take the chance," he said.

It surprised him to hear that her response wasn't normal for her. She had seemed more than into it. Though, she had talked about the tepid chemistry between herself and the man she was engaged to.

There was something wrong with that man, because if he couldn't find chemistry with Emerson, Holden doubted he could find it with anyone.

"Well, of course you're willing to take the chance. You're not the one at risk. You only... Once. I already did three times."

"Which means you have the capacity for more," he said. "At least, that's my professional opinion."

"Professional ranch hand opinion? I didn't know that made you an expert on sex."

He chuckled. "I'm an expert on sex because of vast experience in my personal life, not my professional life. Though, I can tell you I've never considered myself a hobbyist when it came to female pleasure. Definitely a professional."

"Well, then I guess I picked a good man to experiment with."

"Is that what this is? An experiment?"

She rolled over so she was halfway on his body, her breast pressed against his chest, her blue eyes suddenly sincere. "I've never had an orgasm with a man before. I have them on my own. But never with… Never with a partner. I've only been with two men. But… They were my boyfriends. So you would think that if it was this easy they would have figured it out. Or I would have figured it out. And I can't for the life of me figure out why we didn't. Myself included."

"Chemistry," he said, brushing her hair back from her face, surprising himself with the tender gesture. But now she was asking him these wide-eyed innocent questions, when she had done things with him only moments ago that were anything but.

"Chemistry," she said. "I thought it might be something like that. Something magical and strange and completely impossible to re-create in a lab setting, sadly."

"We can re-create it right now."

"But what if I can't ever re-create it again? Although,

I suppose now I know that it's possible for me to feel this way, I…"

"I didn't know that I was your one-man sexual revolution."

"Well, I didn't want to put that kind of pressure on you."

"I thrive under pressure."

It was easy to forget, right now, that she was the daughter of his enemy. That he was here to destroy her family. That her engagement and the lack of chemistry between herself and her fiancé would be the least of her worries in the next week.

In fact, maybe he could spare her from the marriage. Because the optics for the family would be pretty damned reduced, probably beyond the point of healing. Her marriage to an ad exec was hardly going to fix that.

And anyway, the man would probably be much less interested in marrying into the Maxfield dynasty when it was reduced to more of a one-horse outfit and they didn't have two coins to rub together.

Holden waited for there to be guilt. But he didn't feel it.

Instead, he felt some kind of indefinable sense of satisfaction. Like in the past few moments he had collected another chess piece that had once belonged to his enemy. And Emerson was so much more than a pawn.

But he didn't know how to play this victory. Not yet.

And anyway, she didn't feel much like a victory or a conquest lying here in bed with him when he was still naked. He felt more than a little bit conquered himself.

"This is terrifying," she whispered. "Because I shouldn't be here. And I shouldn't be with you at all. And I think this is the most relaxed and maybe even the happiest I've ever felt in my life." She looked up at him, and a tear tracked down her cheek, and just like that, the guilt hit him right in the chest. "And I know that it can't go beyond tonight. I know it can't. Because you have your life... And I have mine."

"And there's no chance those two things could ever cross," he said, the words coming out a hell of a lot more hostile than he intended.

"I'm not trying to be snobby or anything," she said. "But there's expectations about the kind of man that I'll end up with. And what he'll bring to the family."

"Princess, I don't know why you're talking about marriage."

"Well, that's another problem in and of itself, isn't it? I'm at that point. Where marriage has to be considered."

"You're at that point? What the hell does that mean? Are we in the 1800s?"

"In a family like mine, it matters. We have to... My father doesn't have sons. His daughters have to marry well, marry men who respect and uphold the winery. His sons-in-law are going to gain a certain amount of ownership of the place, and that means..."

"His sons-in-law are getting ownership of the business?"

"Yes," she said. "I mean, I'll retain my share as well, so don't think it's that kind of draconian nonsense. But when we marry, Donovan is going to get a share of the winery. As large as mine. When Wren marries, it will be the same. Then there's Cricket, and her husband will get a share as well, though not as large. And by the time that's all finished, my father will only have a portion. A very small portion."

"How does that math work? Cricket gets less?"

"Well, so far Cricket doesn't have any interest in running the place, and she never has. So yes."

"No wonder your father is so invested in controlling who you marry."

"It's for my protection as well. It's not like he wants me getting involved with fortune hunters."

"You really are from another world," he said, disdain in his voice, even though he didn't mean it to be there. Because it didn't matter. Because it wasn't true—he had money, he had status. And because he didn't care about her. Or her opinion. He didn't care that she was as shallow as the rest of her family, as her father. It didn't concern him and, in fact, was sort of helpful given the fact that he had taken pretty terrible advantage of her, that he'd lied to her to get her into bed.

"I can tell that you think I'm a snob," she said. "I'm not, I promise. I wouldn't get naked with a man I thought was beneath me."

"Well, that's BS. It's a pretty well-documented fact that people find slumming to be titillating, Emerson."

"Well, I don't. You're different. And yes, I find that sexy. You're forbidden, and maybe I find that sexy too, but it's not about you being less than me, or less than other men that I've been with. Somehow, you're more, and I don't know what to do with that. That's why it hurts. Because I don't know if I will ever feel as contented, ever again, as I do right now lying in this cabin, and this is not supposed to be..."

"It's not supposed to be anything you aspire to. How could it be? When your mother thinks that what you have is beneath you as it is."

She swallowed and looked away. "My life's not mine. It's attached to this thing my father built from scratch.

This legacy that has meant a life that I'm grateful for, whatever you might think. I don't need to have gone without to understand that what I've been given is extraordinary. I do understand that. But it's an incredible responsibility to bear as well, and I have to be…a steward of it. Whether I want to be or not."

And suddenly, he resented it all. Every last bit. The lies that stood between them, the way she saw him, and his perceived lack of power in this moment. He growled, reversing their positions so he was over her.

"None of that matters just now," he said.

She looked up at him, and then she touched his face. "No," she agreed. "I don't suppose it does."

He reached down and found her red lace bra, touching the flimsy fabric and then looking back at her. He took hold of her wrists, like he'd done earlier, and, this time, secured them tightly with the lace.

"Right now, you're here," he said. "And I'm the only thing you need to worry about. You're mine right here, and there's nothing outside this room, off of this bed, do you understand?"

Her breath quickened, her breasts rising and falling with the motion. She nodded slowly.

"Good girl," he said. "You have a lot of responsibilities outside, but when you're here, the only thing you have to worry about is pleasing me."

This burned away the words of the last few minutes, somehow making it all feel okay again, even if it shouldn't. As if securing her wrists now might help him hold on to this moment a little tighter. Before he had to worry about the rest, before he had to deal with the fallout and what it would mean for Emerson.

This thing that she cared about so deeply, this dynasty, which she was willing to marry a man she didn't care about at all to secure.

He would free her from it, and in the end, it might be a blessing.

He looked at the way her wrists were tied, and suddenly he didn't want to free her at all.

What he wanted was to keep her.

He got a condom from his wallet and returned to her, where she lay on the bed, her wrists bound, her thighs spread wide in invitation.

He sheathed himself and gripped her hips, entering her in one smooth stroke. Her climax was instant, and it was hard, squeezing him tight as he pounded into her without mercy.

And he set about proving to her that there was no limit to the number of times she could find her pleasure.

But there was a cost to that game, one that crystallized in his mind after the third time she cried out his name and settled herself against his chest, her wrists still tightly tied.

She was bound to him now.

And she had betrayed a very crucial piece of information.

And the ways it could all come together for him became suddenly clear.

He knew exactly what he was going to do.

Seven

It had been three days since her night in the cabin with Holden. And he was all she could think about. She knew she was being ridiculous. They had another event happening at the winery tonight, and she couldn't afford to be distracted.

There was going to be an engagement party in the large barn, which had been completely and totally made over into an elegant, rustic setting, with vast open windows that made the most of the view, and elegant chandeliers throughout.

Tonight's event wasn't all on her shoulders. Mostly, it was Wren's responsibility, but Emerson was helping, and she had a feeling that in her current state she wasn't helping much.

All she could do was think about Holden. The things he had done to her body. The things he had taught her about her body.

She felt like an idiot. Spinning fantasies about a man, obsessing about him.

She'd never realized she would be into something like bondage, but he had shown her the absolute freedom there could be in giving up control.

She was so used to controlling everything all the time. And for just a few hours in his bed, he had taken the lead. It was like a burden had been lifted from her.

"Are you there, Emerson? It's me, Wren."

Emerson turned to look at her sister, who was fussing with the guest list in front of her.

"I'm here, and I've been here, helping you obsess over details."

"You're here," Wren said. "But you're not *here*."

Emerson looked down at her left hand and cursed. Because there was supposed to be a ring there. She had taken it off before going to Holden's cabin, but she needed to get it back on before tonight. Before she was circulating in a room full of guests

Tonight's party was different from a brand-related launch. The event was at the heart of the winery itself, and as the manager of the property, Wren was the person taking the lead. When it came to broader brand representation, it was down to Emerson. But Emerson would still be taking discreet photographs of the event to share on social media, as that helped with the broader awareness of the brand.

Their jobs often crossed, as this was a family operation and not a large corporation. But neither of them minded. And in fact, Emerson considered it a good day when she got to spend extra time with her sister. But less so today when Wren was so apparently frazzled.

"What's wrong with you?" Wren asked, and then her

eye fell meaningfully to her left hand. "Did something happen with Donovan?"

"No," Emerson said. "I just forgot to put the ring on."

"That doesn't sound like you. Because you're ever conscious of the fact that a ring like that is a statement."

"I'm well aware of what I'm ever conscious of, *Wren*," she said. "I don't need you to remind me."

"And yet, you forgot something today, so it seems like you need a reminder."

"It's really nothing."

"Except it *is* something. Because if it were nothing, then you wouldn't be acting weird."

"Fine. Don't tell anyone," Emerson said, knowing already that she would regret what she was about to say.

"I like secrets," Wren said, leaning in.

"I had a… I had a one-night stand." Her sister stared at her. Unmoving. "With a man."

Wren huffed a laugh. "Well, I didn't figure you were telling me about the furniture in your bedroom."

"I mean, Donovan and I aren't exclusive, but it didn't feel right to wear his ring while I was…with someone else."

"I had no idea," Wren said, her eyes widening. "I didn't know you were that…"

"Much of a hussy?"

"That *progressive*," she said.

"Well, I'm not. In general. But I was, and am a little thrown off by it. And no one can ever know."

"Solemnly swear."

"You cannot tell Cricket."

"Why would I tell Cricket? She would never be able to look you in the eyes again, and she would absolutely give you away. Not on purpose, mind you."

"No, but it's a secret that she couldn't handle."

"Absolutely."

"Have you met a man that you just…couldn't get out of your head even though he was absolutely unsuitable?"

Wren jolted, her whole body looking like it had been touched by a live wire. "I am very busy with my job."

"Wren."

"Yes. Fine. I do know what it's like to have a sexual obsession with the wrong guy. But I've never…acted on it." The look on her face was so horrified it would have been funny, if Emerson herself hadn't just done the thing that so appalled her sister.

"There's nothing wrong with…being with someone you want, is there? No, I don't really know him, but I knew I wanted him and that seems like a decent reason to sleep with someone, right?"

Wren looked twitchy. "I… Look. Lust and like aren't the same. I get it."

"I like him fine enough," Emerson said. "But we can't ever… *He works for Dad.*"

"Like…in the corporate office?"

"No, like, on the ranch."

"Emersonnnnn."

"What?"

"Are you living out a stable boy fantasy?"

Emerson drew her lip between her teeth and worried it back and forth. "He's not a boy. He's a man. On that you can trust me."

"The question stands."

"Maybe it was sort of that fantasy, I don't know. It was a fantasy, that much I can tell you. But it was supposed to just happen and be done, and I'm obsessing about him instead."

"Who would have ever thought that could happen?" Wren asked in mock surprise.

"In this advanced modern era, I should simply be able to claim my sexuality. Own it! Bring it with me wherever I go. Not…leave it behind in some run-down cabin with the hottest man I've ever seen in my life."

"Those are truly sage words. You should put them on a pretty graphic and post it to your page. Hashtag—girl-boss-of-your-own-sexuality. Put your hair up and screw his brains out!"

Emerson shot her sister a deadly glare. "You know I hate that."

"I also know you never put a toe out of line, and yet here you are, confessing an extremely scandalous transgression."

"This secret goes to your grave with you, or I put you in the ground early, do you understand?"

Wren smirked and seemed to stretch a little taller, as if reminding Emerson she'd outgrown her by two inches when she was thirteen. She and Wren definitely looked like sisters—the same dark hair and blue eyes—but Wren wasn't curvy. She was tall and lean, her hair sleek like her build. She'd honed her more athletic figure with Krav Maga, kickboxing and all other manner of relatively violent exercise.

She claimed it was the only reason she hadn't killed Creed Cooper yet.

She also claimed she liked knowing she *could* kill him if the occasion arose at one of the many different venues where they crossed paths.

Her martial arts skills were yet another reason it was

hilarious for Emerson to threaten her sister. She'd be pinned to the ground in one second flat. Though, as the older sibling, she'd done her part to emotionally scar her sister to the point that, when she'd outgrown her, she still believed on some level Emerson could destroy her.

"In all seriousness," Wren said, "it does concern me. I mean, that you're marrying Donovan, and you're clearly more into whoever this other guy is."

"Right. Because I'm going to marry one of the men that work here. That would go over like... What's heavier than a lead balloon?"

"Does it matter?"

"What kind of ridiculous question is that? Of course it matters."

"Dad has never shown the slightest bit of interest in who I'm dating or not dating."

"You're not the oldest. I think... I think he figures he'll get me out of the way first. And it isn't a matter of him showing interest in who I'm dating. He directly told me that Donovan was the sort of man that I should associate with. He set me up with him."

"You're just going to marry who Dad tells you to marry?"

"Would you do differently, Wren? Honestly, I'm asking you."

"I don't think I could marry a man that I wasn't even attracted to."

"If Dad told you a certain man met with his approval, if he pushed you in that direction...you wouldn't try to make it work?"

Wren looked away. "I don't know. I guess I might have to try, but if after two years I still wasn't interested physically..."

"Marriage is a partnership. Our bodies will change. And sex drives and attraction will all change too. We need to have something in common. I mean, it makes way more sense to marry a man I have a whole host of things in common with than it does to marry one who I just want to be naked with."

"I didn't suggest you marry the ranch hand. But perhaps there's some middle ground. A man you like to talk to, and a man you want to sleep with."

"Well, I have yet to find a middle ground that would be suitable for Dad."

Anyway, Emerson didn't think that Holden could be called a middle ground. Not really. He was something so much more than that. Much too much of an extreme to be called something as neutral as middle ground.

"Maybe you should wait until you do."

"Or maybe I should just do what feels best," Emerson said. "I mean, maybe my marriage won't be the best of the best. Maybe I can't have everything. But we are really lucky, you and I. Look at this life." She gestured around the barn. "We have so much. I can make do with whatever I don't have."

Wren looked sad. "I don't know. That seems…tragic to me."

"What about you? You said you wanted a man and you haven't done anything about it."

"That's different."

"So, there's a man you want, and you can't be with him."

"I don't even like him," she said.

Emerson felt bowled over by that statement. Because there was only one man Emerson knew who Wren hated. And the idea that Wren might want him…

Well, no wonder Wren could barely even speak of it. She hated Creed Cooper more than anything else on earth. If the two of them ever touched…well, they would create an explosion of one kind or another, and Emerson didn't know how she hadn't realized that before.

Possibly because she had never before experienced the kind of intense clash she had experienced just a few nights ago with Holden.

"You do understand, then," Emerson said. "That there is a difference between wanting and having. And having for a limited time." She looked down. "Yes, I'm wildly attracted to this guy, and our chemistry is amazing. But it could never be more than that. Though, as someone who has experienced the temporary fun… You know you could."

Wren affected a full-body shudder.

"I really couldn't. I really, really couldn't."

"Suit yourself. But I'm going to go ahead and say that you're not allowed to give me advice anymore, because you live in a big glass house."

"I do not. It's totally different. I'm not marrying someone I shouldn't."

"Well, I'm marrying someone Dad wants me to. I trust Dad. And at the end of the day, I guess that's it. I'm trusting that it's going to be okay because it's what Dad wants me to do, and he's never… He's never steered me wrong. He's never hurt me. All he's ever done is support me."

Her father wanted the best for her. And she knew it. She was just going to have to trust that in the end, like she trusted him.

"I know," Wren said, putting her arm around Emerson. "At least you have some good memories now."

Emerson smiled. "Really good."

"I don't want details," Wren said, patting Emerson's shoulder.

She flashed back to being tied up in bed with Holden. "I am not giving you details. Those are sacred."

"As long as we're on the same page."

Emerson smiled and went back to the checklist she was supposed to be dealing with. "We are on the same page. Which is currently a checklist. Tonight's party will go off without a hitch."

"Don't jinx it," Wren said, knocking resolutely on one of the wooden tables.

"I'm not going to jinx it. It's one of your parties. So you know it's going to be absolutely perfect."

Eight

The party was going off without a hitch.

Everyone was enjoying themselves, and Emerson was in visual heaven, finding any number of photo opportunities buried in the meticulous decorations that Wren had arranged. With the permission of the couple, she would even share photographs of them, and of the guests. This, at least, served to distract her mildly from the situation with Holden.

Except, there was no *situation*, that was the thing. But it was very difficult for her brain to let go of that truth.

She wanted there to be a situation. But like she had said to Wren earlier, there was really no point in entertaining that idea at all. Marriage was more than just the marriage bed.

And she and Holden might be compatible between the sheets—they were so compatible it made her pulse with desire even thinking about it—but that didn't mean they would be able to make a *relationship*, much less a *marriage*.

They had nothing in common.

You're assuming. You don't actually know that.

Well, it was true. She didn't know, but she could certainly look at the circumstances of his life and make some assumptions.

A passing waiter caught her eye, and she reached out to take hold of a glass of champagne. That was when a couple of things happened all at once. And because they happened so quickly, the reality took her longer to untangle than it might have otherwise.

The first thing she noticed was a man so stunning he took her breath away as he walked into the room.

The second realization was that she knew that man. Even though he looked so different in the sleekly cut black tux he had on his fit body that the name her brain wanted to apply to him couldn't seem to stick.

The third thing that happened was her heart dropping into her feet.

And she didn't even know why.

Because Holden had just walked in wearing a tux.

It might have taken a moment for her brain to link all those details up, but it had now.

She just couldn't figure out what it meant.

That he looked like this. That he was here.

He took a glass of champagne from a tray, and scanned the room. He looked different. But also the same.

Because while he might be clothed in an extremely refined fashion, there was still a ruggedness about him.

Something wild and untamed, even though, on a surface level, he blended in with the people around them.

No, not blended in.

He could never blend in.

He was actually dressed much nicer than anyone else here.

That suit was clearly custom, and it looked horrendously expensive. As did his shoes. As did...everything about him. And could he really be the same man she had happened upon shirtless cutting wood the other day? The same man who had tied her up in his run-down little cabin? The same man who had done desperate, dirty things to her?

And then his eyes collided with hers.

And he smiled.

It made her shiver. It made her ache.

But even so, it was a stranger's smile. It was not the man she knew, and she couldn't make sense of that certainty, even to herself. He walked across the room, acknowledging no one except for her.

And she froze. Like a deer being stalked by a mountain lion. Her heart was pounding in her ears, the sound louder now than the din of chatter going on around her.

"Just the woman I was looking for," he said.

Why did he sound different? He'd been confident in their every interaction. Had never seemed remotely cowed by her position or her money. And maybe that was the real thing she was seeing now.

Not a different man, but one who looked in his element rather than out of it.

"What are you doing here? And where did you get that suit?"

"Would you believe my fairy godmother visited?" The dark humor twisted his lips into a wry smile.

"No," she said, her heart pounding more viciously in her temple.

"Then would you believe that a few of the mice that live in the cabin made the suit for me?"

"Even less likely to believe that. You don't seem like a friend of mice."

"Honey, I'm not really a friend of anyone. And I'm real sorry for what I'm about to do. But if you cooperate with me, things are going to go a whole lot better."

She looked around. As if someone other than him might have answers. Of course, no one offered any if they did. "What do you mean?"

"You see, I haven't been completely honest with you."

"What?"

She couldn't make any sense of this. She looked around the room to see if they were attracting attention, because surely they must be. Because she felt like what was happening between them was shining bright like a beacon on the hill. But somehow they weren't attracting any attention at all.

"Why don't we go outside. I have a meeting with your father in just a few minutes. Unless…unless you are willing to negotiate with me."

"You have a meeting with my father? Negotiate what?"

The thoughts that rolled through her mind sent her into a panic.

He had obviously filmed what had happened between them. He was going to extort money from her family. He was a con man. No *wonder* he didn't want his picture taken.

All those accusations hovered on the edge of her lips, but she couldn't make them. Not here.

"What do you want?" she asked.

He said nothing. The man was a rock in a suit. No more sophisticated than he'd been in jeans. She'd thought he was different, but he wasn't. This was the real man.

And he was harder, darker than the man she'd imagined he'd been.

Funny how dressing up made that clear.

"What do you want?" she asked again.

She refused to move. She felt like the biggest fool on the planet. How had she trusted this man with her body? He was so clearly not who he said, so clearly...

Of course he hadn't actually wanted her. Of course the only man she wanted was actually just playing a game.

"Revenge," he said. "Nothing more. I'm sorry that you're caught in the middle of it."

"Did you film us?" She looked around, trying to see if people had noticed him yet. They still hadn't. "Did you film us together?"

"No," he said. "I'm not posting anything up on the internet, least of all that."

"Are you going to show my father?"

"No," he said, his lip curling. "This isn't about you, Emerson, whether you believe me or not. It isn't. But what I do next is about you. So I need you to come outside with me."

He turned, without waiting to see if she was with him, and walked back out of the barn. Emerson looked around and then darted after his retreating figure.

When they reached the outdoors, it was dim out, just

like the first night they had met. And when he turned to face her, she had the most ridiculous flashback.

He had been in jeans then. With that cowboy hat. And here he was now in a tux. But it was that moment that brought the reality of the situation into focus.

This man was the same man she had been seduced by. Or had she seduced him? It didn't even make sense anymore.

"Tell me what's going on." She looked him up and down. "You clearly aren't actually a ranch hand."

"Your father *did* hire me. Legitimately. So, I guess in total honesty, I do work for your father, and I am a ranch hand."

"What else are you? Are you paparazzi?"

He looked appalled by that. "I'm not a bottom-feeder that makes his living on the misfortunes of others."

"Then what are you? Why are you here?"

"I came here to destroy the winery."

She drew back. The venom in his voice was so intense she could feel the poison sinking down beneath her skin.

He looked her up and down. "But whether or not I do that is up to you now."

"What the hell are you talking about?"

"Your father. Your father had an affair with my sister."

"Your sister? I don't… My father did not have an affair. My father and mother have been married for…more than thirty years. And your sister would have to be…"

"She's younger than you," Holden said. "Younger than you, and incredibly naive about the ways of the world. And your father took advantage of her. When she got pregnant, he tried to pay her to get an abortion, and when she wouldn't, he left. She miscarried, and she's had nothing but health problems since. She's attempted suicide twice and had to be hospitalized. Your father ruined her. Absolutely ruined her."

"No," Emerson said. "It's a mistake. My father would never do that. He would never hurt…"

"I'm not here to argue semantics with you. You can come with me. I'm about to have a meeting with your father, though he doesn't know why. He'll tell you the whole story."

"What does this have to do with me?"

"It didn't have anything to do with you. Until you came to the cabin the other day. I was happy to leave you alone, but you pursued it, and then… And then you told me something very interesting. About the winery. And who'd own it."

Emerson felt like she might pass out. "The man I marry."

"Exactly." He looked at her, those dark eyes blazing. "So you have two choices, really. Let me have that meeting with your father, and you're welcome to attend, where I'll be explaining to him how I've found stacks of NDAs in his employee files. And it doesn't take a genius to figure out why."

"What?"

"Your father has engaged in many, many affairs with workers here on the property. Once I got ahold of the paperwork in his office, I got in touch with some of the women. Most of them wouldn't talk, but enough did. Coercion. And so much of the money for your vineyard comes through all of your celebrity endorsements. Can you imagine the commercial fallout if your father is found to be yet another man who abuses his power? Manipulates women into bed?"

"I don't believe you."

"It doesn't matter whether you believe me or not, Emerson. What matters is that I know I can make other people believe me. And when this is over, you won't be able to give Maxfield wines away with a car wash."

"I don't understand what that gives you," she said, horror coursing through her veins. She couldn't even entertain the idea of this being true. But the truth of it wasn't the thing, not now. The issue was what he could do.

"Revenge," he said, his voice low and hard.

"Revenge isn't a very lucrative business."

"I don't need the revenge to pay. But… I won't lie to you, I find the idea of revenge and a payout very compelling. The idea of owning a piece of this place instead of simply destroying it. So tell me, how does it work? Your husband getting a stake in the business."

"I get married, and then I just call the lawyers, and they'll do the legal paperwork."

His expression became decisive. "Then you and I are getting married."

"And if I don't?"

"I'll publicize the story. I will make sure to ruin the brand. However, if I marry you, what I'll have is ownership of the brand. And you and I, with our united stakes, will have a hell of a lot of decision-making power."

"But to what end?"

"I want your father to know that I ended up owning part of this. And what I do after that…that will depend on what he's willing to do. But I want to make sure he has to contend with me for as long as I want. Yes,

I could ruin the label. But that would destroy everything that you and your sister have worked so hard for, and I'm not necessarily here to hurt you. But gaining a piece of this… Making sure my sister gets something, making sure your father knows that I'm right there… That has value to me."

"What about Donovan?"

"He's not my problem. But it's your call, Emerson. You can marry Donovan. And inherit the smoldering wreckage that I'll leave behind. Or, you marry me."

"How do I know you're telling the truth?"

"Look up Soraya Jane on your favorite social media site."

"I… Wait. I know who she is. She's… She has millions of followers."

"I know," he said.

"She's your sister."

"Yes."

"And…"

"My name is Holden. Holden McCall. I am not famous on the internet, or really anywhere. But I'm one of the wealthiest developers in the state. With my money, my sister gained some connections, got into modeling. Started traveling."

"She's built an empire online," Emerson said.

"I know," he said. "What she's done is nothing short of incredible. But she's lost herself. Your father devastated her. Destroyed her. And I can't let that stand."

"So I… If I don't marry you…you destroy everything. And the reason for me marrying Donovan doesn't even exist anymore."

"That's the size of it."

"And we have to transfer everything before my father realizes what you're doing."

Emerson had no idea what to do. No idea what to think. Holden could be lying to her about all of this, but if he wasn't, then he was going to destroy the winery, and there was really no way for her to be sure about which one was true until it was too late.

"Well, what do we do, then?"

"I told you, that is up to you."

"Okay. So say we get married. Then what?"

"You were already prepared to marry a man you didn't love, might as well be me."

Except… This was worse than marrying a man she didn't love.

She had trusted Holden with something deep and real. Some part of her that she had never shown to anyone else. She had trusted him enough to let him tie her hands.

To let him inside her body.

And now she had to make a decision about marrying him. On the heels of discovering that she didn't know him at all.

"I'll marry you," she said. "I'll marry you."

Nine

The roar of victory in Holden's blood hadn't quieted, not even by the time they boarded his private plane. They'd left the party and were now taking off from the regional airport, bound for Las Vegas, and he was amused by the fact that they both just so happened to be dressed for a wedding, though they hadn't planned it.

"Twenty-four-hour wedding chapels and no waiting period," he said, lifting a glass of champagne, and then extending his hand and offering it to her.

The plane was small, but nicely appointed, and fairly quiet.

He wasn't extraordinarily attached to a great many of the creature comforts that had come with his wealth. But being able to go where he wanted, when he wanted, and without a plane full of people was certainly his favorite.

"You have your own plane," she said, taking the glass

of champagne and downing it quickly. "You are private-plane rich."

She didn't look impressed so much as pissed.

"Yep," he said.

She shook her head, incredulous. "I… I don't even know what to say to that."

"I didn't ask you to say anything."

"No. You asked me to marry you."

"I believe I *demanded* that you marry me or I'd ruin your family."

"My mistake," she said, her tone acerbic. "How could I be so silly?"

"You may not believe me, but I told you, I didn't intend to involve you in this."

"I just conveniently involved myself?"

"If it helps, I found it an inconvenience at first."

"Why? You felt *guilty*? In the middle of your quest to take down my family and our fortune? Yes, that must've been inconvenient for you."

"I didn't want to drag you into it," he said. "Because I'm not your father. And I sure as hell wasn't going to extract revenge by using you for sex. The sex was separate. I only realized the possibilities when you told me about how your husband would be given an ownership stake in the vineyard."

"Right," she said. "Of course. Because I was an idiot who thought that since you had been inside me, I could maybe have a casual conversation with you."

"I'm sorry, but the information was too good for me to let go. And in the end, your family gets off easier."

"Except that you might do something drastic and destroy the winery with your control of the share."

"I was absolutely going to do that, but now I can own

a piece of it instead. And that benefits me. I also have his daughter, right with me."

"Oh, are you going to hold a gun to my head for dramatics?"

"No gun," he said. "In fact, we're on a private plane, and you're drinking champagne. You're not in any danger from me, and I didn't force you to come with me."

"But you did," she said, her voice thick.

"I offered you two choices."

"I didn't like either of them."

"Welcome to life, princess. You not liking your options isn't the same as you not having any."

She ignored that statement. "This is *not* my life."

"It is now." He appraised her for a long moment, the elegant line of her profile. She was staring out the window, doing her very best not to look at him. "The Big Bad Wolf was always going to try and eat you. You know how the fairy tale goes."

"Say whatever you need to say to make yourself feel better," she said. "You're not a wolf. You're just a dick."

"And your father?"

That seemed to kill her desire to banter with him. "I don't know if I believe you."

"But you believe me just enough to be on a plane with me going to Las Vegas to get married, because if I'm right, if I'm telling the truth..."

"It ruins everything. And I don't think I trust anyone quite so much that I would take that chance. Not even my father. I don't trust you at all, but what choice do I have? Because you're right. I was willing to marry a man that I didn't love to support my family. To support the empire. The dynasty. So why the hell wouldn't I do it now?"

"Oh, but you hate me, don't you?"

"I do," she said. "I really do."

He could sense that there was more she wanted to say, but that she wouldn't. And they were silent for the next hour, until the plane touched down in Nevada.

"Did you want an Elvis impersonator?" he asked, when they arrived on the Strip, at the little white wedding chapel he'd reserved before they landed.

"And me without my phone," she said.

"Did you want to take pictures and post them?"

She narrowed her eyes. "I wanted to beat you over the head with it."

"That doesn't answer my question about Elvis."

"Yeah, that would be good. If we don't have an Elvis impersonator, the entire wedding will be ruined."

"Don't tease me, because I will get the Elvis impersonator."

"Get him," she said, making a broad gesture. "Please. Because otherwise this would be *absurd*."

The edge of hysteria in her voice suggested she felt it was already absurd, but he chose to take what she said as gospel.

And he checked the box on the ridiculous paperwork, requesting Elvis, because she thought he was kidding, and she was going to learn very quickly that he was not a man to be trifled with. Even when it came to things like this.

They waited until their names were called.

And sadly, the only impersonator who was available past ten thirty on a Saturday night seemed to be Elvis from the mid-1970s.

"Do you want me to sing 'Burning Love' or 'Can't

Help Falling in Love' at the end of the ceremony?" he asked in all seriousness.

"Pick your favorite," Emerson replied, her face stony.

And Holden knew she had been certain that this level of farce would extinguish the thing that burned between them. Because she hated him now, and he could see the truth of that in her eyes.

But he was happy to accept her challenge. Happy to stand there exchanging vows with an Elvis impersonator as officiant, and a woman in a feathered leotard as witness, because it didn't change the fact that he wanted her.

Desperately.

That all he could think about was when this was finished, he was going to take her up to a lavish suite and have her fifty different ways.

And she might not think she wanted it, but she would.

She might think that she could burn it all out with her anger, but she couldn't. He knew it.

He knew it because he was consumed by it.

He should feel only rage. Should feel only the need for revenge.

But he didn't.

And she wouldn't either.

"You may kiss the bride," Elvis said.

She looked at him with a warning in her eyes, but that warning quickly became a challenge.

She would learn pretty quickly that he didn't back down from a challenge.

He cupped her chin with his hand, and kissed her, hard and fast, but just that light, quick brush of their mouths left them both breathing hard.

And as soon as they separated, the music began to

play and Elvis started singing about how he just couldn't help falling in love.

Well, Holden could sure as hell help falling in love. But he couldn't keep himself from wanting Emerson. That was a whole different situation.

They signed the paperwork quickly, and as soon as they were in the car that had been waiting for them, he handed her his phone. "Call your lawyer."

"It's almost midnight," she said.

"He'll take a call from you, you know it. We need to get everything set into motion so we have it all signed tomorrow morning."

"*She* will take a call from me," she said pointedly. But then she did as he asked. "Hi, Julia. It's Emerson. I just got married." He could hear a voice saying indiscriminate words on the other end. "Thank you. I need to make sure that I transfer the shares of the company into my husband's name. As soon as possible." She looked over at him. "Where are we staying?"

She recited all of the necessary information back to Julia at his direction, including the information about him, before getting off the phone.

"She'll have everything faxed to us by morning."

"And she won't tip off your father?"

"No," she said. "She's the family lawyer, but she must know… She's going to realize that I eloped. And she's going to realize that I'm trying to bypass my father. That I want my husband to have the ownership shares he—I—is entitled to. She won't allow my father to interfere."

"She's a friend of yours, then."

"We became friends, yes. People who aren't liars make friends."

"I'm wounded."

"I didn't think you could wound granite."

"Why did you comply with what I asked you to do so easily?"

Suddenly, her voice sounded very small and tired. "Because. It makes no sense to come here, to marry you, if I don't follow through with the rest. You'll ruin my family if you don't get what you asked for. I'm giving it to you. Protesting now is like tying my own self to the railroad tracks, and damsel in distress isn't my style." She looked at him, her blue eyes certain. "I made my bed. I'll lie in it."

They pulled up to the front of a glitzy casino hotel that was far from his taste in anything.

But what he did like about Las Vegas was the sexual excess. Those who created the lavish hotel rooms here understood exactly why a man was willing to pay a lot of money for a hotel room. And it involved elaborate showers, roomy bathtubs and beds that could accommodate all manner of athletics.

The decor didn't matter to him at all with those other things taken into consideration.

They got out of the car, and he tipped the valet.

"Your secretary called ahead, Mr. McCall," the man said. "You're all checked in and ready to go straight upstairs. A code has been texted to your phone."

Holden put his arm around her, and the two of them began to walk to an elevator. "I hope you don't think… I… We're going to a hotel room and…" Emerson said.

"Do you think you're going to share a space with me tonight and keep your hands off me?"

They got inside the elevator, and the doors closed. "I hate you," she said, shoving at his chest.

"And you want me," he said. "And that might make you hate me even more, but it doesn't make it not true."

"I want to…"

"Go ahead," he said. "Whatever you want."

"I'm going to tear that tux right off your body," she said, her voice low and feral. "Absolutely destroy it."

"Only if I can return the favor," he said, arousal coursing through him.

"You might not be all that confident when I have the most fragile part of you in my hand."

He didn't know why, but that turned him on. "I'll take my chances."

"I don't understand what this is," she said. "I should be…disgusted by you."

"It's too late. You already got dirty with me, honey. You might as well just embrace it. Because you know how good it is between us. And you wanted me when I was nothing other than a ranch hand. Why wouldn't you want me when you know that I'm a rich man with a vengeful streak a mile wide?"

"You forced me into this."

"I rescued you from that boring bowl of oatmeal you called a fiancé. At least you hate me. You didn't feel anything for him."

Her hackles were up by the time they got to the suite door, and he entered his code. The door opened and revealed the lavish room that had all the amenities he wanted out of such a place.

"This is tacky," she said, throwing her purse down on the couch.

"And?"

"Warm," she said.

She reached behind her body and grabbed hold of

her zipper, pulling down the tab and letting her dress fall to the floor.

"I figured you were going to make me work for it."

"Your ego doesn't deserve that. Then you'd get to call it a seduction. I want to fuck you, I can't help myself. But I'm not sure you should be particularly flattered by that. I hate myself for it."

"Feel free to indulge your self-loathing, particularly if at some point it involves you getting that pretty lipstick all over me."

"I'm sure it will. Because I'm here with you. And there's not much I can do about my choices now. We're married. And a stake in the vineyard is close to being transferred into your name. I've already had sex with you. I got myself into this. I might as well have an orgasm."

"We can certainly do better than one orgasm," he said.

She looked good enough to eat, standing there in some very bridal underwear, all white and lacy, and unintentionally perfect for the moment, still wearing the red high heels she'd had on with her dress.

He liked her like this.

But he liked her naked even better.

She walked over to where he stood, grabbed hold of his tie and made good on her promise.

She wrenched the knot loose, then tore at his shirt, sending buttons scattering across the floor. "I hope that was expensive," she said, moving her hand over his bare chest.

"It was," he said. "Very, very expensive. But sadly for you, expensive doesn't mean anything to me. I could buy ten more and not notice the expense."

He could see the moment when realization washed over her. About who had the power. She was so very comfortable with her financial status and she'd had an idea about his, and what that meant, and even though she'd seen the plane, seen him in the tux, the reality of who he'd been all along was just now hitting her.

"And to think," she said, "I was very worried about taking advantage of you that night we were together."

"That says more about you and the way you view people without money than it does about me, sweetheart."

"Not because of that. You work for my father. By extension, for me, since I own part of the winery. And I was afraid that I might be taking advantage of you. But here you were, so willing to blackmail me."

"Absolutely. Life's a bastard, and so am I. That's just the way of things."

"Here I thought she was a bitch. Which I've always found handy, I have to say." She pushed his shirt off his shoulders, and he shed it the rest of the way onto the floor, and then she unhooked his belt, pulling it through the loops.

He grinned. "Did you want to use that?"

"What?"

"You know, you could tie me down if you wanted," he said. "If it would make you feel better. Make you feel like you have some control."

Something flared in her eyes, but he couldn't quite read it. "Why would I want that? That wouldn't give me more control. It would just mean I was doing most of the work." She lifted her wrists up in supplication, her eyes never leaving his. "You can tie my wrists, and I'll still have the control."

He put the tip of the leather through the buckle, and looped it over her wrists, pulling the end tight before he looped it through the buckle again, her wrists held fast together. Then, those blue eyes never leaving his, she sank down onto her knees in front of him.

Ten

She had lost her mind, or something. Her heart was pounding so hard, a mixture of arousal, rage and shame pouring over her.

She should have told him no. She should have told him he was never touching her again. But something about her anger only made her want to play these games with him even more, and she didn't know what that said about her.

But he was challenging her, with everything from his marriage proposal to the Elvis at the chapel. This room itself was a challenge, and then the offer to let her tie him up.

All of it was seeing if he could make her or break her, and she refused to break. Because she was Emerson Maxfield, and she excelled at everything she did. And if this was the way she was going to save her family's dynasty, then she was going to save it on her knees in front of Holden McCall.

"You think I'm just going to give you what you want?" he asked, stroking himself through his pants. She could see the aggressive outline of his arousal beneath the dark fabric, and her internal muscles pulsed.

"Yes," she said. "Because I don't think you're strong enough to resist me."

"You might be right about that," he said. "Because I don't do resisting. I spent too much of my life wanting, and that's not something that I allow. I don't want anymore. I have."

He unhooked the closure on his pants, slid the zipper down slowly and then freed himself.

He wrapped his hand around the base, holding himself steady for her. She arched up on her knees and took him into her mouth, keeping her eyes on his the entire time.

With her hands bound as they were, she allowed him to guide her, her hair wrapped around his fist as he dictated her movements.

It was a game.

She could get out of the restraints if she wanted to. Could leave him standing there, hard and aching. But she was submitting to this fiction that she was trapped, because somehow, given the marriage—which she truly was trapped in—this felt like power.

This choice.

Feeling him begin to tremble as she took him in deep, feeling his power fracture as she licked him, tasted him.

She was the one bound, but he couldn't have walked away from her now if he wanted to, and she knew it.

They both did.

He held all the power outside this room, outside this moment. But she'd claimed her own here, and she was going to relish every second.

She teased him. Tormented him.

"Stand up," he said, the words scraping his throat raw.

She looked up at him, keeping her expression serene. "Are you not enjoying yourself?"

"Stand up," he commanded. "I want you to walk to the bed."

She stood slowly, her hands still held in that position of chosen obedience. Then with her eyes never leaving his, she walked slowly toward the bedroom. She didn't turn away from him until she had to, and even then, she could feel his gaze burning into her. Lighting a fire inside of her.

Whatever this was, it was bigger than them both.

Because he hated her father, and whether or not the reasons that he hated James Maxfield were strictly true or not, the fact was he did.

And she didn't get the impression that he was excited to find himself sexually obsessed with her. But he was.

She actually believed that what he wanted from her in terms of the winery was separate from him wanting her body, because this kind of intensity couldn't be faked.

And most important, it wasn't only on his side.

That had humiliated her at first.

The realization that she had been utterly captivated by this man, even while he was engaged in a charade.

But the fact of the matter was, he was just as enthralled with her.

They were both tangled in it.

Whether they wanted to be or not.

She climbed onto the bed, positioning herself on her back, her arms held straight down in front of her, covering her breasts, covering that space between her thighs. And she held that pose when he walked in.

Hunger lit his gaze and affirmed what she already knew to be true in her heart. He wanted her.

He hated it.

There was something so deliciously wicked about the contrast.

About this control she had over him even now.

A spark flamed inside her stomach.

He doesn't approve of this, or of you. But he can't help himself.

She arched her hips upward unconsciously, seeking some kind of satisfaction.

It was so much more arousing than it had any right to be. This moment of triumph.

Because it was private. Because it was secret.

Emerson lived for appearances.

She had been prepared to marry a man for those appearances.

And yet, this moment with Holden was about nothing more than the desire between two people. That he resented their connection? That only made it all feel stronger, hotter.

He removed his clothes completely as he approached the bed.

She looked down at her own body, realizing she was still wearing her bra and panties, her high heels.

"You like me like this," she whispered.

"I like you any way I can get you," he said, his voice low and filled with gravel.

"You like this, don't you? You had so much commentary on me wanting to slum it with a ranch hand. I think you like something about having a rich girl. Though, now I don't know why."

"Is there any man on earth who doesn't fantasize about corrupting the daughter of his enemy?"

"Did you corrupt me? I must've missed the memo."

"If I haven't yet, honey, then it's going to be a long night." He scooted her up the mattress, and lifted her arms, looping them back over her head, around one of the posts on the bed frame. Her hands parted, the leather from the belt stretching tight over the furniture, holding her fast. "At my mercy," he said.

He took his time with her then.

Took her high heels off her feet slowly, kissing her ankle, her calf, the inside of her thigh. Then he teased the edges of her underwear before pulling them down slowly, kissing her more intimately. He traveled upward, to her breasts, teasing her through the lace before removing the bra and casting it to the floor. And then he stood back, as if admiring his hard work.

"As fun as this is," he said, "I want your hands on me."

She could take her own hands out of the belt, but she refused. Refused to break the fiction that had built between the two of them.

So she waited. Waited as he slowly, painstakingly undid the belt and made a show of releasing her wrists. Her entire body pulsed with need for him. And thankfully, it was Vegas, so there were condoms on the bedside table.

He took care of the necessities, quickly, and then joined her on the bed, pinning her down on the mattress.

She smiled up at him, lifting her hand and tracing the line of his jaw with her fingertip. "Let's go for a ride," she whispered.

He growled, gripped her hips and held her steady as he entered her in one smooth stroke.

She gasped at the welcome invasion, arching against his body as he tortured them both mercilessly, drove them both higher than she thought she could stand.

And when she looked into his eyes, she saw the man she had been with that first night, not a rich stranger.

Holden.

His last name didn't matter. It didn't matter where he was from. What was real was *this*.

And she knew it, because their desire hadn't changed, even if their circumstances had. If anything, their desire had sharpened, grown in intensity.

And she believed with her whole soul that what they'd shared in his bed had never been about manipulating her.

Because the intensity was beyond them. Beyond sex in a normal sense, so much deeper. So much more terrifying.

She took advantage of her freedom. In every sense of the word.

The freedom of her hands to explore every ridge of muscle on his back, down his spine, to his sculpted ass.

And the freedom of being in this moment. A moment that had nothing to do with anything except need.

This…this benefited no one. In fact, it was a short road off a cliff, but that hadn't stopped either of them.

They couldn't stop.

He lowered his head, growling again as he thrust into her one last time, his entire body shaking with his release.

And she followed him over the edge.

She let out a hoarse cry, digging her fingernails into

his skin as she crested that wave of desire over and over again.

She didn't think it would end.

She thought she might die.

She thought she might not mind, if this was heaven, between the sheets with him.

And when her orgasm passed, she knew she was going to have to deal with the fact that he was her husband.

With the reality of what her father would think.

With Holden, her father's enemy, owning a share in the winery.

But those realizations made her head pound and her heart ache.

And she would rather focus on the places where her body burned with pleasure.

Tomorrow would come soon enough, and there would be documents to fax and sign, and they would have to fly back to Oregon.

But that was all for later.

And Emerson had no desire to check her phone. No desire to have any contact with the outside world.

No desire to take a picture to document anything.

Because none of this could be contained in a pithy post. None of it could even be summed up in something half so coherent as words.

The only communication they needed was between their bodies.

Tomorrow would require words. Explanations. Probably recriminations.

But tonight, they had this.

And so Emerson shut the world out, and turned to him.

Eleven

By the time he and his new wife were on a plane back to Oregon, Emerson was looking sullen.

"It's possible he'll know what happened by the time we get there," she said.

"But you're confident there's nothing he can do to stop it?"

She looked at him, prickles of irritation radiating off her. A sharp contrast to the willing woman who had been in his bed last night.

"Why do you care? It works out for you either way."

"True. But it doesn't work out particularly well for you."

"And you care about that?"

"I married you."

"Yeah, I still don't really get that. What exactly do you think is going to happen now?"

"We'll have a marriage. Why not?"

"You told me you didn't believe in marriage."

"I also told you I was a ranch hand."

"Have you been married before?" She frowned.

"No. Would it matter if I had?"

"In a practical sense, obviously nothing is a deal breaker, since I'm already married to you, for the winery. So no. But yes. Actually, it does."

"Never been married. No kids."

"Dammit," she said. "It didn't even occur to me that you might have children."

"Well, I don't."

"Thank God."

"Do you want to have some?"

The idea should horrify him. But for some reason, the image of Emerson getting round with his baby didn't horrify him at all. In fact, the side effect of bringing her into his plans pleased him in ways he couldn't quite articulate.

The idea of simply ruining James Maxfield had been risky. Because there was every chance that no matter how hard Holden tried there would be no serious blow-back for the man who had harmed Holden's sister the way that he had.

Wealthy men tended to be tougher targets than young women. Particularly young women who traded on the image of their beauty.

Not that Holden wasn't up to the task of trying to ruin the man.

Holden was powerful in his own right, and he was ruthless with it.

But there was something deeply satisfying about owning a piece of his enemy's legacy. And not only that, he got James's precious daughter in the bargain.

This felt right.

"I can't believe that you're suggesting we…"

"You wanted children, right?"

"I… Yes."

"So, it's not such an outrageous thought."

"You think we're going to stay married?"

"You didn't sign a prenuptial agreement, Emerson. You leave me, I still get half of your shares of the vineyard."

"You didn't sign one either. I have the impression half of what's yours comes out to an awful lot of money."

"Money is just money. I'll make more. I don't have anything I care about half as much as you care about the vineyard. About the whole label."

"Well, why don't we wait to discuss children until I decide how much I hate you."

"You hate me so much you climbed on me at least five times last night."

"Yes, and in the cold light of day that seems less exciting than it did last night. The chemistry between us doesn't have anything to do with…our marriage."

"It has everything to do with it," he said, his tone far darker and more intense than he'd intended it to be.

"What? You manufactured this chemistry so we could…"

"No. The marriage made sense because of our chemistry. I was hardly going to let you walk away from me and marry another man, Emerson. Let him get his hands on your body when he has had all this time? He's had the last two years and he did nothing? He doesn't deserve you. And your father doesn't get to use you as a pawn."

"My father…"

"He's not a good man. Whether you believe me or not, it's true. But I imagine that when we impart the happy news to him today... You can make that decision for yourself."

"Thanks. But I don't need your permission to make my own decisions about my father or anything else."

But the look on her face was something close to haunted, and if he were a man prone to guilt, he might feel it now. They landed not long after, and his truck was there, still where he'd left it.

When they paused in front of it, she gave it a withering stare. "This thing is quite the performance."

It was a pretty beat-up truck. But it was genuinely his.

"It's mine," he said.

"From when?"

"Well, I got it when I was about...eighteen. So going on fifteen years ago."

"I don't even know how old you are. I mean, I do now, because I can do math. But really, I don't know anything about you, Holden."

"Well, I'll be happy to give you the rundown after we meet with your father."

"Well, looking forward to all that."

She was still wearing her dress from last night. He had found a replacement shirt in the hotel shop before they'd left, and it was too tight on his shoulders and not snug enough in the waist. When they arrived at the winery and entered the family's estate together, he could only imagine the picture they made.

Him in part of a tux, and her in last night's gown.

"Is my father in his study yet?" she questioned one of the first members of the household staff who walked by.

"Yes," the woman said, looking between Emerson and him. "Shall I see if he's receiving visitors?"

"He doesn't really have a choice," Holden said. "He'll make time to see us."

He took Emerson's hand and led her through the house, their footsteps loud on the marble floors. And he realized as they approached the office, what a pretentious show this whole place was.

James Maxfield wasn't that different from Holden. A man from humble beginnings hell-bent on forging a different path. But the difference between James and Holden was that Holden hadn't forgotten where he'd come from. He hadn't forgotten what it was to be powerless, and he would never make anyone else feel that kind of desperation.

James seemed to enjoy his position and all the power that came with it.

You don't enjoy it? Is that why you're standing here getting ready to walk through that door with his daughter and make him squirm? Is that why you forced Emerson to marry you?

He pushed those thoughts aside. And walked into the office without knocking, still holding tightly to Emerson.

Her father looked up, looked at him and then at Emerson. "What the hell is this?" he asked.

"I…"

"A hostile takeover," Holden said. "You ruined my sister's life. And now I'm here to make yours very, very difficult. And only by your daughter's good grace am I leaving you with anything other than a smoldering pile of wreckage. Believe me when I say it's not for your sake. But for the innocent people in your family who don't deserve to lose everything just because of your sins."

"Which sins are those?"

"My sister. Soraya Jane."

The silence in the room was palpable. Finally, James spoke.

"What is it you intend to do?"

"You need to guard your office better. I know you think this house isn't a corporation so you don't need high security, but you're such a damned narcissist you didn't realize you'd hired someone who was after the secrets you keep in your home. And now I have them. And thanks to Emerson, I now have a stake in this winery too. You can contest the marriage and my ownership, but it won't end well for you. It might not be my first choice now, but I'm still willing to detonate everything if it suits me."

James Maxfield's expression remained neutral, and his focus turned to his daughter.

"Emerson," her father said, "you agreed to this? You are allowing him to blackmail us?"

"What choice did I have?" she asked, a thread of desperation in her voice. "I trust you, Dad. I do. But he planned to destroy us. Whether his accusations are true or not, that was his intent. He gave me no time, and he didn't give me a lot of options. This marriage was the only way I could salvage what we've built, because he was ready to wage a campaign against you, against our family, at any cost. He was going to come at us personally and professionally. I couldn't take any chances. I couldn't. I did what I had to do. I did what you would have done, I'm sure. I did what needed doing."

"You were supposed to marry Donovan," James said, his tone icy.

"I know," Emerson said. "But what was I supposed to do when the situation changed? This man…"

"Have you slept with him?"

Emerson drew back, clearly shocked that her father had asked her that question. "I don't understand what that has to do with anything."

"It certainly compromises the purity of your claims," James returned. "You say you've been blackmailed into this arrangement, but if you're in a relationship with him…"

"Did you sleep with his sister?" she asked. "All those… All those other women in the files. Did you… Did you cheat on Mom?"

"Emerson, there are things you don't need to know about, and things you don't understand. My relationship with your mother works, even if it's not traditional."

"You *did*." She lowered her voice to a near whisper. "His sister. She's younger than me."

"Emerson…"

Holden took a step toward James's desk. "Men like you always think it won't come back on you. You think you can take advantage of women who are young, who are desperate, and no one will come for you. But I am here for you. This empire of yours? It serves me now. Your daughter? She's mine too. And if you push me, I swear I will see it all ruined and everyone will know what you are. How many people do you think will come here for a wedding, or parties, then? What of the brand worldwide? Who wants to think about sexual harassment, coercion and the destruction of a woman young enough to be your daughter when they have a sip of your merlot?"

Silence fell, tense and hard between them.

"The brand is everything," James said finally. "I've done everything I can to foster that family brand, as has your mother. What we do in private is between us."

"And the gag order you had my sister sign, and all those other women? Soraya has been institutionalized because of all of this. Because of the fallout. And she might have signed papers, but I did not. And now I don't need to tell the world about your transgressions to have control over what you've built. And believe me, in the years to come, I will make your life hell." Holden leaned forward, placing his palms on the desk. "Emerson was your pawn. You were going to use her as a wife to the man you wanted as part of this empire. But Emerson is with me now. She's no longer yours."

"*Emerson* is right here," Emerson said, her voice vibrating with emotion. "And frankly, I'm disgusted by the both of you. I don't belong to either of you. Dad, I did what I had to do to save the vineyard. I did it because I trusted you. I trusted that Holden's accusations were false. But you did all of this, didn't you?"

"It was an affair," James said. "It looks to me like you are having one of your own, so it's a bit rich for you to stand in judgment of me."

"I hadn't made vows to Donovan. And I never claimed to love him. He also knows…"

"Your mother knows," James said. "The terms of a marriage are not things you discuss with your children. You clearly have the same view of relationships that I do, and here you are lecturing me."

"It's not the same," she said. "And as for you," she

said, turning to Holden. "I married you because it was the lesser of two evils. But that doesn't make me yours. You lied to me. You made me believe you were someone you weren't. You're no different from him."

Emerson stormed out of the room, and left Holden standing there with James.

"She makes your victory ring hollow," James said.

"Even if she divorces me, part of the winery is still mine. We didn't have a prenuptial agreement drafted between us, something I'm sure you were intending to take care of when she married that soft boy from the East Coast."

"What exactly are you going to do now?"

"I haven't decided yet. And the beauty of this is I have time. You can consider me the sword of Damocles hanging over your head. And one day, you know the thread will break. The question is when."

"And what do you intend to do to Emerson?"

"I've done it already. She's married to me. She's mine."

Those words burned with conviction, no matter her protests before storming out. And he didn't know why he felt the truth of those words deeper than anything else.

He had married her. It was done as far as he was concerned.

He went out of the office, and saw Emerson standing there, her hands planted firmly on the balustrade, overlooking the entry below.

"Let's talk," he said.

She turned to face him. "I don't want to talk. You should go talk with my father some more. The two of you seemed to be enjoying that dialogue."

"*Enjoy* is a strong word."

"You betrayed me," she said.

"I don't know you, Emerson. You don't know me. We hadn't ever made promises to each other. I didn't betray you. Your *father* betrayed you."

She looked stricken by that, and she said nothing.

"I want you to come live with me."

"Why would I do that?"

"Because we're married. Because it's not fake."

"Does that mean you love me?" she asked, her tone scathing.

"No. But there's a lot of mileage between love and fake. And you know it."

"I live here. I work here. I can't leave."

"Handily, I have bought a property on the adjacent mountain. You won't have to leave. I do have another ranch in Jackson Creek, and I'd like to visit there from time to time. I do a bit of traveling. But there's no reason we can't be based here, in Gold Valley."

"You'll have to forgive me. I'm not understanding the part of your maniacal plan where we try to pretend we're a happy family."

"The vineyard is more yours now than it was before. I have no issue deferring to you on a great many things."

"You're not just going to…let it get run into the ground?"

"If I wanted to do that, I wouldn't have to own a piece. I own part of your father's legacy. And that appeases me.

"So," he concluded, "shall we go?"

Twelve

Emerson looked around the marble halls of the Max-field estate, and for the very first time in all her life, she didn't feel like she was home.

The man in the office behind her was a stranger.

The man in front of her was her husband, whether or not he was a stranger.

And his words kept echoing in her head.

I didn't betray you. Your father betrayed you.

"Let's go," she said. Before she could think the words through.

She found herself bundled back up into his truck, still wearing the dress she had been wearing at yesterday's party. His house was a quick drive away from the estate, a modern feat of design built into the hillside, all windows to make the most of the view.

"Tell me about your sister," she said, standing in the

drive with him, feeling decidedly flat and more than a bit defeated.

"She's my half sister," Holden said, taking long strides toward the front entry. He entered a code, opened the door and ushered her into a fully furnished living area.

"I had everything taken care of already," he said. "It's ready for us."

Ready for us.

She didn't know why she found that comforting. She shouldn't. She was unaccountably wounded by his betrayal, had been forced into this marriage. And yet, she wanted him. She couldn't explain it.

And her old life didn't feel right anymore, because it was even more of a lie than this one.

"My mother never had much luck with love," Holden said, his voice rough. "I had to take care of her. Because the men she was with didn't. They would either abuse her outright or manipulate her, and she wasn't very strong. Soraya came along when I was eight. About the cutest thing I'd ever seen. And a hell of a lot of trouble. I had to get her ready, had to make sure her hair was brushed for school. All of that. But I did it. I worked, and I took care of them, and once I got money, I made sure they had whatever they wanted." He looked away from her, a muscle jumping in his jaw. "It was after Soraya had money that she met your father. I don't think it takes a genius to realize she's got daddy issues. And he played each and every one of them. She got pregnant. He tried to get her to terminate. She wouldn't. She lost the baby anyway. And she lost her mind right along with it."

Hearing those words again, now knowing that they were true…they hit her differently.

She sat down on the couch, her stomach cramping with horror.

"You must love her a lot," she said. "To do all of this for her."

She thought about her father, and how she had been willing to marry a stranger for him. And then how she had married Holden to protect the winery, to protect her family, her father. And now she wasn't entirely convinced she shouldn't have just let Holden do what he wanted.

He frowned. "I did what had to be done. Like I always do. I take care of them."

"Because you love them," she said.

"Because no one else takes care of them." He shook his head. "My family wasn't loving. They still aren't. My mother is one of the most cantankerous people on the face of the planet, but you do what you do. You keep people going. When they're your responsibility, there's no other choice."

"Oh," she said. She took a deep, shuddering breath. "You see, I love my father. I love my mother. That's why her disapproval hurts. That's why his betrayal... I didn't know that he was like this. That he could have done those things to someone like your sister. It hurts me to know it. You're right. He is the one who betrayed me. And I will never be able to go into the estate again and look at it, at him, the same way. I'll never be able to look at him the same. It's just all broken, and I don't think it can ever be put back together."

"We'll see," he said. "I never came here to put anything back together. Because I knew it was all broken beyond the fixing of it. I came here to break *him*, because he broke Soraya. And I don't think she's going to be fixed either." He came to stand in front of Emerson, his hands shoved into his pockets, his expression grim. "And I'm sorry that you're caught up in the middle of this, because I don't have any stake in breaking you. But here's what I know about broken things. They can't be put back together exactly as they were. I think you can make something new out of them, though."

"Are you giving me life advice? Really? The man who blackmailed me into marriage?" He was still so absurdly beautiful, so ridiculously gorgeous and compelling to her. It was wrong. But she didn't know how to fix it. How to change it. Like anything else in her life. And really, right at the moment, it was only one of the deeply messed up things in her reality.

That she felt bonded to him even as the bonds that connected her to her family were shattered.

"You can take it or not," he said. "That doesn't change the fact that it's true. Whether or not I exposed him, your father is a predator. This is who he is. You could have lived your life without knowing the truth, but I don't see how that's comforting."

It wasn't. It made a shiver race down her spine, made her feel cold all over. "I just… I trusted him. I trusted him so much that I was willing to marry a man he chose for me. I would have done anything he asked me to do. He built a life for me, and he gave me a wonderful childhood, and he made me the woman that I am. For better or for worse. He did a whole host of wonderful things for me, and I don't know how to reconcile that with what else I now know about him."

"All *I* know is your father is a fool. Because the way you believe in him… I've never believed in anyone that way. Anyone or anything. And the way my sister believed in him… He didn't deserve that, from either of you. And if just one person believed in me the way that either of you believed in him, the way that I think your mother believes in him, your sisters… I wouldn't have done anything to mess that up."

Something quiet and sad bloomed inside of her. And she realized that the sadness wasn't for losing her faith in her father. Not even a little.

"I did," she said.

"What?"

"I did. Believe in you like that. Holden Brown. That ranch hand I met not so long ago. I don't know what you think about me, or women like me. But it mattered to me that I slept with you. That I let you into my body. I've only been with two other men. For me, sex is an intimate thing. And I've never shared it with someone outside of a relationship. But there was something about you. I trusted you. I believed what you told me about who you were. And I believed in what my body told me about what was between us. And now what we shared has kind of turned into this weird and awful thing, and I just… I don't think I'll ever trust myself again. Between my father and you…"

"I didn't lie to you." His voice was almost furious in its harshness. "Not about wanting you. Nothing that happened between you and me in bed was a lie. Not last night, and not the first night. I swear to you, I did not seduce you to get revenge on your father. Quite the opposite. I told myself when I came here that I would never touch you. You were forbidden to me, Emerson, because I didn't want to do the same thing your father had done. Because I didn't want to lie to you or take advantage of you in any way. When I first met you in that vineyard, I told myself I was disgusted by you. Because you had his blood in your veins. But no matter how much I told myself that, I couldn't make it true. You're not your father. And that's how I feel. This thing between us is separate, and real."

"But the marriage is for revenge."

"Yes. But I wouldn't have taken the wedding *night* if I didn't want you."

"Can I believe in you?"

She didn't know where that question came from, all vulnerable and sad, and she wasn't entirely sure that she liked the fact that she'd asked it. But she needed to grab on to something. In this world where nothing made sense, in this moment when she felt rootless, because not even her father was who she thought he was, and she didn't know how she was going to face having that conversation with Wren, or with Cricket. Didn't know what she was going to say to her mother, because no matter how difficult their own relationship was, this gave Emerson intense sympathy for her mother.

Not to mention her sympathy for the young woman her father had harmed. And the other women who were like her. How many had there been just like Soraya? It made Emerson hurt to wonder.

She had no solid ground to stand on, and she was desperate to find purchase.

If Holden was telling the truth, if the chemistry between them was as real to him as it was to her, then she could believe in that if nothing else. And she needed to believe in it. Desperately.

"If I… If I go all in on this marriage, Holden, on this thing between us, if we work together to make the vineyard…ours—Wren and Cricket included—promise me that you'll be honest with me. That you will be faithful to me. Because right now, I'll pledge myself to you, because I don't know what the hell else to believe in. I'm angry with you, but if you're telling me the truth about wanting me, and you also told me the truth about my father, then you are the most real and honest thing in my life right now, and I will... I'll bet on that. But only if you promise me right now that you won't lie to me."

"I promise," he said, his eyes like two chips of obsidian, dark and fathomless. Hard.

And in her world that had proven to be built on a shifting sand foundation, his hardness was something steady. Something real.

She needed something real.

She stood up from her position on the couch, her legs wobbling when she closed the distance between them. "Then take me to bed. Because the only thing that feels good right now is you and me."

"I notice you didn't say it's the only thing that makes sense," he said, his voice rough. He cupped her cheek, rubbing his thumb over her cheekbone.

"Because it doesn't make sense. I should hate you. But I can't. Maybe it's just because I don't have the energy right now. Because I'm too sad. But this...whatever we have, it feels *real*. And I'm not sure what else is."

"This *is* real," he said, taking her hand and putting it on his chest. His heart was raging out of control, and she felt a surge of power roll through her.

It was real. Whatever else wasn't, the attraction between them couldn't be denied.

He carried her to the bed, and they said vows to each other's bodies. And somehow, it felt right. Somehow, in the midst of all that she had lost, her desire for Holden felt like the one right thing she had done.

Marrying him. Making this real.

Tonight, there were no restraints, no verbal demands. Just their bodies. Unspoken promises that she was going to hold in her heart forever.

And as the hours passed, a feeling welled up in her chest that terrified her more than anything else.

It wasn't hate. Not even close.

But she refused to give it a name. Not yet. Not now.

She would have a whole lot of time to sort out what she felt for this man.

She'd have the rest of her life.

Thirteen

The day he put Maxfield Vineyards as one of the assets on his corporate holdings was sadistically satisfying. He was going to make a special new label of wine as well. Soraya deserved to be indelibly part of the Maxfield legacy

Because James Maxfield was indelibly part of Soraya's. And Holden's entire philosophy on the situation was that James didn't deserve to walk away from her without being marked by the experience.

Holden was now a man in possession of a very powerful method through which to dole out if not traditional revenge, then a steady dose of justice.

He was also a man in possession of a wife.

That was very strange indeed. But he counted his marriage to Emerson among the benefits of this arrangement.

Her words kept coming back to him. Echoing inside of him. All day, and every night when he reached for her.

Can I believe in you?

He found that he wanted her to believe in him, and he couldn't quite figure out why. Why should it matter that he not sweep Emerson into a web of destruction?

Why had he decided to go about marrying her in the first place when he could have simply wiped James Maxfield off the map?

But no. He didn't want to question himself.

Marrying her was a more sophisticated power play. And at the end of the day, he liked it better.

He had possession of the man's daughter. He had a stake in the man's company.

The sword of Damocles.

After all, ruination could be accomplished only once, but this was a method of torture that could continue on for a very long time.

His sense of satisfaction wasn't just because of Emerson.

He wasn't so soft that he would change direction because of a woman he'd slept with a few times.

Though, every night that he had her, he felt more and more connected to her.

He had taken great pleasure a few days ago when she broke the news to her fiancé.

The other man had been upset, but not about Emerson being with another man, rather about the fact that he was losing his stake in the Maxfield dynasty. In Holden's estimation that meant the man didn't deserve Emerson at all. Of course, he didn't care what anyone deserved, not in this scenario. *He* didn't deserve Emerson either, but he wanted her. That was all that mattered to him.

It was more than her ex-fiancé felt for her.

There was one person he had yet to call, though. Soraya. She deserved to know everything that had happened.

He was one of her very few approved contacts. She was allowed to speak to him over the phone.

They had done some very careful and clever things to protect Soraya from contact with the outside world. He, his mother and Soraya's therapists were careful not to cut her off completely, but her social media use was monitored.

They had learned that with people like her, who had built an empire and a web of connections in the digital world, they had to be very careful about cutting them off entirely, or they felt like they had been cast into darkness.

But then, a good amount of their depression often came from that public world.

It was a balance. She was actually on her accounts less now than she had been when she'd first been hospitalized.

He called, and it didn't take long for someone to answer.

"This is Holden McCall. I'm calling for Soraya."

"Your sister is just finishing an art class. She should be with you in a moment."

In art class. He would have never picked something like that for her, but then, her sense of fashion was art in and of itself, he supposed. The way she framed her life and the scenes she found herself in. It was why she was so popular online. That she made her life into art.

It pleased him to know she had found another way to express that. One that was maybe about her more than it was about the broader world.

"Holden?" Her voice sounded less frantic, more relaxed than he was used to.

"Yes," he said. "It's me."

"I haven't heard from you in a while." She sounded a bit petulant, childlike and accusing. Which, frankly, was the closest to her old self he'd heard her sound in quite some time.

"I know. I'm sorry. I've been busy. But I have something to tell you. And I hope this won't upset you. I think it might make you happy."

"What is happy?" She said it a bit sharply, and he wondered if she was being funny. It was almost impossible to tell with her anymore.

He ignored that question, and the way it landed inside of him. The way that it hollowed him out.

"I got married," he said.

"Holden," she said, sounding genuinely pleased. "I'm so glad. Did you fall in love? Love is wonderful. When it isn't terrible."

He swallowed hard. "No. I've married James Maxfield's daughter."

She gasped, the sound sharp in his ear, stabbing him with regret. "Why?"

"Well, that's the interesting part," he said. "I now own some of Maxfield Vineyards. And, Soraya, I'm going to make a wine and name it after you. Because he shouldn't be able to forget you, or what he did to you."

There was silence. For a long moment. "And I'm the one that's locked up because I'm crazy."

"What?"

"Did you hear yourself? You sound… You married somebody you don't love."

"It's not about love. It's about justice. He didn't deserve to get away with what he did to you."

"But he has," she said. "He has because he doesn't care."

"And I've made him care. His daughter knows what kind of man he is now. He's lost a controlling share in his own winery. He's also lost an alliance that he was hoping to build by marrying Emerson off to someone else."

"And the cost of those victories is your happiness. Because you aren't with a woman you love."

"I was never going to fall in love," he said. "It's not in me."

"Yeah, that's what I said too. Money was the only thing I loved. Until it wasn't." There was another long stretch of silence.

"I thought you would be happy. I'm getting a piece of this for you."

"I don't… I don't want it."

"You don't…"

"You have to do what you have to do," she said.

"I guess so." He didn't know what to say to that, and for the first time since he'd set out on this course, he questioned himself.

"Holden, where is my baby? They won't answer me."

Rage and grief seized up in his chest. She had sounded better, but she wasn't. "Sweetheart," he said. "You lost the baby. Remember?"

The silence was shattering. "I guess I did. I'm sorry. That's silly. It doesn't seem real. I don't seem real sometimes."

And he knew then, that no matter what she said, whether or not she accepted this gift he'd won for her, he didn't regret it. Didn't regret doing this for his sister, who slid in and out of terrible grief so often, and then had to relive her loss over and over again. At least this time she had accepted his response without having a breakdown. But talking about Maxfield cut her every time, he knew.

"Take care of yourself," he said.

"I will," she said.

And he was just thankful that there was someone there to take care of her, because whatever she said, he worried she wouldn't do it for herself.

And he was resolved then that what he'd done was right.

It had nothing to do with Emerson, or his feelings for her.

James deserved everything that he got and more.

Holden refused to feel guilt about any of it.

Very little had been said between herself and Wren about her elopement. And Emerson knew she needed to talk to her sister. Both of her sisters. But it was difficult to work up the courage to do it.

Because explaining it to them required sharing secrets about their father, secrets she knew would devastate them. She also knew devastating them would further her husband's goals.

Because she and Holden currently had the majority ownership in the vineyard. And with her sisters, they could take absolute control, which she knew was what Holden wanted ultimately.

Frankly, it all made her very anxious.

But anxious or not, talking with her sisters was why she had invited them to have lunch with her down in Gold Valley.

She walked into Bellissima, and the hostess greeted her, recognizing her instantly, and offering her the usual table.

There wasn't much in the way of incredibly fancy dining in Gold Valley, but her family had a good relationship with the restaurants, since they often supplied wine to them, and while they weren't places that required reservations or anything like that, a Maxfield could always count on having the best table in the house.

She sat at her table with a view, morosely perusing the menu while her mouth felt like it was full of sawdust. That was when Cricket and Wren arrived.

"You're actually taking a lunch break," Wren said. "Something must be wrong."

"We need to talk," Emerson said. "I thought it might be best to do it over a basket of bread."

She pushed the basket to the center of the table, like a very tasty peace offering.

Wren eyeballed it "Things must be terrible if you're suggesting we eat carbs in the middle of the day."

"I eat carbs whenever I want," Cricket said, sitting down first, Wren following her younger sister's lead.

"I haven't really talked to you guys since—"

"Since you defied father and eloped with some guy that none of us even know?" Wren asked.

"Yeah, since that."

"Is he the guy?" Wren asked.

"*What* guy?" Cricket asked.

"She cheated on Donovan, had a one-night stand with some guy that I now assume is the guy she married. And the reason she disappeared from my party the other night."

"You did *what*?" Cricket asked.

"I'm sorry, now you're going to be more shocked about my one-night stand and about my random marriage?"

Cricket blinked. "Well. Yes."

"Yes. It is the same guy."

"Wow," Wren said. "I didn't take you for a romantic, Emerson. But I guess I was wrong."

"No," Emerson said. "I'm not a romantic."

But somehow, the words seemed wrong. Especially with the way her feelings were jumbled up inside of her.

"Then what happened?"

"That's what I need to talk to you about," she said. "It is not a good story. And I didn't want to talk to either of you about it at the winery. But I'm not sure bringing you into a public space to discuss it was the best choice either."

"You do have your own house now," Cricket pointed out.

"Yes. And Holden is there. And… Anyway. It'll all become clear in a second."

Before the waitress could even bring menus to her sisters, Emerson spilled out everything. About their father. About Holden's sister. And about the ultimatum that had led to her marriage.

"You just went along with it?" Wren asked.

"There was no *just* about it," Emerson responded. "I didn't know what he would do to the winery if I didn't comply. And I wasn't sure about Dad's piece in it until… until I talked to him. Holden and I. Dad didn't deny any of it. He says that him and Mom have an understanding, and of course it's something he wouldn't talk about with any of us. But I don't even know if that's true. And my only option is going to Mom and potentially hurting her if I want to find out that truth. So here's what I know so far. That Dad hurt someone. Someone younger than me, someone my new husband loves very much."

"But he's only your husband because he wants to get revenge," Cricket pointed out.

"I… I think that's complicated too. I hope it is."

"You're not in love with him, are you?" Wren asked.

She decided to dodge that question and continue on with the discussion. "I love Dad. And I don't want to believe any of this, but I have to because…it's true."

Cricket looked down. "I wish that I could say I'm surprised. But it's different, being me. I mean, I feel like I see the outside of things. You're both so deep on the inside. Dad loves you, and he pays all kinds of attention to you. I'm kind of forgotten. Along with Mom. And when you're looking at him from a greater distance, I think the cracks show a lot more clearly."

"*I'm* shocked," Wren said sadly. "I've thrown my whole life into this vineyard. Into supporting him. And I… I can't believe that the man who encouraged me, treated me the way he did, could do that to someone else. To many women, it sounds like."

"People and feelings are very complicated," Emerson said slowly. "Nothing has shown me that more than my relationship with Holden."

"You do love him," Wren said.

Did she? Did she love a man who wanted to ruin her family?

"I don't know," Emerson said. "I feel something for him. Because you know what, you're right. I would never have just let him blackmail me into marriage if on some level I didn't... I... It's a real marriage." She felt her face getting hot, which was silly, because she didn't have any hang-ups about that sort of thing normally. "But I'm a little afraid that I'm confusing...well, that part of our relationship being good with actual love."

"I am not the person to consult about that kind of thing," Cricket said, taking a piece of bread out of the basket at the center of the table and biting into it fiercely.

"Don't look at me," Wren said. "We've already had the discussion about my own shameful issues."

Cricket looked at Wren questioningly, but didn't say anything.

"Well, the entire point of this lunch wasn't just to talk about me. Or my feelings. Or Dad. It's to discuss what we are going to do. Because the three of us can band together, and we can make all the controlling decisions for the winery. We supersede my husband even. We can protect the label, keep his actions in check and make our own mark. You're right, Cricket," Emerson said. "You have been on the outside looking in for too long. And you deserve better."

"I don't actually want to do anything at the winery," Cricket said. "I got a job."

"You did?"

"Yes. At Sugar Cup."

"Making coffee?"

"Yes," Cricket said proudly. "I want to do something different. Different from the whole Maxfield thing. But I'm with you, in terms of banding together for decision-making. I'll be a silent partner, and I'll support you."

"I'm in," Wren said. "Although, you realize that your

husband has the ace up his sleeve. He could just decide to ruin us anyway."

"Yes, he could," Emerson said. "But now he owns a piece of the winery, and I think ownership means more to him than that."

"And he has you," Wren pointed out.

"I know," Emerson said. "But what can I do about it?"

"You do love him," Cricket said, her eyes getting wide. "I never thought you were sentimental enough."

"To fall in love? I have a heart, Cricket."

"Yes, but you were going to marry when you didn't love your fiancé. It's so patently obvious that you don't have any feelings for Donovan at all, and you were just going to marry him anyway. So, I assumed it didn't matter to you. Not really, and now you've gone and fallen in love with this guy... Someone who puts in danger the very thing you care about most. The thing you were willing to marry that bowl of oatmeal for."

"He wasn't a bowl of oatmeal," Emerson said.

"You're right," Wren said. "He wasn't. Because at least a person might want to eat a bowl of oatmeal, even if it's plain. You'd never want to eat him."

"Oh, for God's sake."

"Well," Wren said. "It's true."

"What matters is that the three of us are on the same page. No matter what happens. We are stronger together."

"Right," Wren and Cricket agreed.

"I felt like the rug was pulled out from under me when I found out about Dad. The winery didn't feel like it would ever seem like home again. I felt rootless, drifting. But we are a team. *We* are the Maxfield label. We are the Maxfield name. Just as much as he is."

"Agreed," Wren said.

"Agreed," said Cricket.

And their agreement made Emerson feel some sense of affirmation. Some sense of who she was.

She didn't have the relationship with her father she'd thought she had. She didn't have the father she'd thought she had.

Her relationship with Holden was...

Well, she was still trying to figure it out. But her relationship with Wren and Cricket was real. And it was strong. Strong enough to weather this, any of it.

And eventually she would have to talk to her mother. And maybe she would find something there that surprised her too. Because if there was one thing she was learning, it was that it didn't matter how things appeared. What mattered was the truth.

Really, as the person who controlled the brand of an entire label using pictures on the internet, she should have known better from the start. But somehow, she had thought that because she was so good at manipulating those images, that she might be immune to falling for them.

Right at this moment she believed in two things: her sisters, and the sexual heat between herself and Holden. Those seemed to be the only things that made any sense. The only things that had any kind of authenticity to them.

And maybe how you feel about him.

Well. Maybe.

But the problem was she couldn't be sure if he felt the same. And just at the moment she was too afraid to take a chance at being hurt. Because she was already raw and wounded, and she didn't know if she could stand anything more.

But she had her sisters. And she would rest in that for now.

Fourteen

The weeks that followed were strange. They were serene in some ways, which Emerson really hadn't expected. Her life had changed, and she was surprised how positive she found the change.

Oh, losing her respect for her father wasn't overly positive. But working more closely with her sisters was. She and Wren had always been close, but both of them had always found it a bit of a challenge to connect with Cricket, but it seemed easier now.

The three of them were a team. It wasn't Wren and Emerson on Team Maxfield, with Cricket hanging out on the sidelines.

It was a feat to launch a new sort of wine on the heels of the select label, which they had only just released. But the only demand Holden had made of the company so far was that they release a line of wines under his sister's name.

Actually, Emerson thought it was brilliant. Soraya had such a presence online—even if she wasn't in the public at the moment—and her image was synonymous with youth. Soraya's reputation gave Emerson several ideas for how to market wines geared toward the youthful jet-set crowd who loved to post photographs of their every move.

One of the first things Emerson had done was consult a graphic designer about making labels that were eminently postable, along with coming up with a few snappy names for the unique blends they would use. And of course, they would need for the price point to be right. They would start with three—Tempranillo Tantrum, Chardonyay and No Way Rosé.

Cricket rolled her eyes at the whole thing, feeling out of step with other people her age, as she had no desire to post on any kind of social media site, and found those puns ridiculous. Wren, while not a big enthusiast herself, at least understood the branding campaign. Emerson was ridiculously pleased. And together the three of them had enjoyed doing the work.

Cricket, true to her word, had not overly involved herself, given that she was in training down at the coffee shop. Emerson couldn't quite understand why her sister wanted to work there, but she could understand why Cricket felt the need to gain some independence.

Being a Maxfield was difficult.

But it was also interesting, building something that wasn't for her father's approval. Sure, Holden's approval was involved on some level, but…this was different from any other work she'd done.

She was doing this as much for herself as for him,

and he trusted that she would do a good job. She knew she would.

It felt…good.

The prototype labels, along with the charms she had chosen to drape elegantly over the narrow neck of each bottle, came back from production relatively quickly, and she was so excited to show Holden she could hardly contain herself.

She wasn't sure why she was so excited to show him, only that she was.

It wasn't as if she wanted his approval, the way she had with her father. It was more that she wanted to share what she had created. The way she felt she needed to please him. This was more of an excitement sort of feeling.

She wanted to please Holden in a totally different way. Wanted to make him… Happy.

She wondered what would make a man like him happy. If he *could* be happy.

And suddenly, she was beset by the burning desire to try.

He was a strange man, her husband, filled with dark intensity, but she knew that part of that intensity was an intense capacity to love.

The things that he had done for his sister…

All of her life, really. And for his mother.

It wasn't just this, though it was a large gesture, but everything.

He had protected his mother from her endless array of boyfriends. He had made sure Soraya had gotten off to school okay every day. He had bought his mother and sister houses the moment he had begun making money.

She had done research on him, somewhat covertly,

in the past weeks. And she had seen that he had donated large amounts of money, homes, to a great many people in need.

He hid all of that generosity underneath a gruff, hard exterior. Knowing what she knew now, she continually came back to that moment when he had refused to say his plan for revenge was born out of love for his sister. As if admitting to something like love would be disastrous for him.

She saw the top of his cowboy hat through the window of the tasting room, where she was waiting with the Soraya-branded wines.

He walked in, and her heart squeezed tight.

"I have three complete products to show you. And I hope you're going to like them."

She held up the first bottle—the Tempranillo Tantrum—with a little silver porcupine charm dangling from the top. "Because porcupines are grumpy," she said.

"Are they?"

"Well, do you want to hassle one and find out how grumpy they are? Because I don't."

"Very nice," he said, brushing his fingers over the gold foil on the label.

"People will want to take pictures of it. Even if they don't buy it, they're going to post and share it."

He looked at the others, one with a rose-gold unicorn charm, the next with a platinum fox. And above each of the names was *Soraya*.

"She'll love this," he said, his voice suddenly soft.

"How is she doing?"

"Last I spoke to her? I don't know. A little bit better. She didn't seem as confused."

"Do they know why she misremembers sometimes?" He had told her about how his sister often didn't remember she'd had a fairly late-term miscarriage. That sometimes she would call him scared, looking for a baby that she didn't have.

It broke Emerson's heart. Knowing everything Soraya had gone through. And she supposed there were plenty of young women who could have gone through something like that and not ended up in such a difficult position, but Soraya wasn't one of them. And the fact that Emerson's father had chosen someone so vulnerable, and upon learning how vulnerable she was, had ignored the distress she was in...

If Emerson had been on the fence about whether or not her father was redeemable...the more she knew about the state Holden's sister had been left in, the less she thought so.

"Her brain is protecting her from the trauma. Though, it's doing a pretty bad job," he said. "Every time she has to hear the truth again...it hurts her all over."

"Well, I hope this makes her happy," she said, gesturing to the wine. "And that it makes her feel like... she is part of this. Because she's part of the family now. Because of you. My sisters and I... We care about what happens to her. People do care."

"You've done an amazing job with this," he said, the sincerity in his voice shocking her. "I could never have figured out how to make this wine something she specifically would like so much, but this... She's going to love it." He touched one of the little charms. "She'll think those are just perfect."

"I'm glad. I'd like to meet her. Someday. When she is feeling well enough for something like that."

"I'm sure we can arrange it."

After that encounter, she kept turning her feelings over and over inside of her.

She was changing. What she wanted was changing.

She was beginning to like her life with Holden. More than like it. There was no denying the chemistry they shared. That what happened between them at night was singular. Like nothing else she had ever experienced. But it was moments like that one—the little moments that happened during the day—that surprised her.

She liked him.

And if she were really honest with herself, she more than liked him.

She needed…

She needed to somehow show him that she wanted more.

Of course, she didn't know what more there was, considering the fact that they were already married.

She was still thinking about what she wanted, what she could do, when she saw Wren later that day.

"Have you ever been in love?"

Wren looked at her, jerking her head abruptly to the side. "No," she said. "Don't you think you would have known if I'd ever been in love?"

"I don't know. We don't really talk about that kind of stuff. We talk about work. You don't know if I've ever been in love."

"Well, other than Holden? You haven't been. You've had boyfriends, but you haven't been in love."

"I didn't tell you I was in love with Holden."

"But you are," Wren said. "Which is why I assume you're asking me about love now."

"Yes," Emerson said. "Okay. I am. I'm in love with

Holden, and I need to figure out a way to tell him. Because how do you tell a man that you want more than marriage?"

"You tell him that you love him."

"It doesn't feel like enough. Anyone can say anything anytime they want. That doesn't make it real. But I want him to see that the way I feel has changed."

"Well, I don't know. Except… Men don't really use words so much as…"

"Sex. Well, our sex life has been good. Very good."

"Glad to hear it," Wren said. "But what might be missing from that?"

Emerson thought about that. "Our wedding night was a bit unconventional." Tearing tuxedos and getting tied up with leather belts might not be everyone's idea of a honeymoon. Though, Emerson didn't really have any complaints.

There had been anger between them that night. Anger that had burned into passion. And since then, they'd had sex in all manner of different ways, because she couldn't be bored when she shared a bed with someone she was so compatible with, and for whatever reason she felt no inhibition when she was with him. But they hadn't had a real wedding night.

Not really.

One where they gave themselves to each other after saying their vows.

That was it. She needed to make a vow to him. With her body, and then with her words.

"I might need to make a trip to town," she said.

"For?"

"Very bridal lingerie."

"I would be happy to knock off work early and help you in your pursuit."

"We really do make a great team."

When she and Wren returned that evening, Emerson was triumphant in her purchases, and more than ready to greet her husband.

Now she just had to hope he would understand what she was saying to him.

And she had to hope he would want the same thing she did.

When Holden got back to the house that night, it was dark.

That was strange, because Emerson usually got home before he did. He was discovering his new work at the winery to be fulfilling, but he also spent a good amount of time dealing with work for his own company, and that made for long days.

He looked down at the floor, and saw a few crimson spots, and for a moment, he knew panic. His throat tightened.

Except... It wasn't blood. It was rose petals.

There was a trail of them, leading from the living room to the stairwell, and up the stairs. He followed the path, down the dimly lit hall, and into the master bedroom that he shared with Emerson.

The rose petals led up to the bed, and there, perched on the mattress, was his wife.

His throat went dry, all the blood in his body rushing south. She was wearing... It was like a bridal gown, but made entirely of see-through lace that gave peeks at her glorious body underneath. The straps were thin, the neckline plunging down between her breasts, which were spilling out over the top of the diaphanous fabric.

She looked like temptation in the most glorious form he'd ever seen.

"What's all this?"

"I... I went to town for a few things today."

"I see that."

"It's kind of a belated wedding gift," she said. "A belated wedding night."

"We had a wedding night. I remember it very clearly."

"Not like this. Not..." She reached next to her, and pulled out a large velvet box. "And we're missing something."

She opened it up, and inside was a thick band of metal next to a slimmer one.

"They're wedding bands," she said. "One for you and one for me."

"What brought this on?"

He didn't really know what to say. He didn't know what to think about this at all.

The past few weeks had been good between the two of them, that couldn't be denied. But he felt like she was proposing to him, and that was an idea he could barely wrap his mind around.

"I want to wear your ring," she said. "And I guess... I bought the rings. But this ring is mine," she said, pulling out the man's ring. "And I want you to wear it. This ring is yours. I want to wear it." She took out the slim band and placed it on her finger, and then held the thicker one out for him.

"I've never been one for jewelry."

"You've never been one for marriage either, but here

we are. I know we had a strange start, but this has… It's been a good partnership so far, hasn't it?"

The work she had done on his sister's wine had been incredible, it was true. The care she had put into it had surprised him. It hadn't simply been a generic nod to Soraya. Emerson had made something that somehow managed to capture his sister's whole personality, and he knew Emerson well enough to know that she had done it by researching who Soraya was. And when Emerson asked him about his sister, he knew that she cared. Their own mother didn't even care that much.

But she seemed to bleed with her caring, with her regret that Soraya had been hurt. And now Emerson wanted rings. Wanted to join herself to him in a serious way.

And why not? She's your wife. She should be wearing your ring.

"Thanks," he said, taking the ring and putting it on quickly.

Her shoulders sagged a little, and he wondered if she had wanted this to go differently, but he was wearing the ring, so it must be okay. She let out a shaking breath. "Holden, with this ring, I take you as my husband. To have and to hold. For better or for worse. For richer or poorer. Until death separates us."

Those vows sent a shiver down his spine.

"We took those vows already."

"I took those vows with you because I had to. Because I felt like I didn't have another choice. I'm saying them now because I choose to. Because I want to. And because I mean them. If all of this, the winery, everything, goes away, I still want to be partners with you. In our lives. Not just in business. I want this to be about more than my father, more than your sister. I want it to be about us. And so that's my promise to you with my words. And I want to make that official with my body."

There were little ties at the center of the dress she was wearing, and she began to undo the first one, the fabric parting between her breasts. Then she undid the next one, and the next, until it opened, revealing the tiny pair of panties she had on underneath. She slipped the dress from her shoulders and then she began to undress him.

It was slow, unhurried. She'd torn the clothes from his body before. She had allowed him to tie her hands. She had surrendered herself to him in challenging and intense ways that had twisted the idea of submission on its head, because when her hands were tied, he was the one that was powerless.

But this was different. And he felt…

Owned.

By that soft, sweet touch, by the brush of her fingertips against him as she pushed his shirt up over his head. By the way her nimble fingers attacked his belt buckle, removing his jeans.

And somehow, *he* was the naked one then, and she was still wearing those panties. There was something generous about what she was doing now. And he didn't know why that word came to the front of his mind.

But she was giving.

Giving from a deep place inside of her that was more than just a physical gift. Without asking for anything in return. She lay back on the bed, lifting her hips slightly and pushing her panties down, revealing that tempting triangle at the apex of her thighs, revealing her whole body to him.

He growled, covering her, covering her mouth with his own, kissing her deep and hard.

And she opened to him. Pliant and willing.

Giving.

Had anyone ever given to him before?

He'd had nothing like this ever. That was the truth.

Everyone in his life had taken from him from the very beginning. But not her. And she had no reason to give to him. And if this were the same as all their other sexual encounters, he could have put it off to chemistry.

Because everybody was a little bit wild when there was sexual attraction involved, but this was more.

Sex didn't require vows.

It didn't require rings.

And it didn't feel like this.

This was more.

It touched him deeper, in so many places deep inside, all the way to his soul.

And he didn't know what to say, or feel, so he just kissed her. Because he knew how to do that. Knew how to touch her and make her wet. Knew how to make her come.

He knew how to find his pleasure in her.

But he didn't know how to find the bottom of this deep, aching need that existed inside of him.

He settled himself between her thighs, thrust into her, and she cried out against his mouth. Then her gaze met his, and she touched him, her fingertips skimming over his cheekbone.

"I love you." The words were like an arrow straight through his chest.

"Emerson..."

She clung to him, grasping his face, her legs wrapped

around his. "I love you," she said, rocking up into him, taking him deeper.

And he would have pulled away, done something to escape the clawing panic, but his desire for her was too intense.

Love.

Had anyone ever said those words to him? He didn't think so. He should let go of her, he should stop. But he was powerless against the driving need to stay joined to her. It wasn't even about release. It was about something else, something he couldn't name or define.

Can't you?

He ignored that voice. He ignored that burning sensation in his chest, and he tried to block out the words she'd said. But she said them over and over again, and something in him was so hungry for them, he didn't know how to deny himself.

He looked down, and his eyes met hers, and he was sure she could see straight inside of him, and that what she saw there would be woefully empty compared to what he saw in hers.

He growled, lowering his head and chasing the pleasure building inside of him, thrusting harder, faster, trying to build up a pace that would make him forget.

Who he was.

What she'd said.

What he wanted.

What he couldn't have.

But when her pleasure crested, his own followed close behind, and he made the mistake of looking at her again. Of watching as pleasure overtook her.

He had wanted her from the beginning.

It had never mattered what he could get by marrying her.

It had always been about her. Always.

Because he had seen her, and he could not have her, from the very first.

He had told himself he should hate her because she had Maxfield blood in her veins. Then he had told himself that he needed her, and that was why it had to be marriage.

But he was selfish, down to his core.

And he had manipulated, used and blackmailed her. He was no different than her father, and now here she was, professing her love. And he was a man who didn't even know what that was.

All this giving. All this generosity from her. And he didn't deserve it. Couldn't begin to.

And he deserved it from her least of all.

Because he had nothing to give back.

He shuddered, his release taking him, stealing his thoughts, making it impossible for him to feel anything but pleasure. No regrets. No guilt. Just the bliss of being joined to her. And when it was over, she looked at him, and she whispered one more time, "I love you."

And that was when he pulled away.

Fifteen

She had known it was a mistake, but she hadn't been able to hold it back. The declaration of love. Because she did love him. It was true. With all of herself. And while she had been determined to show him, with her body, with the vows she had made and with the rings she had bought, it wasn't enough.

She had thought the words by themselves wouldn't be enough, but the actions without the words didn't mean anything either. Not to her. Not when there was this big shift inside her, as real and deep as anything ever had been. She had wanted for so long to do enough that she would be worthy. And she felt like some things had crystallized inside of her. Because all of those things she craved, that approval, it was surface. It was like a brand. The way that her father saw brand. That as long as the outside looked good, as long as all the external things were getting done, that was all that mattered.

But it wasn't.

Because what she felt, who she was in her deepest parts, those were the things that mattered. And she didn't have to perform or be good to be loved. She, as a person, was enough all on her own. And that was what Holden had become to her. And that was what she wanted. For her life, for her marriage. Not something as shallow as approval for a performance. A brand was meaningless if there was no substance behind it. A beautiful bottle of wine didn't matter if what was inside was nothing more than grape juice.

A marriage was useless if love and commitment weren't at the center.

It was those deep things, those deep connections, and she hadn't had them, not in all her life. Not really. She was beginning to forge them with her sisters, and she needed them from Holden.

And if that meant risking disapproval, risking everything, then she would. She had. And she could see that her declaration definitely hadn't been the most welcome.

Since she'd told him she loved him, everything about him was shut down, shut off. She knew him well enough to recognize that.

"I don't know what you expect me to say."

"Traditionally, people like to hear 'I love you too.' But I'm suspecting I'm not going to get that. So, here's the deal. You don't have to say anything. I just… I wanted you to know how I felt. How serious I am. How much my feelings have changed since I first met you."

"Why?"

"Because," she said. "Because you…you came into my life and you turned it upside down. You uncovered so many things that were hidden in the dark for so long. And yes, some of that uncovering has been painful. But more than that, you made me realize what I really wanted from life. I thought that as long as everything looked okay, it would be okay. But you destroyed that. You destroyed the illusions all around me, including the ones I had built for myself. Meeting you, feeling that attraction for you, it cut through all this…bullshit. I thought I could marry a man I didn't even feel a temptation to sleep with. And then I met you. I felt more for you in those few minutes in the vineyard that night we met than I had felt for Donovan in the two years we'd been together. I couldn't imagine not being with you. It was like an obsession, and then we were together, and you made me want things, made me do things that I never would have thought I would do. But *those* were all the real parts of me. All that I am.

"I thought that if I put enough makeup on, and smiled wide enough, and put enough filters on the pictures, that I could be the person I needed to be, but it's not who I am. Who I am is the woman I am when I'm with you. In your arms. In your bed. The things you make me feel, the things you make me want. That's real. And it's amazing, because none of this is about optics, it's not about pleasing anyone, it's just about me and you. It's so wonderful. To have found this. To have found you."

"You didn't find me, honey. I found you. I came here to get revenge on your father. This isn't fate. It was calculated through and through."

"It started that way," she said. "I know it did. And I would never call it fate. Because I don't believe that it was divine design that your sister was injured the way that she was. But what I do believe is that there has to be a way to make something good out of something broken, because if there isn't, then I don't know what future you and I could possibly have."

"There are things that make sense in this world," he said. "Emotion isn't one of them. Money is. What we can do with the vineyard, that makes sense. We can build that together. We don't need any of the other stuff."

"The other stuff," she said, "is only everything. It's only love. It took me until right now to realize that. It's the missing piece. It's what I've been looking for all this time. It really is. And I... I love you. I love you down to my bones. It's real. It's not about a hashtag or a brand. It's about what I feel. And how it goes beyond rational and reasonable. How it goes beyond what should be possible. I love you. I love you and it's changed the way that I see myself."

"Are you sure you're not just looking for approval from somewhere else? You lost the relationship with your father, and now..."

"You're not my father. And I'm not confused. Don't try to tell me that I am."

"I don't do love," he said, his voice hard as stone.

"Somehow I knew you would say that. You're so desperate to make me believe that, aren't you? Mostly because I think you're so desperate to make yourself believe it. You won't even admit that you did all of this because you love your sister."

"Because you are thinking about happy families, and you're thinking about people who share their lives. That's never been what I've had with my mother and sister. I take care of them. And when I say that, I'm telling you the truth. It's not... It's not give-and-take."

"You loving them," she said, "and them being selfish with that love has nothing to do with who you are. Or what you're capable of. Why can't we have something other than that? Something other than me trying to earn approval and you trying to rescue? Can't we love each other? Give to each other? That's what I want. I think our bodies knew what was right all along. I know why you were here, and what you weren't supposed to want. And I know what I was supposed to do. But I think we were always supposed to be with each other. I do. From the deepest part of my body. I believe that."

"Bodies don't know anything," he said. "They just know they want sex. That's not love. And it's not anything worth tearing yourself apart over."

"But I... I don't have another choice. I'm torn apart by this. By us. By what we could be."

"There isn't an us. There is you and me. And we're married, and I'm willing to make that work. But you have to be realistic about what that means to a man like me."

"No," Emerson said. "I refuse to be realistic. Nothing in my life has ever been better because I was realistic. The things that have been good happened because I stepped out of my comfort zone. I don't want to be trapped in a one-sided relationship. To always be trying to earn my place. I've done that. I've lived it. I don't want to do it anymore."

"Fair enough," he said. "Then we don't have to do this."

"No," she said. "I want our marriage. I want..."

"You want me to love you, and I can't. I'm sorry. But I can't, I won't. And I..." He reached out, his callused fingertips skimming her cheek. "Honey, I appreciate you saying I'm not like your father, but it's pretty clear that I am. I'm not going to make you sign a nondisclosure agreement or anything like that. I'm going to ask one thing of you. Keep the Soraya wine going for my sister. But otherwise, my share of the winery goes to you."

"What?"

"I'm giving it back. I'm giving it to you. Because it's yours, it's not mine."

"You would rather…do all of that than try to love me?"

"I never meant to hurt you," he said. "That was never my goal, whether you believe it or not. I don't have strong enough feelings about you to want to hurt you."

And those words were like an arrow through her heart, piercing deeper than any other cruelty that could have come out of his mouth.

It would've been better, in fact, if he had said that he hated her. If he had threatened to destroy the winery again. If her ultimatum had made him fly into a rage. But it didn't. Instead, he was cold, closed off and utterly impassive. Instead, he looked like a man who truly didn't care, and she would've taken hatred over that any day, because it would have meant that at least he felt something. But she didn't get that. Instead, she got a blank wall of nothing.

She couldn't fight this. Couldn't push back against nothing. If he didn't want to fight, then there was nothing for her to do.

"So that's it," she said. "You came in here like a thunderstorm, ready to destroy everything in your path, and now you're just…letting me go?"

"Your father is handled. The control of the winery is with you and your sisters. I don't have any reason to destroy you."

"I don't think that you're being chivalrous. I think you're being a coward."

"Cowards don't change their lives, don't make something of themselves the way I did. Cowards don't go out seeking justice for their sisters."

"Cowards *do* run when someone demands something that scares them, though. And that's what you're doing. Make no mistake. You can pretend you're a man without fear. You're hard in some ways, and I know it. But all that hardness is just to protect yourself. I wish I knew why. I wish I knew what I could do."

"It won't last," he said. "Whatever you think you want to give me, it won't last."

"Why do you think that?"

"I've never actually seen anyone want to do something that wasn't ultimately about serving themselves. Why would you be any different?"

"It's not me that's different. It's the feelings."

"But you have to be able to put your trust in feelings in order to believe in something like that, and I don't. I believe in the things you can see, in the things you can buy."

"I believe in us," she said, pressing her hand against her chest.

"You believe wrong, darlin'."

Pain welled up inside of her. "You're not the Big Bad Wolf after all," she said. "At least he had the courage to eat Red Riding Hood all up. You don't even have the courage to do that."

"You should be grateful."

"You don't get to break my heart and tell me I should be grateful because you didn't do it a certain way. The end result is the same. And I hope that someday you realize you broke your own heart too. I hope that someday you look back on this and realize we had love, and you were afraid to take it. And I hope you ask yourself why it was so much easier for you to cross a state because of rage than it was for you to cross a room and tell someone you love them."

She started to collect her clothes, doing her very best to move with dignity, to keep her shoulders from shaking, to keep herself from dissolving. And she waited. As she collected her clothes. Waited for her big, gruff cowboy to sweep her up in his arms and stop her from leaving. But he didn't. He let her gather her clothes. And he let her walk out the bedroom door. Let her walk out of the house. Let her walk out of his life. And as Emerson stood out in front of the place she had called home with a man she had come to love, she found herself yet again unsure of what her life was.

Except… Unlike when the revelations about her father had upended everything, this time she had a clear idea of who *she* was.

Holden had changed her. Had made her realize the depth of her capacity for pleasure. For desire. For love. Had given her an appreciation of depth.

An understanding of what she could feel if she dug deep, instead of clinging to the perfection of the surface.

And whatever happened, she would walk away from this experience changed. Would walk away from this wanting more, wanting better.

He wouldn't, though.

And of all the things that broke her heart in this moment, that truth was the one that cut deepest.

Emerson knew she couldn't avoid having a conversation with her mother any longer. There were several reasons for that. The first being that she'd had to move back home. The second being that she had an offer to make her father. But she needed to talk to her mom about it first.

Emerson took a deep breath, and walked into the sitting room, where she knew she would find her mother at this time of day.

She always took tea in the sitting room with a book in the afternoon.

"Hi," she said. "Can we talk?"

"Of course," her mom said, straightening and setting her book down. "I didn't expect to see you here today."

"Well. I'm kind of…back here. Because I hit a rough patch in my marriage. You know, by which I mean my husband doesn't want to be married to me anymore."

"That is a surprise."

"Is it? I married him quickly, and really not for the best reasons."

"It seemed like you cared for him quite a bit."

"I did. But the feeling wasn't mutual. So there's not much I can do about that in any case."

"We all make choices. Although, I thought you had finally found your spine with this one."

Emerson frowned. "My spine?"

"Emerson, you have to understand, the reason I've always resisted your involvement in the winery is because I didn't want your father to own you."

"What are you talking about?"

"I know you know. The way that he is. It's not a surprise to me, I've known it for years. He's never been faithful to me. But that's beside the point. The real issue is the way that he uses people."

"You've known. All along?"

"Yes. And when I had you girls the biggest issue was

that if I left, he would make sure that I never saw you again. That wasn't a risk I could take. And I won't lie to you, I feared poverty more than I should have. I didn't want to go back to it. And so I made some decisions that I regret now. Especially as I watched you grow up. And I watched the way he was able to find closeness with you and with Wren. When I wasn't able to."

"I just… No matter what I did, you never seemed like you thought I did enough. Or like I had done it right."

"And I'm sorry about that. I made mistakes. In pushing you, I pushed you away, and I think I pushed you toward your father. Which I didn't mean to do. I was afraid, always, and I wanted you to be able to stand on your own feet because I had ended up hobbling myself. I was dependent on his money. I didn't know how to do anything separate from this place, separate from him that could keep me from sinking back into the poverty that I was raised in. I was trapped in many ways by my own greed. I gave up so much for this. For him." Her eyes clouded over. "That's another part of the problem. When I chose your father over… When I chose your father, it was such a deep, controversial thing, it caused so much pain, to myself included, in many ways, and I'm too stubborn and stiff-necked to take back that kind of thing."

"I don't understand."

She ran a hand over her lined brow, pushing her dark hair off her face. "I was in love with someone else. There was a misunderstanding between us, and we broke up. Then your father began to show an interest, because of a rivalry he had with my former beau. I figured that I would use that. And it all went too far. This is the life I made for myself. And what I really wanted, to try and atone for my sins, was to make sure you girls had it different. But then he was pushing you to marry... So when you came back from Las Vegas married to Holden, what I hoped was that you had found something more."

Emerson was silent for a long moment, trying to process all this information. And suddenly, she saw everything so clearly through her mother's eyes. Her fears, the reason she had pushed Emerson the way she had. The way she had disapproved of Emerson pouring everything into the winery.

"I do love Holden," Emerson said. "But he...he says he doesn't love me."

"That's what happened with the man I loved. And I got angry, and I went off on my own. Then I went to someone else. I've always regretted it. Because I've never loved your father the way that I loved him. Then it was too late. I held on to pride, I didn't want to lower myself to beg him to be with me, but now I wish I had. I wish I had exhausted everything in the name of love. Rather than giving so much to stubbornness and spite. To financial security. Without love, these sorts of places just feel like a mausoleum. A crypt for dead dreams." She smiled sadly, looking around the vast, beautiful room that seemed suddenly so much darker. "I have you girls. And I've never regretted that. I have regretted our lack of closeness, Emerson, and I know that it's my fault."

"It's mine too," Emerson said. "We've never really talked before, not like this."

"There wasn't much I could tell you. Not with the way you felt about your father. And... You have to understand, while I wanted to protect you, I also didn't want to shatter your love for him. Because no matter what else he has done, he does love his daughters. He's a flawed man, make no mistake. But what he feels for you is real."

"I don't know that I'm in a place where that can matter much to me."

"No, I don't suppose you are. And I don't blame you."

"I want to buy Dad out of the winery," Emerson said. "When Holden left, he returned his stake to me. I want to buy Dad out. I want to run the winery with Wren and Cricket. And there will be a place here for you, Mom. But not for him."

"He's never going to agree to that."

"If he doesn't, I'll expose him myself. Because I won't sit by and allow the abuse of women and of his power to continue. He has two choices. He can leave of his own accord, or I'll burn this place to the ground around me, but I won't let injustice go on."

"I didn't have to worry about you after all," her mother said. "You have more of a spine than I've ever had."

"Well, now I do. For this. But when it comes to Holden…"

"Your pride won't keep you warm at night. And you can't trade one man for another, believe me, I've tried. If you don't put it all on the line, you'll regret it. You'll have to sit by while he marries someone else, has children with her. And everything will fester inside of you until it turns into something dark and ugly. Don't let that be you. Don't make the mistakes that I did."

"Mom… Who…"

"It doesn't matter now. It's been so long. He probably doesn't remember me anyway."

"I doubt that."

"All right, he remembers me," she said. "But not fondly."

"I love him," Emerson said. "I love him, and I don't know what I'm going to do without him. Which is silly, because I've lived twenty-nine years without him. You would think that I would be just fine."

"When you fall in love like that, you give away a piece of yourself," her mom said. "And that person always has it. It doesn't matter how long you had them for. When it's real, that's how it is."

"Well, I don't know what I'm supposed to do."

"Hope that he gave you a piece of him. Hope that whatever he says, he loves you just the way you love him. And then do more than hope. You're strong enough to come in here and stand up to your father. To do what's right for other people. Do what's right for you too."

Emerson nodded slowly. "Okay." She looked around, and suddenly laughter bubbled up inside of her.

"What?"

"It's just… A few weeks ago, at the launch for the select label, I was thinking how bored I was. Looking forward to my boring future. My boring marriage. I would almost pay to be bored again, because at least I wasn't heartbroken."

"Oh, trust me," her mom said. "As painful as it is, love is what gets you through the years. Even if you don't have it anymore. You once did. Your heart remembers that it exists in the world, and then suddenly the world looks a whole lot more hopeful. Because when you can believe that two people from completely different places can come together and find something that goes beyond explanation, something that goes beyond what you can see with your eyes…that's the thing that gives you hope in your darkest hour. Whatever happens with him…"

"Yeah," Emerson said softly. "I know."

She did. Because he was the reason she was standing here connecting with her mother now. He was the reason she was deciding to take this action against her father.

And she wouldn't be the reason they didn't end up together. She wouldn't give up too soon.

She didn't care how it looked. She would go down swinging.

Optics be damned.

Sixteen

Holden wasn't a man given to questioning himself. He acted with decisiveness, and he did what had to be done. But his last conversation with Emerson kept replaying itself in his head over and over again. And worse, it echoed in his chest, made a terrible, painful tearing sensation around his heart every time he tried to breathe. It felt like… He didn't the hell know. Because he had never felt anything like it before. He felt like he had cut off an essential part of himself and left it behind and it had nothing to do with revenge.

He was at the facility where his sister lived, visiting her today, because it seemed like an important thing to do. He owed her an apology.

He walked through the manicured grounds and up to the front desk. "I'm here to see Soraya Jane."

The facility was more like high-end apartments, and

his sister had her rooms on the second floor, overlooking the ocean. When he walked in, she was sitting there on the end of the bed, her hair loose.

"Good to see you," he said.

"Holden."

She smiled, but she didn't hug him.

They weren't like that.

"I came to see you because I owe you an apology."

"An apology? That doesn't sound like you."

"I know. It doesn't."

"What happened?"

"I did some thinking and I realized that what I did might have hurt you more than it helped you. And I'm sorry."

"You've never hurt me," she said. "Everything you do is just trying to take care of me. And nobody else does that."

He looked at his sister, so brittle and raw, and he realized that her issues went back further than James Maxfield. She was wounded in a thousand ways, by a life that had been more hard knocks than not. And she was right. No one had taken care of her but him. And he had been the oldest, so no one had taken care of him at all.

And the one time that Soraya had tried to reach out, the one time she had tried to love, she had been punished for it.

No wonder it had broken her the way it had.

"I abandoned my revenge plot. Emerson and I are going to divorce."

"You don't look happy," she said.

"I'm not," he said. "I hurt someone I didn't mean to hurt."

"Are you talking about me or her?"

He was quiet for a moment. "I didn't mean to hurt either of you."

"Did you really just marry her to get back at her father?"

"No. Not only that. I mean, that's not why I married her."

"You look miserable."

"I am, but I'm not sure what that has to do with anything."

"It has to do with love. This is how love is. It's miserable. It makes you crazy. And I can say that."

"You're not crazy," he said, fiercely. "Don't say that about yourself, don't think it."

"Look where I am."

"It's not a failure. And it doesn't… Soraya, there's no shame in having a problem. There's no shame in getting help."

"Fine. Well, what's your excuse then? I got help and you ruined your life."

"I'm not in love."

"You're not? Because you have that horrible look about you. You know, like someone who just had their heart utterly ripped out of their chest."

He was quiet for a moment, and he took a breath. He listened to his heart beat steadily in his ears. "My heart is still there," he said.

"Sure. But not your *heart* heart. The one that feels things. Do you love her?"

"I don't know how to love people. How would we know what real, healthy love looks like? I believe that you loved James Maxfield, but look where it got you. Weird… We are busted up and broken from the past, how are we supposed to figure out what's real?"

"If it feels real, it is real. I don't think there's anything all that difficult to understand about love. When you feel like everything good about you lives inside another person, and they're wandering around with the best of you in their chest, you just want to be with them all the time. And you're so afraid of losing them, because if you do, you're going to lose everything interesting and bright about you too."

He thought of Emerson, of the way she looked at him. And he didn't know if what Soraya said was true. If he felt like the best of him was anywhere at all. But what he knew for sure was that Emerson made him want to be better. She made him want something other than money or success. Something deep and indefinable that he couldn't quite grasp.

"She said she loved me," he said, his voice scraped raw, the admission unexpected.

"And you left her?"

"I forced her to marry me. I couldn't…"

"She loves you. She's obviously not being forced into anything."

"I took advantage…"

"You know, if you're going to go worrying about taking advantage of women, it might be helpful if you believe them when they tell you what they want. You deciding that you know better than she does what's in her heart is not enlightened. It's just more of some man telling a woman what she ought to be. And what's acceptable for her to like and want."

"I…" He hadn't quite expected that from his sister.

"She loves you. If she loves you, why won't you be with her?"

"I…"

He thought about what Emerson had said. When she called him a coward.

"Because I'm afraid I don't know how to be in love," he said finally.

It was the one true thing he'd said on the matter. He hadn't meant to lie, he hadn't known that he had. But it was clear as day to him now.

"Look at how we were raised. I don't know a damn thing about love."

"You're the only one who ever did," Soraya said. "Look what you've done for me. Look at where I am. It's not because of me."

"No," he said. "It's because of me. I got you started on all the modeling stuff, and you went to the party where you met James…"

"That's not what I meant. I meant the reason that I'm taken care of now, the reason that I've always been taken care of, is because of you. The reason Mom has been taken care of… That's you. All those families you gave money to, houses to. And I know I've been selfish. Being here, I've had a lot of time to think. And I know that sometimes I'm not…lucid. But sometimes I am, and when I am, I think a lot about how much you gave. And no one gave it back to you. And I don't think it's that you don't know how to love, Holden. I think it's that you don't know what it's like when someone loves you back. And you don't know what to do with it."

He just sat and stared, because he had never thought of himself the way that his sister seemed to. But she made him sound…well, kind of like not a bad guy. Maybe even like someone who cared quite a bit.

"I don't blame you for protecting yourself. But this isn't protecting yourself. It's hurting yourself."

"You might be right," he said, his voice rough. "You know, you might be right."

"Do you love her?"

He thought about the way Emerson had looked in the moments before he had rejected her. Beautiful and bare. His wife in every way.

"Yes," he said, his voice rough. "I do."

"Then none of it matters. Not who her father is, not being afraid. Just that you love her."

"Look what it did to you to be in love," he said. "Don't you think I'm right to be afraid of it?"

"Oh," she said. "You're definitely right to be afraid of it. It's terrifying. And it has the power to destroy everything in its path. But the alternative is this. This kind of gray existence. The one that I'm in. The one that you're in. So maybe it won't work out. But what if it did?"

And suddenly, he was filled with a sense of determination. With a sense of absolute certainty. There was no what-if. Because he could make it turn out with his actions. He was a man who had—as Emerson had pointed out— crossed the state for revenge.

He could sure as hell do the work required to make love last. It was a risk. A damn sight bigger risk than being angry.

But he was willing to take it.

"Thank you," he said to his sister.

"Thank you too," she said. "For everything. Even the revenge."

"Emerson is making a wine label for you," he said. "It's pretty brilliant."

Soraya smiled. "She is?"

"Yes."

"Well, I can't wait until I can come and celebrate with the both of you."

"Neither can I."

And now all that was left was for him to go and make sure he had Emerson, so the two of them could be together for the launch of the wine label, and for the rest of forever.

Emerson was standing on the balcony to her bedroom, looking out over the vineyard.

It was hers now, she supposed. Hers and Wren's and Cricket's. The deal with her father had been struck, and her mother had made the decision to stay there at the winery, and let James go off into retirement. The move would cause waves; there was no avoiding it. Her parents' separation, and her father removing himself from the label.

But Emerson had been the public face of Maxfield for so long that it would be a smooth enough transition.

The moonlight was casting a glow across the great fields, and Emerson sighed, taking in the simple beauty of it.

Everything still hurt, the loss of Holden still hurt. But she could already see that her mother was right. Love was miraculous, and believing in the miraculous, having experienced it, enhanced the beauty in the world, even as it hurt.

And then, out in the rows, she was sure that she saw movement.

She held her breath, and there in the moonlight she saw the silhouette of a cowboy.

Not just a cowboy. *Her* cowboy.

For a moment, she thought about not going down.

She thought about staying up in her room. But she couldn't. She had to go to him.

Even if it was foolish.

She stole out and padded down the stairs, out the front door of the estate and straight out to the vines.

"What are you doing here?"

"I know I'm not on the guest list," he said.

"No," she said. "You're not. In fact, you were supposed to have ridden off into the sunset."

"Sorry about that. But the sun has set."

"Holden…"

"I was wondering if you needed a ranch hand."

"What?"

"The winery is yours. I want it to stay yours. Yours and your sisters'. I certainly don't deserve a piece of it. And I just thought… The one time I had it right with you when I worked here. When it was you and me, and not all this manipulation. So I thought maybe I would just offer me."

"Just you?"

"Yeah," he said. "Just me."

"I mean, you still have your property development money, I assume."

"Yeah," he said. "But… I also love you. And I was sort of hoping that you still love me."

She blinked hard, her heart about to race out of her chest. "Yes," she said. "I love you still. I do. And all I need is you. Not anything else."

"I feel the same way," he said. "You. Just the way you are. It quit being about revenge, and when it quit being about revenge, I didn't have an excuse to stay anymore, and it scared the hell out of me. Because I never thought that I would be the kind of man that wanted forever. And wanting it scared me. And I don't like being scared."

"None of us do. But I'm so glad that you came here, though," she said. "Because if you hadn't... I thought as long as everything looked good, then it was close enough to being good. I had no idea that it could be like this."

"And if I had never met you, then I would never have had anything but money and anger. And believe me, compared to this, compared to you, that's nothing."

"You showed me my heart," she said. "You showed me what I really wanted."

"And you showed me mine. I was wrong," he said. "When I said things couldn't be fixed. They can be. When I told my sister that I came here to get revenge, she wasn't happy. It's not what she needed from me. She needed love. Support. Revenge just destroys, love is what builds. I want to love you and build a life with you. Forever."

"So do I." She threw herself into his arms, wrapped her own around his neck and kissed him. "So do I."

Emerson Maxfield knew without a shadow of a doubt, as her strong, handsome husband held her in his arms, that she was never going to be bored with her life again.

Because she knew now that it wasn't a party, a launch, a successful campaign that was going to bring happiness or decide who she was.

No, that came from inside of her.

And it was enough.

Who she was loved Holden McCall. And whatever came their way, it didn't scare her. Because they would face it together.

She remembered that feeling she'd had, adrift, like she had nowhere to go, like her whole life had been untethered.

But she had found who she was, she had found her heart, in him.

And she knew that she would never have to question where she belonged again. Because it was wherever he was.

Forever.

* * * * *

Read more from New York Times *bestselling author Maisey Yates and Harlequin Desire!*

Take Me, Cowboy
Seduce Me, Cowboy
Claim Me, Cowboy
Want Me, Cowboy
Need Me, Cowboy

HOLD ME, COWBOY

To KatieSauce, the sister I was always waiting for.
What a joy it is to have you in my life.

One

"Creative photography," Madison West muttered as she entered the security code on the box that contained the key to the cabin she would be staying in for the weekend

She looked across the snowy landscape to see another home situated *far* too close to the place she would be inhabiting for the next couple of days. The photographs on the vacation-rental website hadn't mentioned that she would be sharing the property with anyone else.

And obviously, the example pictures had been taken from inventive angles.

It didn't matter. Nothing was going to change her plans. She just hoped the neighbors had earplugs. Because she was having sex this weekend. Nonstop sex.

Ten years celibate, and it was ending tonight. She had finally found *the one*. Not the one she was going to marry, obviously. *Please*. Love was for other people. People who hadn't been tricked, manipulated and humiliated when they were seventeen.

No, she had no interest in love and marriage. But she had abundant interest in orgasms. So much interest. And she had found the perfect man to deliver them.

All day, all night, for the next forty-eight hours.

She was armed with a suitcase full of lingerie and four bottles of wine. Neighbors be damned. She'd been hoping for a little more seclusion, but this was fine. It would be fine.

She unlocked the door and stepped inside, breathing a sigh of relief when she saw that the interior, at least, met with her expectations. But it was a little bit smaller than it had looked online, and she could only hope that wasn't some sort of dark portent for the rest of her evening.

She shook her head; she was not going to introduce that concern into the mix, thank you very much. There was enough to worry about when you were thinking about breaking ten years of celibacy without adding such concerns.

Christopher was going to arrive soon, so she figured she'd better get upstairs and start setting a scene. She made her way to the bedroom, then opened her suitcase and took out the preselected bit of lace she had chosen for their first time. It was red, which looked very good on her, if a bit obvious. But she was aiming for obvious.

Christopher wasn't her boyfriend. And he wasn't going to be. He was a very nice equine-vitamin-supplement salesman she'd met a few weeks ago when he'd come by the West estate. She had bought some products for her horses, and they'd struck up a conversation, which had transitioned into a flirtation.

Typically, when things began to transition into flirtation, Maddy put a stop to them. But she hadn't with him. Maybe because he was special. Maybe because ten years was just way too long. Either way, she had kept on flirting with him.

They'd gone out for drinks, and she'd allowed him to kiss her. Which had been a lot more than she'd allowed any other guy in recent years. It had reminded her how much she'd enjoyed that sort of thing once upon a time. And once she'd been reminded…well.

He'd asked for another date. She'd stopped him. Because wouldn't a no-strings physical encounter be way better?

He'd of course agreed. Because he was a man.

But she hadn't wanted to get involved with anyone in town. She didn't need anyone seeing her at a hotel or his house or with his car parked at her little home on her parents' property.

Thus, the cabin-weekend idea had been born.

She shimmied out of her clothes and wiggled into the skintight lace dress that barely covered her backside. Then she set to work fluffing her blond hair and applying some lipstick that matched the lingerie.

She was not answering the door in this outfit, however.

She put her long coat back on over the lingerie, then gave her reflection a critical look. It had been a long time since she had dressed to attract a man. Usually, she was more interested in keeping them at a distance.

"Not tonight," she said. "*Not* tonight."

She padded downstairs, peering out the window and

seeing nothing beyond the truck parked at the small house across the way and a vast stretch of snow, falling harder and faster.

Typically, it didn't snow in Copper Ridge, Oregon. You had to drive up to the mountains—as she'd done today—to get any of the white stuff. So, for her, this was a treat, albeit a chilly one. But that was perfect, since she planned to get her blood all heated and stuff.

She hummed, keeping an eye on the scene outside, waiting for Christopher to pull in. She wondered if she should have brought a condom downstairs with her. Decided that she should have.

She went back upstairs, taking them two at a time, grateful that she was by herself, since there was nothing sexy about her ascent. Then she rifled through her bag, found some protection and curled her fingers around it before heading back down the stairs as quickly as possible.

As soon as she entered the living area, the lights flickered, then died. Suddenly, everything in the house seemed unnaturally quiet, and even though it was probably her imagination, she felt the temperature drop several degrees.

"Are you kidding me?" she asked, into the darkness.

There was no answer. Nothing but a subtle creak from the house. Maybe it was all that heavy snow on the roof. Maybe it was going to collapse. That would figure.

A punishment for her thinking she could be normal and have sex.

A shiver worked its way down her spine, and she jolted.

Suddenly, she had gone from hopeful and buoyant

to feeling a bit flat and tragic. That was definitely not the best sign.

No. She wasn't doing this. She wasn't sinking into self-pity and tragedy. Been there, done that for ten years, thank you.

Madison didn't believe in signs. *So there.* She believed in fuses blowing in bad weather when overtaxed heaters had to work too hard in ancient houses. Yes, *that* she believed in. She also believed that she would have to wait for Christopher to arrive to fix the problem.

She sighed and then made her way over to the kitchen counter and grabbed hold of her purse as she deposited the two condoms on the counter. She pulled her phone out and grimaced when she saw that she had no signal.

Too late, she remembered that she had thought the lack of cell service might be an attraction to a place like this. That it would be nice if both she and Christopher could be cut off from the outside world while they indulged themselves.

That notion seemed really freaking stupid right now. Since she couldn't use the phone in the house thanks to the outage, and that left her cut off from the outside world all alone.

"Oh no," she said, "I'm the first five minutes of a crime show. I'm going to get ax-murdered. And I'm going to die a born-again virgin."

She scowled, looking back out at the resolutely blank landscape. Christopher still wasn't here. But it looked like the house across the way had power.

She pressed her lips together, not happy about the idea of interrupting her neighbor. Or of meeting her neighbor, since the whole point of going out of town was so they could remain anonymous and not see people.

She tightened the belt on her coat and made her way slowly out the front door, bracing herself against the arctic wind.

She muttered darkly about the cold as she made her way across the space between the houses. She paused for a moment in front of the larger cabin, lit up and looking all warm and toasty. Clearly, this was the premium accommodation. While hers was likely beset by rodents that had chewed through relevant cords.

She huffed, clutching her coat tightly as she knocked on the door. She waited, bouncing in place to try to keep her blood flowing. She just needed to call Christopher and find out when he would be arriving and, if he was still a ways out, possibly beg her neighbor for help getting the power going. Or at least help getting a fire started.

The front door swung open and Madison's heart stopped. The man standing there was large, so tall that she only just came up to the middle of his chest. He was broad, his shoulders well muscled, his waist trim. He had the kind of body that came not from working out but from hard physical labor.

Then she looked up. Straight nose, square jaw, short brown hair and dark eyes that were even harder than his muscles. And far too familiar.

"What are *you* doing here?"

Sam McCormack gritted his teeth against the sharp tug of irritation that assaulted him when Madison West asked the question that had been on his own lips.

"I rented the place," he responded, not inviting her in. "Though I could ask you the same question."

She continued to do a little bounce in place, her arms

folded tight against her body, her hands clasped beneath her chin. "And you'd get the same answer," she said. "I'm across the driveway."

"Then you're at the wrong door." He made a move to shut said door, and she reached out, stopping him.

"Sam. Do you always have to be this unpleasant?"

It was a question that had been asked of him more than once. And he gave his standard answer. "Yes."

"Sam," she said, sounding exasperated. "The power went out, and I'm freezing to death. Can I come in?"

He let out a long-suffering sigh and stepped to the side. He didn't like Madison West. He never had. Not from the moment he had been hired on as a farrier for the West estate eight years earlier. In all the years since he'd first met Madison, since he'd first started shoeing her horses, he'd never received one polite word from her.

But then, he'd never given one either.

She was sleek, blonde and freezing cold—and he didn't mean because she had just come in from the storm. The woman carried her own little snow cloud right above her head at all times, and he wasn't a fan of ice princesses. Still, something about her had always been like a burr beneath his skin that he couldn't get at.

"Thank you," she said crisply, stepping over the threshold.

"You're rich and pretty," he said, shutting the door tight behind her. "And I'm poor. And kind of an ass. It wouldn't do for me to let you die out there in a snowdrift. I would probably end up getting hung."

Madison sniffed, making a show of brushing snowflakes from the shoulders of her jacket. "I highly doubt you're poor," she said drily.

She wasn't wrong. A lot had changed since he'd gone

to work for the Wests eight years ago. Hell, a lot had changed in the past year.

The strangest thing was that his art had taken off, and along with it the metalwork and blacksmithing business he ran with his brother, Chase.

But now he was busier coming up with actual fine-art pieces than he was doing daily grunt work. One sale on a piece like that could set them up for the entire quarter. Strange, and not where he'd seen his life going, but true.

He still had trouble defining himself as an artist. In his mind, he was just a blacksmith cowboy. Most at home on the family ranch, most proficient at pounding metal into another shape. It just so happened that for some reason people wanted to spend a lot of money on that metal.

"Well," he said, "perception is everything."

She looked up at him, those blue eyes hitting him hard, like a punch in the gut. That was the other obnoxious thing about Madison West. She was pretty. She was more than pretty. She was the kind of pretty that kept a man up all night, hard and aching, with fantasies about her swirling in his head.

She was also the kind of woman who would probably leave icicles on a man's member after a blow job.

No, thank you.

"Sure," she said, waving her hand. "Now, I *perceive* that I need to use your phone."

"There's no cell service up here."

"Landline," she said. "I have no power. And no cell service. The source of all my problems."

"In that case, be my guest," he responded, turning

away from her and walking toward the kitchen, where the lone phone was plugged in.

He picked up the receiver and held it out to her. She eyed it for a moment as though it were a live snake, then snatched it out of his hand. "Are you just going to stand there?"

He shrugged, crossing his arms and leaning against the doorframe. "I thought I might."

She scoffed, then dialed the number, doing the same impatient hop she'd been doing outside while she waited for the person on the other end to answer. "Christopher?"

The physical response Sam felt to her uttering another man's name was not something he ever could have anticipated. His stomach tightened, dropped, and a lick of flame that felt a hell of a lot like jealousy sparked inside him.

"What do you mean you can't get up here?" She looked away from him, determinedly so, her eyes fixed on the kitchen floor. "The road is closed. Okay. So that means I can't get back down either?" There was a pause. "Right. Well, hopefully I don't freeze to death." Another pause. "No, you don't need to call anybody. I'm not going to freeze to death. I'm using the neighbor's phone. Just forget it. I don't have cell service. I'll call you if the power comes back on in my cabin."

She hung up then, her expression so sharp it could have cut him clean through.

"I take it you had plans."

She looked at him, her eyes as frosty as the weather outside. "Did you figure that out all by yourself?"

"Only just barely. You know blacksmiths aren't known for their deductive reasoning skills. Mostly we're famous for hitting heavy things with other heavy things."

"Kind of like cavemen and rocks."

He took a step toward her. "Kind of."

She shrank back, a hint of color bleeding into her cheeks. "Well, now that we've established that there's basically no difference between you and a Neanderthal, I better get back to my dark, empty cabin. And hope that you aren't a secret serial killer."

Her sharp tongue left cuts behind, and he had to admit he kind of enjoyed it. There weren't very many people who sparred with him like this. Possibly because he didn't talk to very many people. "Is that a legitimate concern you have?"

"I don't know. The entire situation is just crazy enough that I might be trapped in a horror movie with a tortured artist blacksmith who is also secretly murdery."

"I guarantee you I'm not murdery. If you see me outside with an ax, it will only be because I'm cutting firewood."

She cocked her head to the side, a glint in her blue eyes that didn't look like ice making his stomach—and everything south of there—tighten. "Well, that's a relief. Anyway. I'm going. Dark cabin, no one waiting for me. It promises to be a seriously good time."

"You don't have any idea why the power is out, or how to fix it?" he asked.

"No," she said, sounding exasperated, and about thirty seconds away from stamping her foot.

Well, damn his conscience, but he wasn't letting her go back to an empty, dark, cold cabin. No matter that she had always treated him like a bit of muck she'd stepped in with her handmade riding boots.

"Let me have a look at your fuse box," he said.

"You sound like you'd rather die," she said.

"I pretty much would, but I'm not going to let *you* die either." He reached for his black jacket and the matching black cowboy hat hanging on a hook. He put both on and nodded.

"Thank you," she muttered, and he could tell the little bit of social nicety directed at him cost her dearly.

They headed toward the front door and he pushed it open, waiting for her to go out first. Since he had arrived earlier today, the temperature had dropped drastically. He had come up to the mountain to do some planning for his next few art projects. It pained him to admit, even to himself, that solitude was somewhat necessary for him to get a clear handle on what he was going to work on next.

"So," he said, making conversation not so much for the sake of it but more to needle her and see if he could earn one of her patented death glares, "Christopher, huh? Your boyfriend?" That hot spike drove its way through his gut again and he did his best to ignore it.

"No," she said tersely. "Just a friend."

"I see. So you decided to meet a man up here for a friendly game of Twister?"

She turned slightly, arching one pale brow. "Yahtzee, actually. I'm very good at it."

"And I'm sure your…*friend* was hoping to get a full house."

She rolled her eyes and looked forward again, taking quick steps over the icy ground, and somehow managing to keep sure footing. Then she opened the door to her cabin. "Welcome," she said, extending her arm.

"Please excuse the shuddering cold and oppressive darkness."

"Ladies first," he said.

She shook her head, walking into the house, and he followed behind, closing the door against the elements. It was already cold in the dark little room. "You were just going to come back here and sit in the dark if I hadn't offered to fiddle with the circuit breaker?"

"Maybe I know how to break my own circuits, Sam. Did you ever think of that?"

"Oh, but you said you didn't, Madison."

"I prefer Maddy," she said.

"Sorry, Madison," he said, tipping his hat, just to be a jerk.

"I should have just frozen to death. Then there could have been a legend about my tragic and beautiful demise in the mountains." He didn't say anything. He just looked at her until she sighed and continued talking. "I don't know where the box thingy is. You're going to have to hunt for it."

"I think I can handle that." He walked deeper into the kitchen, then stopped when he saw two purple packets sitting on the kitchen counter. That heat returned with a vengeance when he realized exactly what they were, and what they meant. He looked up, his eyes meeting her extremely guilty gaze. "Yahtzee, huh?"

"That's what the kids call it," she said, pressing her palm over the telling packets.

"Only because they're too immature to call it fucking."

Color washed up her neck, into her cheeks. "Or not crass enough."

In that moment, he had no idea what devil possessed

him, and he didn't particularly care. He turned to face
her, planting his hands on the countertop, just an inch
away from hers. "I don't know about that. I'm betting
that you could use a little crassness in your life, Madison West."

"Are you trying to suggest that I need *you*?" she
asked, her voice choked.

Lightning streaked through his blood, and in that
moment, he was lost. It didn't matter that he thought
she was insufferable, a prissy little princess who didn't
appreciate any damn thing she had. It didn't matter that
he'd come up here to work.

All that mattered was he hadn't touched a woman
in a long time, and Madison West was so close all he
would have to do was shift his weight slightly and he'd
be able to take her into his arms.

He looked down pointedly at her hand, acting as
though he could see straight through to the protection
beneath. "Well," he said, "you have a couple of the essential ingredients to have yourself a pretty fun evening.
All you seem to be missing is the man. But I imagine
the guy you invited up here is *nice*. I'm not very nice,
Madison," he said, leaning in, "but I could damn sure
show you a good time."

Two

The absolute worst thing was the fact that Sam's words sent a shiver down her spine. Sam McCormack. Why did it have to be Sam McCormack? He was the deadly serpent to her Indiana Jones.

She should throw him out. Throw him out and get back to her very disappointing evening where all orgasms would be self-administered. So, basically a regular Friday night.

She wanted to throw herself on the ground and wail. It was not supposed to be a regular Friday night. She was supposed to be breaking her sex fast. Maybe this was why people had flings in the spring. Inclement weather made winter flings difficult. Also, mostly you just wanted to keep your socks on the whole time. And that wasn't sexy.

Maybe her libido should hibernate for a while. Pop

up again when the pear trees were blooming or something.

She looked over at Sam, and her libido made a dash to the foreground. That was the problem with Sam. He irritated her. He was exactly the kind of man she didn't like. He was cocky. He was rough and crude.

Whenever she'd given him very helpful pointers about handling the horses when he came to do farrier work at the estate, he was always telling her to go away and in general showing no deference.

And okay, if he'd come and told her how to do her job, she would have told him where he could stick his hoof nippers. But still. Her animals. So she was entitled to her opinions.

Last time she'd walked into the barn when he was doing shoes, he hadn't even looked up from his work. He'd just pointed back toward the door and shouted, *out!*

Yeah, he was a jerk.

However, there was something about the way he looked in a tight T-shirt, his muscles bulging as he did all that hard labor, that made a mockery of that very certain hatred she felt burning in her breast.

"Are you going to take off your coat and stay awhile?" The question, asked in a faintly mocking tone, sent a dart of tension straight down between her thighs.

She could *not* take off her coat. Because she was wearing nothing more than a little scrap of red lace underneath it. And now that was all she could think of. About how little stood between Sam and her naked body.

About what might happen if she just went ahead and dropped the coat now and revealed all of that to him.

"It's cold," she snapped. "Maybe if you went to work

getting the electricity back on rather than standing there making terrible double entendres, I would be able to take off my coat."

He lifted a brow. "And then do you think you'll take me up on my offer to show you a good time?"

"If you can get my electricity back on, I will consider a good time shown to me. Honestly, that's all I want. The ability to microwave popcorn and not turn into a Maddycicle."

The maddening man raised his eyebrows, shooting her a look that clearly said *Suit yourself,* then set about looking for the fuse box.

She stood by alone for a while, her arms wrapped around her midsection. Then she started to feel like an idiot just kind of hanging out there while he searched for the source of all power. She let out an exasperated sigh and followed his path, stopping when she saw him leaning up against a wall, a little metal door fixed between the logs open as he examined the small black switches inside.

"It's not a fuse. That means there's something else going on." He slammed the door shut. Then he turned back to look at her. "You should come over to my cabin."

"No!" The denial was a little bit too enthusiastic. A little bit too telling. "I mean, I can start a fire here—it's going to be fine. I'm not going to freeze."

"You're going to curl up by the fire with a blanket? Like a sad little pet?"

She made a scoffing sound. "No, I'm going to curl up by the fire like the Little Match Girl."

"That makes it even worse. The Little Match Girl froze to death."

"What?"

"How did you not know that?"

"I saw it when I was a kid. It was a *cartoon*. She really died?" Maddy blinked. "What kind of story is that to present to children?"

"An early lesson, maybe? Life is bleak, and then you freeze to death alone?"

"Charming," she said.

"Life rarely is." He kept looking at her. His dark gaze was worrisome.

"I'm fine," she said, because somebody had to say something.

"You are not. Get your suitcase—come over to the cabin. We can flip the lights on, and then if we notice from across the driveway that your power's on again, you can always come back."

It was stupid to refuse him. She knew him, if not personally, at least well enough to know that he wasn't any kind of danger to her.

The alternative was trying to sleep on the couch in the living room while the outside temperatures hovered below freezing, waking up every few hours to keep the fire stoked.

Definitely, going over to his cabin made more sense. But the idea filled her with a strange tension that she couldn't quite shake. Well, she knew exactly what kind of tension it was. *Sexual tension.*

She and Sam had so much of it that hung between them like a fog whenever they interacted. Although, maybe she read it wrong. Maybe on his end it was just irritation and it wasn't at all tinged with sensual shame.

"Why do you have to be so damned reasonable?" she asked, turning away from him and stalking toward the stairs.

"Where are you going?"

She stopped, turning to face him. "To change. Also, to get my suitcase. I have snacks in there."

"Are snacks a euphemism for something interesting?" he asked, arching a dark brow.

She sputtered, genuinely speechless. Which was unusual to downright unheard of. "No," she said, her tone sounding petulant. "I have *actual snacks*."

"Come over to my place. Bring the snacks."

"I will," she said, turning on her heel, heading toward the stairs.

"Maybe bring the Yahtzee too."

Those words hit her hard, with all the impact of a stomach punch. She could feel her face turning crimson, and she refused to look back at him. Refused to react to that bait at all. He didn't want *that*. He did not want to play euphemistic board games with her. And she didn't want to play them with him.

If she felt a little bit…on edge, it was just because she had been anticipating sex and she had experienced profound sex disappointment. That was all.

She continued up the stairs, making her way to the bedroom, then changed back into a pair of jeans and a sweatshirt as quickly as possible before stuffing the little red lace thing back in the bag and zipping everything up.

She lugged it back downstairs, her heart slamming against her breastbone when Sam was in her line of sight again. Tall, broad shouldered and far too sexy for his own good, he promised to be the antidote to sexual disappointment.

But an emotionless hookup with a guy she liked well enough but wouldn't get emotionally involved with was one thing. Replacing him at the last moment with a guy she didn't even like? No, that was out of the question.

Absolutely and completely out of the question.

"Okay," she said, "let's go."

By the time she got settled in the extra room in the cabin, she was feeling antsy. She could hide, but she was hungry. And Maddy didn't believe in being hungry when food was at hand. Yes, she had some various sugar-based items in her bag, but she needed protein.

In the past, she had braved any number of her father's awkward soirees to gain access to bacon-wrapped appetizers.

She could brave Sam McCormack well enough to root around for sustenance. She would allow no man to stand between herself and her dinner.

Cautiously, she made her way downstairs, hoping that maybe Sam had put himself away for the night. The thought made her smile. That he didn't go to bed like a normal person but closed himself inside...not a coffin. But maybe a scratchy, rock-hewn box that would provide no warmth or comfort. It seemed like something he would be into.

In fairness, she didn't really know Sam McCormack that well, but everything she did know about him led her to believe that he was a supremely unpleasant person. Well, except for the whole him-not-letting-her-die-of-frostbite-in-her-powerless-cabin thing. She supposed she had to go ahead and put that in the Maybe He's Not Such a Jackass column.

Her foot hit the ground after the last stair silently, and she cautiously padded into the kitchen.

"Looking for something?"

She startled, turning around and seeing Sam standing there, leaning in the doorway, his muscular arms crossed over his broad chest. She did her best to look cool. Composed. Not interested in his muscles. "Well—" she tucked her hair behind her ear "—I was hoping to find some food."

"You brought snacks," he said.

"Candy," she countered.

"So, that made it okay for you to come downstairs and steal my steak?"

Her stomach growled. "You have steak?"

"It's *my* steak."

She hadn't really thought of that. "Well, my…you know, *the guy*. He was supposed to bring food. And I'm sorry. I didn't exactly think about the fact that whatever food is in this fridge is food that you personally provided. I was protein blind." She did her best to look plaintive. Unsurprisingly, Sam did not seem moved by her plaintiveness.

"I mean, it seems cruel to eat steak in front of you, Madison. Especially if I'm not willing to share." He rubbed his chin, the sounds of his whiskers abrading his palm sending a little shiver down her back. God knew why.

"You *would* do that. You would… You would tease me with your steak." Suddenly, it was all starting to sound a little bit sexual. Which she had a feeling was due in part to the fact that everything felt sexual to her right about now.

Which was because of the other man she had been about to sleep with. Not Sam. Not really.

A slow smile crossed his face. "I would never tease

you with my steak, Madison. If you want a taste, all you have to do is ask. Nicely."

She felt her face getting hotter. "May I please have your steak?"

"Are you going to cook it for me?"

"Did you want it to be edible?"

"That would be the goal, yes," he responded.

She lifted her hands up, palms out. "These hands don't cook."

His expression shifted. A glint of wickedness cutting through all that hardness. She'd known Sam was mean. She'd known he was rough. She had not realized he was wicked. "What do those hands do, I wonder?"

He let that innuendo linger between them and she practically hissed in response. "Do you have salad? I will fix salad. *You* cook steak. Then we can eat."

"Works for me, but I assume you're going to be sharing your candy with me?"

Seriously, everything sounded filthy. She had to get a handle on herself. "Maybe," she said, "but it depends on if your behavior merits candy." That didn't make it better.

"I see. And what, pray tell, does Madison West consider candy-deserving behavior?"

She shrugged, making her way to the fridge and opening it, bending down and opening the crisper drawer. "I don't know. Not being completely unbearable?"

"Your standards are low."

"Luckily for you."

She looked up at him and saw that that had actually elicited what looked to be a genuine grin. The man was a mystery. And she shouldn't care about that. She should not want to unlock, unravel or otherwise solve him.

The great thing about Christopher was that he was simple. He wasn't connected to her life in any way. They could come up and have an affair and it would never bleed over to her existence in Copper Ridge. It was the antithesis of everything she had experienced with David. David, who had blown up her entire life, shattered her career ambitions and damaged her good standing in the community.

This thing with Christopher was supposed to be sex. Sex that made nary a ripple in the rest of her life.

Sam would not be rippleless.

The McCormack family was too much a part of the fabric of Copper Ridge. More so in the past year. Sam and his brother, Chase, had done an amazing job of revitalizing their family ranch, and somewhere in all of that Sam had become an in-demand artist. Though he would be the last person to say it. He still showed up right on schedule to do the farrier work at her family ranch. As though he weren't raking in way more money with his ironwork.

Sam was… Well, he was kind of everywhere. His works of art appearing in restaurants and galleries around town. His person appearing on the family ranch to work on the horses. He was the exact wrong kind of man for her to be fantasizing about.

She should be more gun-shy than this. Actually, she had spent the past decade being more gun-shy than this. It was just that apparently now that she had allowed herself to remember she had sexual feelings, it was difficult for her to turn them off. Especially when she was trapped in a snowstorm with a man for whom the term *rock-hard body* would be a mere description and not hyperbole.

She produced the salad, then set about to preparing it. Thankfully, it was washed and torn already. So her responsibility literally consisted of dumping it from bag to bowl. That was the kind of cooking she could get behind. Meanwhile, Sam busied himself with preparing two steaks on the stovetop. At some point, he took the pan from the stovetop and transferred it to the oven.

"I didn't know you had actual cooking technique," she said, not even pretending to herself that she wasn't watching the play of his muscles in his forearms as he worked.

Even at the West Ranch, where she always ended up sniping at him if they ever interacted, she tended to linger around him while he did his work with the horses because his arms put on quite a show. She was hardly going to turn away from him now that they were in an enclosed space, with said arms very, very close. And no one else around to witness her ogling.

She just didn't possess that kind of willpower.

"Well, Madison, I have a lot of eating technique. The two are compatible."

"Right," she said, "as you don't have a wife. Or a girlfriend…" She could have punched her own face for that. It sounded so leading and obvious. As if she cared if he had a woman in his life.

She didn't. Well, she kind of did. Because honestly, she didn't even like to ogle men who could be involved with another woman. Once bitten, twice shy. By which she meant once caught in a torrid extramarital affair with a man in good standing in the equestrian community, ten years emotionally scarred.

"No," he said, tilting his head, the cocky look in his eye doing strange things to her stomach, "I don't."

"I don't have a boyfriend. Not an actual boyfriend." Oh, good Lord. She was the desperate worst and she hated herself.

"So you keep saying," he returned. "You really want to make sure I know Christopher isn't your boyfriend." She couldn't ignore the implication in his tone.

"Because he isn't. Because we're not... Because we've never. This was going to be our first time." Being forthright and making people uncomfortable with said forthrightness had been a very handy shield for the past decade, but tonight it was really obnoxious.

"Oh really?" He suddenly looked extremely interested.

"Yes," she responded, keeping her tone crisp, refusing to show him just how off-kilter she felt. "I'm just making dinner conversation."

"This is the kind of dinner conversation you normally make?"

She arched her brow. "Actually, yes. Shocking people is kind of my modus operandi."

"I don't find you that shocking, Madison. I do find it a little bit amusing that you got cock-blocked by a snowbank."

She nearly choked. "Wine. Do you have wine?" She turned and started rummaging through the nearest cabinet. "Of course you do. You probably have a baguette too. That seems like something an artist would do. Set up here and drink wine and eat a baguette."

He laughed, a kind of short, dismissive sound. "Hate to disappoint you. But my artistic genius is fueled by Jack." He reached up, opening the cabinet nearest to his head, and pulled down a bottle of whiskey. "But I'm happy to share that too."

"You have diet soda?"

"Regular."

"My, this *is* a hedonistic experience. I'll have regular, then."

"Well, when a woman was expecting sex and doesn't get it, I suppose regular cola is poor consolation, but it is better than diet."

"Truer words were never spoken." She watched him while he set about to making a couple of mixed drinks for them. He handed one to her, and she lifted it in salute before taking a small sip. By then he was taking the steak out of the oven and setting it back on the stovetop.

"Perfect," he remarked when he cut one of the pieces of meat in half and gauged the color of the interior.

She frowned. "How did I never notice that you aren't horrible?"

He looked at her, his expression one of mock surprise. "Not horrible? You be careful throwing around compliments like that, missy. A man could get the wrong idea."

She rolled her eyes. "Right. I just mean, you're funny."

"How much of that whiskey have you had?"

"One sip. So it isn't even that." She eyeballed the food that he was now putting onto plates. "It might be the steak. I'm not going to lie to you."

"I'm comfortable with that."

He carried their plates to the table, and she took the lone bottle of ranch dressing out of the fridge and set it and her drink next to her plate. And then, somehow, she ended up sitting at a very nicely appointed dinner table with Sam McCormack, who was not the man she was supposed to be with tonight.

Maybe it was because of the liquored-up soda. Maybe it was neglected hormones losing their ever-loving minds in the presence of such a fine male specimen. Maybe it was just as simple as want. Maybe there was no justification for it at all. Except that Sam was actually beautiful. And she had always thought so, no matter how much he got under her skin.

That was the honest truth. It was why she found him so off-putting, why she had always found him so off-putting from the moment he had first walked onto the West Ranch property. Because he was the kind of man a woman could make a mistake with. And she had thought she was done making mistakes.

Now she was starting to wonder if a woman was entitled to one every decade.

Her safe mistake, the one who would lift out of her life, hadn't eventuated. And here in front of her was one that had the potential to be huge. But very, very good.

She wasn't so young anymore. She wasn't naive at all. When it came right down to it, she was hot for Sam. She had been for a long time.

She'd had so much caution for so long. So much hiding. So much *not doing*. Well, she was tired of that.

"I was very disappointed about Christopher not making it up here," she said, just as Sam was putting the last bite of steak into his mouth.

"Sure," he said.

"Very disappointed."

"Nobody likes blue balls, Maddy, even if they don't have testicles."

She forced a laugh through her constricted throat. "That's hilarious," she said.

He looked up at her slowly. "No," he said, "it wasn't."

She let out a long, slow breath. "Okay," she said, "it wasn't that funny. But here's the thing. The reason I was so looking forward to tonight is that I hadn't had sex with Christopher before. In fact, I haven't had sex with anyone in ten years. So. Maybe you could help me with that?"

Three

Sam was pretty sure he must be hallucinating. Because there was no way Madison West had just propositioned him. Especially not on the heels of admitting that it had been ten years since she'd had sex.

Hell, he was starting to think that *he* was the celibacy champion. But clearly, Maddy had him beat. Or she didn't, because there was no way in hell that she had actually said any of that.

"Are you drunk, Madison?" It was the first thing that came to mind, and it seemed like an important thing to figure out.

"After one Jack Daniel's and Coke? Absolutely not. I am a West, dammit. We can hold our liquor. I am... reckless, opportunistic and horny. A lot horny. I just... I need this. Sam, do you know what it's like to go *ten years* without doing something? It becomes a whole thing. Like, a whole big thing that starts to define you, even if it shouldn't. And you don't want anyone to know. Oh, my gosh, can you even imagine if my friends knew that it has been ten years since I have seen an actual…?" She took a deep breath, then forged on. "I'm rambling and I just *really* need this."

Sam felt like he had been hit over the head with a metric ton of iron. He had no idea how he was supposed to respond to this—the strangest of all propositions— from a woman who had professed to hate him only a few moments ago.

He had always thought Madison was a snob. A pain in his ass, even if she was a pretty pain in the ass. She was always looming around, looking down her nose at him while he did his work. As though only the aristocracy of Copper Ridge could possibly know how to do the lowly labor he was seeing to. Even if they hadn't the ability to do it themselves.

The kinds of people who professed to have strengths in "management." People who didn't know how to get their hands dirty.

He hated people like that. And he had never been a fan of Madison West.

He, Sam McCormack, should not be interested in taking her up on her offer. No, not in any way. However, Sam McCormack's dick was way more interested in it than he would've liked to admit.

Immediately, he was rock hard thinking about what it would be like to have her delicate, soft hands skimming over him. He had rough hands. Workman's hands. The kind of hands that a woman like Madison West had probably never felt against her rarefied flesh.

Hell, the fact that it had been ten years since she'd

gotten any made that even more likely. And damn if that didn't turn him on. It was kind of twisted, a little bit sick, but then, it was nothing short of what he expected from himself.

He was a lot of things. Good wasn't one of them.

Ready to explode after years of repressing his desires, after years of pushing said desire all down and pretending it wasn't there? He was that.

"I'm not actually sure you want this," he said, wondering what the hell he was doing. Giving her an out when he wanted to throw her down and make her his.

Maddy stood up, not about to be cowed by him. He should have known that she would take that as a challenge. Maybe he had known that. Maybe it was why he'd said it.

That sounded like him. That sounded a lot more like him than trying to do the honorable thing.

"You don't know what I want, Sam," she said, crossing the space between them, swaying her hips just a little bit more than she usually did.

He would be a damn liar if he said that he had never thought about what it might be like to grab hold of those hips and pull Maddy West up against him. To grind his hardness against her soft flesh and make her feel exactly what her snobby-rich-girl mouth did to him.

But just because he'd fantasized about it before, didn't mean he had ever anticipated doing it. It didn't mean that he should take her up on it now.

Still, the closer she got to him, the less likely it seemed that he was going to say no.

"I think that after ten years of celibacy a man could make the argument that you don't know what you want, Madison West."

Her eyes narrowed, glittering blue diamonds that looked like they could cut a man straight down to the bone. "I've always known what I wanted. I may not have always made the best decisions, but I was completely certain that I wanted them. At the time."

His lips tipped upward. "I'm just going to be another *at the time*, Maddy. Nothing else."

"That was the entire point of this weekend. For me to have something that didn't have consequences. For me to get a little bit of something for myself. Is that so wrong? Do I have to live a passionless existence because I made a mistake once? Am I going to question myself forever? I just need to… I need to rip the Band-Aid off."

"The Band-Aid?"

"The sex Band-Aid."

He nodded, pretending that he understood. "Okay."

"I want this," she said, her tone confident.

"Are you…suggesting…that I give you…sexual healing?"

She made a scoffing sound. "Don't make it sound cheesy. This is very serious. I would never joke about my sexual needs." She let out an exasperated sigh. "I'm doing this wrong. I'm just…"

Suddenly, she launched herself at him, wrapping her arms around his neck and pressing her lips against his. The moment she did it, it was like the strike of a hammer against hot iron. As rigid as he'd been before—in that moment, he bent. And easily.

Staying seated in the chair, he curved himself around Madison, wrapping his arms around her body, sliding his hands over her back, down to the sweet indent of her waist, farther still to the flare of those pretty hips.

The hips he had thought about taking hold of so many times before.

There was no hesitation now. None at all. There was only this. Only her. Only the soft, intoxicating taste of her on his tongue. Sugar, Jack Daniel's and something that was entirely Maddy.

Too rich for his blood. Far too expensive for a man like him. It didn't matter what he became. Didn't matter how much money he had in his bank account, he would always be what he was. There was no escaping it. Nobody knew. Not really. Not the various women who had graced his bed over the years, not his brother, Chase.

Nobody knew Sam McCormack.

At least, nobody alive.

Neither, he thought, would Madison West. This wasn't about knowing anybody. This was just about satisfying a need. And he was simple enough to take her up on that.

He wedged his thigh up between her legs, pressing his palm down on her lower back, encouraging her to flex her hips in time with each stroke of his tongue. Encouraging her to satisfy that ache at the apex of her thighs.

Her head fell back, her skin flushed and satisfaction grabbed him by the throat, gripping him hard and strong. It would've surprised him if he hadn't suspected he was the sort of bastard who would get off on something like this.

Watching this beautiful, classy girl coming undone in his arms.

She was right. This weekend could be out of time. It could be a moment for them to indulge in things they would never normally allow themselves to have. The kinds of things that he had closed himself off from years ago.

Softness, warmth, touch.

He had denied himself all those things for years. Why not do this now? No one would know. No one would ever have to know. Maddy would see to that. She would never, no chance in hell, admit that she had gotten down and dirty with a man who was essentially a glorified blacksmith.

No way in hell.

That made them both safe. It made this safe. Well, as safe as fire this hot could be.

She bit his lip and he growled, pushing his hands up underneath the hem of her shirt, kissing her deeper as he let his fingertips roam to the line of her elegant spine, then tracing it upward until he found her bra, releasing it with ease, then dragging it and her top up over her head, leaving her naked from the waist up.

"I…" Her face was a bright shade of red. "I… I have lingerie. I wasn't going to…"

"I don't give a damn about your lingerie. I just want this." He lowered his head, sliding his tongue around the perimeter of one of her tightened nipples. "I want your skin." He closed his lips over that tight bud, sucking it in deep.

"I had a seduction plan," she said, her voice trembling. He wasn't entirely sure it was a protest, or even a complaint.

"You don't plan passion, baby," he said.

At least, he didn't. Because if he were thinking clearly, he would be putting her top back on and telling her to go back to her ice-cold cabin, where she would be safe.

"I do," she said, her teeth chattering in spite of the fact that it was very warm in the kitchen. "I plan everything."

"Not this. You're a dirty girl now, Madison West," he said, sliding his thumb over her damp nipple, moving it in a slow circle until she arched her back and cried out. "You were going to sleep with another man this weekend, and you replaced him so damn easily. With me. Doesn't even matter to you who you have. As long as you get a little bit. Is that how it is?"

She whimpered, biting her lip, rolling her hips against him.

"Good girl," he said, his gut tightening, his arousal so hard he was sure he was going to burst through the front of his jeans. "I like that. I like you being dirty for me."

He moved his hands then, curving his fingers around her midsection, his thumbs resting just beneath the swell of her breasts. She was so soft, so smooth, so petite and fragile. Everything he should never be allowed to put his hands on. But for some reason, instead of feeling a bolt of shame, he felt aroused. Hotter and harder than he could ever remember being. "You like that? My hands are rough. Maybe a little bit too rough for you."

"No," she said, and this time the protest was clear. "Not too rough for me at all."

He slid his hands down her back, taking a moment to really revel in how soft she was and how much different he must feel to her. She squirmed against him, and he took that as evidence that she really did like it.

That only made him hotter. Harder. More impatient.

"You didn't bring your damn candy and forget the condoms, did you?"

"No," she said, the denial coming quickly. "I brought the condoms."

"You always knew we would end up like this, didn't you?"

She looked away from him, and the way she refused to meet his eyes turned a throwaway game of a question into something deadly serious.

"Madison," he said, his voice hard. She still didn't look at him. He grabbed hold of her chin, redirecting her face so that she was forced to make eye contact with him. "You knew this would happen all along, didn't you?"

She still refused to answer him. Refused to speak.

"I think you did," he continued. "I think that's why you can never say a kind word to me. I think that's why you acted like a scalded cat every time I walked into the room. Because you knew it would end here. Because you wanted this. Because you wanted me."

Her expression turned even more mutinous.

"Madison," he said, a warning lacing through the word. "Don't play games with me. Or I'm not going to give you what you want. So you have to tell me. Tell me that you've always wanted me. You've always wanted my dirty hands on you. That's why you hate me so damn much, isn't it? Because you want me."

"I…"

"Madison," he said, his tone even more firm, "tell me—" he rubbed his hand over her nipple "—or I stop."

"I wanted you," she said, the admission rushed but clear all the same.

"More," he said, barely recognizing his own voice. "Tell me more."

It seemed essential suddenly, to know she'd wanted him. He didn't know why. He didn't care why.

"I've always wanted you. From the moment I first saw you. I knew that it would be like this. I knew that I would climb up into your lap and I would make a fool of myself rubbing all over you like a cat. I knew that from the beginning. So I argued with you instead."

He felt a satisfied smile that curved his lips upward. "Good girl." He lowered his hands, undoing the snap on her jeans and drawing the zipper down slowly. "You just made us both very happy." He moved his fingertips down beneath the waistband of her panties, his breath catching in his throat when he felt hot wetness beneath his touch. It had been way too long since he felt a silky-smooth desirable woman. Had been way too long in his self-imposed prison.

Too long since he'd wanted at all.

But Madison wasn't Elizabeth. And this wasn't the same.

He didn't need to think about her. He wasn't going to. Not for the rest of the night.

He pushed every thought out of his mind and instead exulted in the sound that Madison made when he moved his fingers over that place where she was wet and aching for him. When he delved deeper, pushing one finger inside her, feeling just how close she was to the edge, evidenced by the way her internal muscles clenched around him. He could thrust into her here. Take her hard and fast and she would still come. He knew that she would.

But she'd had ten years of celibacy, and he was pushing on five. They deserved more. They deserved better. At the very least they deserved a damn bed.

With that in mind, he wrapped his arms more tightly around her, moving his hands to cup her behind as he lifted her, wrapping her legs tightly around him as he carried them across the kitchen and toward the stairs.

Maddy let out an inelegant squeak as he began to ascend toward the bedrooms. "This is really happening," she said, sounding slightly dazed.

"I thought you said you weren't drunk."

"I'm not."

"Then try not to look so surprised. It's making me question things. And I don't want to question things. I just want you."

She shivered in his hold. "You're not like most men I know."

"Pretty boys with popped collars and pastel polo shirts? I must be a real disappointment."

"Obviously you aren't. Obviously I don't care about men in pastel polo shirts or I would've gotten laid any number of times in the past decade."

He pushed open the bedroom door, threw her down over the simply appointed bed that was far too small for the kind of acrobatics he wanted to get up to tonight. Then he stood back, admiring her, wearing nothing but those half-open jeans riding low on her hips, her stomach dipping in with each breath, her breasts thrust into greater prominence at the same time.

"Were you waiting for me?" He kept the words light, taunting, because he knew that she liked it.

She had always liked sparring with him. That was what they'd always done. Of course she would like it now. Of course he would like it now. Or maybe it had nothing to do with her. Maybe it had everything to do with the fact that he had years' worth of dirty in him that needed to be let out.

"Screw you," she said, pushing herself back farther up the mattress so that her head was resting on the pillow. Then she put her hands behind her head, her blue gaze sharp. "Come on, cowboy. Get naked for me."

"Oh no, Maddy, you're not running the show."

"Ten years," she said, her gaze level with his. "Ten years, Sam. That's how long it's been since I've seen a naked man. And let me tell you, I have never seen a naked man like you." She held up a finger. "One man. One insipid man. He wasn't even that good."

"You haven't had sex for ten years and your last lover wasn't even good? I was sort of hoping that it had been so good you were waiting for your knees to stop shaking before you bothered to go out and get some again."

"If only. My knees never once shook. In fact, they're shaking harder now and you haven't even gotten out of those pants yet."

"You give good dirty talk."

She lifted a shoulder. "I'm good at talking. That's about the thing I'm best at."

"Oh, I hope not, baby. I hope that mouth is good for a lot of other things too."

He saw her breasts hitch. Her eyes growing round. Then he smiled, grabbing hold of the hem of his shirt and stripping it off over his head. Her reaction was more satisfying than he could've possibly anticipated. It'd been a long time since he'd seen a woman looking at him that way.

Sure, women checked him out. That happened all the time. But this was different. This was raw, open hunger. She wasn't bothering to hide it. Why would she? They were both here to do this. No holds barred, no clothes, no nothing. Why bother to be coy? Why bother to pretend this was about anything other than satisfying lust. And if that was all it was, why should either of them bother to hide that lust.

"Keep looking at me like that, sweetheart, this is gonna end fast."

"Don't do that," she said, a wicked smile on her lips. "You're no good to me in that case."

"Don't worry, babe. I can get it up more than once."

At least, he could if he remembered correctly.

"Good thing I brought about three boxes of condoms."

"For two days? You did have high hopes for the weekend."

"Ten years," she reiterated.

"Point taken."

He moved his hands down, slowly working at his belt. The way that she licked her lips as her eyes followed his every movement ratcheting up his arousal another impossible notch.

Everything felt too sharp, too clear, every rasp of fabric over his skin, every downward flick of her eyes, every small, near-imperceptible gasp on her lips.

He hadn't been in a bedroom alone with a woman in a long damn time. And it was all catching up with him now.

Shutting down, being a mean bastard who didn't let anyone close? That was easy enough. It made it easy to forget. He shut the world out, stripped everything away. Reverted back to the way he had been just after his parents had died and it had been too difficult to feel anything more than his grief.

That was what he had done in the past five years. That was what he had done with his new, impossible loss that never should have happened. Wouldn't have if he'd had a shred of self-control and decency.

And now, tonight, he was proving that he probably still didn't have any at all. Oh well, just as well. Because he was going to do this.

He was going to do her.

He pushed his jeans down his lean hips, showing her the extent of his desire for her, reveling in the way her eyes widened when he revealed his body completely to her hungry gaze.

"I have never seen one that big before," she said.

He laughed. "Are you just saying that because it's what you think men need to hear?"

"No, I'm saying that because it's the biggest I've ever seen. And I want it."

"Baby," he said, "you can have it."

Maddy turned over onto her stomach and crawled across the bed on all fours in a move that damn near gave him a heart attack. Then she moved to the edge of the mattress, straightening up, raking her nails down over his torso before she leaned in, flicking her tongue over the head of his arousal.

He jerked beneath her touch, his length twitching as her tongue traced it from base to tip, just before she engulfed him completely in the warm heat of her mouth. She hummed, the vibration moving through his body, drawing his balls up tight. He really was going to lose it. Here and now like a green teenage boy if he didn't get a grip on himself. Or a grip on her.

He settled for the second option.

He reached back, grabbing hold of her hair and jerking her lips away from him. "You keep doing that and it really will end."

The color was high in her cheeks, her eyes glittering. "I've never, ever enjoyed it like that before."

She was so good for his ego. Way better than a man like him deserved. But damned if he wasn't going to take it.

"Well, you can enjoy more of that. Later. Right now? I need to be inside you."

"Technically," she said, her tone one of protest, "you were inside me."

"And as much as I like being in that pretty mouth of yours, that isn't what I want right now." He gritted his teeth, looking around the room. "The condoms."

She scrambled off the bed and shimmied out of her jeans and panties as she made her way across the room and toward her suitcase. She flipped it open, dug through it frantically and produced the two packets he had seen earlier.

All things considered, he felt a little bit triumphant to be the one getting these condoms. He didn't know Christopher, but that sad sack was sitting at home with a hard-on, and Sam was having his woman. He was going to go ahead and enjoy the hell out of that.

Madison turned to face him, the sight of that enticing, pale triangle at the apex of her thighs sending a shot straight down to his gut. She kept her eyes on his as she moved nearer, holding one of the condoms like it was a reward he was about to receive.

She tore it open and settled back onto the bed, then leaned forward and rolled it over his length. Then she took her position back up against the pillows, her thighs parting, her heavily lidded gaze averted from his now that she was in that vulnerable position.

"Okay," she said, "I'm ready."

She wasn't. Not by a long shot.

Ten years.

And he had been ready to thrust into her with absolutely no finesse. A woman who'd been celibate for ten years deserved more than that. She deserved more than one orgasm. Hell, she deserved more than two.

He had never been the biggest fan of Madison West, but tonight they were allies. Allies in pleasure. And he was going to hold up his end of the bargain so well that if she was celibate after this, it really would be because she was waiting for her legs to work again.

"Not quite yet, Maddy," he said, kneeling down at the end of the bed, reaching forward and grabbing hold of her hips, dragging her down toward his face. He brought her up against his mouth, her legs thrown over his shoulders, that place where she was warm and wet for him right there, ready for him to taste her.

"Sam!" Maddy squeaked.

"There is no way you're a prude, Maddy," he said. "I've had too many conversations with you to believe that."

"I've never... No one has ever..."

"Then it's time somebody did."

He lowered his head, tasting her in long, slow passes, like she was an ice-cream cone that he just had to take the time to savor. Like she was a delicacy he couldn't get enough of.

Because she was.

She was all warmth and sweet female, better than he had ever remembered a woman being. Or maybe she was just better. It was hard to say. He didn't really care which. It didn't matter. All that mattered was this.

If he could lose himself in any moment, in any time, it would be this one.

It sure as hell wouldn't be pounding iron, trying to hammer the guilt out of his body. Certainly wouldn't be in his damn sculptures, trying to figure out what to make next, trying to figure out how to satisfy the customer. This deeply personal thing that had started being given to the rest of the world, when he wasn't sure he wanted the rest of the world to see what was inside him.

Hell, *he* didn't want to see what was inside him.

He made a hell of a lot of money, carving himself out, making it into a product people could buy. And he sure as hell liked the money, but that didn't make it a pleasant experience.

No, none of that mattered. Not now. Not when there was Maddy. And that sweet sugar-whiskey taste.

He tasted her until she screamed, and then he thrust his fingers inside her, fast and rough, until he felt her pulse around him, until her orgasm swept through them both.

Then he moved up, his lips almost touching hers. "Now," he said, his voice husky, "now you're ready."

Four

Maddy was shaking from head to toe, and she honestly didn't know if she could take any more. She had never—not in her entire life—had an orgasm like that. It was still echoing through her body, creating little waves of sensation that shivered through her with each and every breath she took.

And there was still more. They weren't done. She was glad about that. She didn't want to be done. But at the same time she wasn't sure if she could handle the rest. But there he was, above her, over her, so hot and hard and male that she didn't think she could deny him. She didn't want to deny him.

She looked at him, at the broad expanse of his shoulders and chest, the way it tapered down to his narrow waist, those flat washboard abs that she could probably actually wash her clothes on.

He was everything a man should be. If the perfect fantasy man had been pulled straight out of her deepest fantasies, he would look like this. It hit her then that Christopher had not even been close to being a fantasy man. And that was maybe why he had been so safe. It was why Sam had always been so threatening.

Because Christopher had the power to make a ripple. Sam McCormack possessed the power to engulf her in a tidal wave.

She had no desire to be swept out to sea by any man. But in this instance she had a life preserver. And that was her general dislike of him. The fact that their time together was going to be contained to only this weekend. So what did it matter if she allowed herself to get a little bit storm tossed. It didn't. She was free. Free to enjoy this as much as she wanted.

And she wanted. *Wanted* with an endless hunger that seemed to growl inside her like a feral beast.

He possessed the equipment to satisfy it. She let her eyes drift lower than just his abs, taking in the heart, the unequivocal evidence, of his maleness. She had not been lying when she said it was the biggest one she'd ever seen. It made her feel a little bit intimidated. Especially since she had been celibate for so very long. But she had a few days to acclimate.

The thought made her giddy.

"Now," she said, not entirely certain that she was totally prepared for him now but also unable to wait for him.

"You sure you're ready for me?" He leaned forward, bracing his hand on the headboard, poised over her like the very embodiment of carnal temptation. Just out of reach, close enough that she did easily inhale his masculine scent. Far enough away that he wasn't giving her what she needed. Not yet.

She felt hollow. Aching. And that, she realized, was how she knew she was going to take all of him whether or not it seemed possible. Because the only other option was remaining like this. Hollowed out and empty. And she couldn't stand that either. Not for one more second.

"Please," she said, not caring that she sounded plaintive. Not caring that she was begging. Begging Sam, the man she had spent the past several years harassing every time he came around her ranch.

No, she didn't care. She would make a fool out of herself if she had to, would lower herself as far down as she needed to go, if only she could get the kind of satisfaction that his body promised to deliver.

He moved his other hand up to the headboard, gripping it tight. Then he flexed his hips forward, the blunt head of his arousal teasing the slick entrance to her body. She reached up, bracing her palms flat against his chest, a shiver running through her as he teased her with near penetration.

She cursed. The sound quivering, weak in the near silence of the room. She had no idea where hard-ass Maddy had gone. That tough, flippant girl who knew how to keep everyone at a distance with her words. Who knew how to play off every situation as if it weren't a big deal.

This was a big deal. How could she pretend that it wasn't? She was breaking apart from the inside out; how could she act as though she weren't?

"Please," she repeated.

He let go of the headboard with one hand and pressed his hand down next to her face, then repeated the motion with the other as he rocked his hips forward more fully, entering her slowly, inch by tantalizing inch. She gasped when he filled her all the way, the intense stretching sensation a pleasure more than it was a pain.

She slid her hands up to his shoulders, down his back, holding on to him tightly there before locking her legs around his lean hips and urging him even deeper.

"Yes," she breathed, a wave of satisfaction rolling over her, chased on the heels by a sense that she was still incomplete. That this wasn't enough. That it would never be enough.

Then he began to move. Ratcheting up the tension between them. Taking her need, her arousal, to greater heights than she had ever imagined possible. He was measured at first, taking care to establish a rhythm that helped her move closer to completion. But she didn't need the help. She didn't want it. She just wanted to ride the storm.

She tilted her head to the side, scraping her teeth along the tendon in his neck that stood out as a testament to his hard-won self-control.

And that did it.

He growled low in his throat. Then his movements became hard, harsh. Following no particular rhythm but his own. She loved it. Gloried in it. He grabbed hold of her hips, tugging her up against him every time he thrust down, making it rougher, making it deeper. Making it hurt. She felt full with it, full with him. This was exactly what she needed, and she hadn't even realized it. To be utterly and completely overwhelmed. To have this man consume her every sensation, her every breath.

She fused her lips to his, kissing him frantically as he continued to move inside her and she held on to him tighter, her nails digging into his skin. But she knew he didn't mind the pain. She knew it just as she didn't mind it. Knew it because he began to move harder, faster, reaching the edge of his own control as he pushed her nearer to the edge of hers.

Suddenly, it gripped her fiercely, down low inside her, a force of pleasure that she couldn't deny or control. She froze, stiffening against him, the scream that lodged itself in her throat the very opposite of who she usually was. It wasn't calculated; it wasn't pretty; it wasn't designed to do anything. It simply was. An expression of what she felt. Beyond her reach, beyond her completely.

She was racked with her desire for him, with the intensity of the orgasm that swept through her. And then, just as she was beginning to find a way to breathe again, he found his own release, his hardness pulsing deep inside her as he gave himself up to it.

His release—the intensity of it—sent another shattering wave through her. And she clung to him even more tightly, needing him to anchor her to the bed, to the earth, or she would lose herself completely.

And then in the aftermath, she was left there, clinging to a stranger, having just shown the deepest, most hidden parts of herself to him. Having just lost her control with him in a way she never would have done with someone she knew better. Perhaps this was the only way she could have ever experienced this kind of freedom. The only way she could have ever let her guard down enough. What did she have to lose with Sam? His opinion of her was already low. So if he thought that she was a sex-hungry maniac after this, what did it matter?

He moved away from her and she threw her arm

over her face, letting her head fall back, the sound of her fractured breathing echoing in the room.

After she had gulped in a few gasps of air, she removed her arm, opened her eyes and realized that Sam wasn't in the room anymore. Probably off to the bathroom to deal with necessities. Good. She needed some space. She needed a moment. At least a few breaths.

He returned a little bit quicker than she had hoped he might, all long lean muscle and satisfied male. It was the expression on his face that began to ease the tension in her chest. He didn't look angry. He didn't look like he was judging her. And he didn't look like he was in love with her or was about to start making promises that she didn't want him to make.

No, he just looked satisfied. A bone-deep satisfaction that she felt too.

"Holy hell," he said, coming to lie on the bed next to her, drawing her naked body up against his. She felt a smile curve her lips. "I think you about blew my head off."

"You're so romantic," she said, smiling even wider. Because this was perfect. Absolutely perfect.

"You don't want me to be romantic," he returned.

"No," she said, feeling happy, buoyant even. "I sure as hell don't."

"You want me to be bad, and dirty, and to be your every fantasy of slumming it with a man who is so very beneath you."

That, she took affront to a little bit. "I don't think you're beneath me, Sam," she said. Then he grabbed hold of her hips and lifted her up off the mattress before bringing her down over his body. A wicked smile crossed his face.

"I am now."

"You're insatiable. And terrible."

"For a weekend fling, honey, that's all you really need."

"Oh, dammit," she said, "what if the roads open up, and Christopher tries to come up?"

"I'm not really into threesomes." He tightened his grip on her. "And I'm not into sharing."

"No worries. I don't have any desire to broaden my experience by testing him out."

"Have I ruined you for him?"

The cocky bastard. She wanted to tell him no, but she had a feeling that denting the masculine ego when a man was underneath you wasn't the best idea if you wanted to have sex with said man again.

"Ruined me completely," she responded. "In fact, I should leave a message for him."

Sam snagged the phone on the nightstand and thrust it at her. "You can leave him a message now."

"Okay," she said, grimacing slightly.

She picked up the phone and dialed Christopher's number quickly. Praying that she got his voice mail and not his actual voice.

Of course, if she did, that meant he'd gone out. Which meant that maybe he was trying to find sex to replace the sex that he'd lost. Which she had done; she couldn't really be annoyed about that. But she had baggage.

"Come on," she muttered as the phone rang endlessly. Then she breathed a sigh of relief when she got his voice mail. "Hi, Christopher, it's Madison. Don't worry about coming up here if the roads clear up. If that happens, I'm probably just going to go back to Copper Ridge.

The weekend is kind of ruined. And…and maybe you should just wait for me to call you?" She looked up at Sam, who was nearly vibrating with forcibly contained laughter. She rolled her eyes. "Anyway, sorry that this didn't work out. Bye."

"That was terrible," he said. "But I think you made it pretty clear that you don't want to hear from him."

"I said I would call him," she said in protestation.

"Are you going to?"

"*Hell* no."

Sam chuckled, rolling her back underneath him, kissing her deep, hard. "Good thing I only want a weekend."

"Why is that?"

"God help the man that wants more from you."

"Oh, please, that's not fair." She wiggled, luxuriating in the hard feel of him between her thighs. He wanted her again already. "I pity the woman that falls for you, Sam McCormack."

A shadow passed over his face. "So do I."

Then, as quickly as they had appeared, those clouds cleared and he was smiling again, that wicked, intense smile that let her know he was about ready to take her to heaven again.

"It's a good thing both of us only want a weekend."

Five

"How did the art retreat go?"

Sam gritted his teeth against his younger brother's questioning as Chase walked into their workshop. "Fine," he returned.

"Fine?" Chase leaned against the doorframe, crossing his arms, looking a little too much like Sam for his own comfort. Because he was a bastard, and he didn't want to see his bastard face looking back at him. "I thought you were going to get inspiration. To come up with the ideas that will keep the McCormack Ranch flush for the next several years."

"I'm not a machine," Sam said, keeping his tone hard. "You can't force art."

He said things like that, in that tone, because he knew that no one would believe that cliché phrase, even if it was true. He didn't like that it was true.

But there wasn't much he was willing to do about it either.

"Sure. And I feel a slight amount of guilt over pressuring you, but since I do a lot of managing of your career, I consider it a part of my job."

"Stick to pounding iron, Chase—that's where your talents lie."

"I don't have talent," Chase said. "I have business sense. Which you don't have. So you should be thankful for me."

"You say that. You say it a lot. I think mostly because you know that I actually shouldn't be all that thankful for your meddling."

He was being irritable, and he knew it. But he didn't want Chase asking how the weekend was. He didn't want to explain the way he had spent his time. And he really didn't want to get into why the only thing he was inspired to do was start painting nudes.

Of one woman in particular.

Because the only kind of grand inspirational moments he'd had were when he was inside Maddy. Yeah, he wasn't going to explain that to his younger brother. He was never going to tell anybody. And he had to get his shit together.

"Seriously, though, everything is going okay? Anna is worried about you."

"Your wife is meddlesome. I liked her better when she was just your friend and all she did was come by for pizza a couple times a week. And she didn't worry too much about what I was doing or whether or not I was happy."

"Yeah, sadly for you she has decided she loves me. And by extension she has decided she loves you, which means her getting up in your business. I don't think she knows another way to be."

"Tell her to go pull apart a tractor and stop digging around in my life."

"No, thanks, I like my balls where they are. Which means I will not be telling Anna what to do. Ever."

"I liked it better when you were miserable and alone."

Chase laughed. "Why, because you're miserable and alone?"

"No, that would imply that I'm uncomfortable with the state of things. I myself am quite dedicated to my solitude and my misery."

"They say misery loves company," Chase said.

"Only true if you aren't a hermit."

"I suppose that's true." His brother looked at him, his gaze far too perceptive for Sam's liking. "You didn't used to be this terrible."

"I have been for a while." But worse with Maddy. She pushed at him. At things and needs and desires that were best left in the past.

He gritted his teeth. She pushed at him because he turned her on and that made her mad. He... Well, it was complicated.

"Yes," Chase said. "For a while."

"Don't psychoanalyze me. Maybe it's a crazy artist thing. Dad always said that it would make me a pussy."

"You aren't a pussy. You're a jerk."

"Six of one, half dozen of the other. Either way, I have issues."

Chase shook his head. "Well, deal with them on your own time. You have to be over at the West Ranch in less than an hour." Chase shook his head. "Pretty soon we'll be released from the contract. But you know until then we could always hire somebody else to go. You don't have to do horseshoes if you don't want. We're kind of beyond that now."

Sam gritted his teeth. For the first time he was actually tempted to take his brother up on the offer. To replace his position with someone else. Mostly because the idea of seeing Madison again filled him with the kind of reckless tension that he knew he wouldn't be able to do anything about once he saw her again.

Oh, not because of her. Not because of anything to do with her moral code or protestations. He could demolish those easily enough. It was because he couldn't afford to waste any more time thinking about her. Because he couldn't afford to get in any deeper. What had happened over the past weekend had been good. Damn good. But he had to leave it there.

Normally, he relished the idea of getting in there and doing grunt work. There was something about it that fulfilled him. Chase might not understand that.

But Sam wasn't a paperwork man. He wasn't a business mind. He needed physical exertion to keep himself going.

His lips twitched as he thought about the kind of physical exertion he had indulged in with Maddy. Yeah, it kind of all made sense. Why he had thrown himself into the blacksmithing thing during his celibacy. He needed to pound something, one way or another. And since he had been so intent on denying himself female companionship, he had picked up a hammer instead.

He was tempted to back out. To make sure he kept his distance from Maddy. He wouldn't, because he was also far too tempted to go. Too tempted to test his control and see if there was a weak link. If he might end up with her underneath him again.

It would be the better thing to send Chase. Or to call in and say they would have to reschedule, then hire somebody else to take over that kind of work. They could more than afford it. But as much as he wanted to avoid Maddy, he wanted to see her again.

Just because.

His body began to harden just thinking about it.

"It's fine. I'm going to head over. You know that I like physical labor."

"I just don't understand why," Chase said, looking genuinely mystified.

But hell, Chase had a life. A wife. Things that Sam was never going to have. Chase had worked through his stuff and made them both a hell of a lot of money, and Sam was happy for him. As happy as he ever got.

"You don't need to understand me. You just have to keep me organized so that I don't end up out on the street."

"You would never end up out on the streets of Copper Ridge. Mostly because if you stood out there with a cardboard sign, some well-meaning elderly woman would wrap you in a blanket and take you back to her house for casserole. And you would rather die. We both know that."

That made Sam smile reluctantly. "True enough."

"So, I guess you better keep working, then."

Sam thought about Maddy again, about her sweet, supple curves. About how seeing her again was going to test him in the best way possible. Perhaps that was why he should go. Just so he could test himself. Push up against his control. Yeah, maybe that was what he needed.

Yeah, that justification worked well. And it meant he would see her again.

It wasn't feelings. It was just sex. And he was starting to think just sex might be what he needed.

"I plan on it."

Maddy took a deep breath of clean salt air and arena dirt. There was something comforting about it. Familiar. Whenever things had gone wrong in her life, this was what she could count on. The familiar sights and sounds of the ranch, her horses. Herself.

She never felt stronger than when she was on the back of a horse, working in time with the animal to move from a trot to a walk, a walk to a halt. She never felt more understood.

A funny thing. Because, while she knew she was an excellent trainer and she had full confidence in her ability to keep control over the animal, she knew that she would never have absolute control. Animals were unpredictable. Always.

One day, they could simply decide they didn't want to deal with you and buck you off. It was the risk that every person who worked with large beasts took. And they took it on gladly.

She liked that juxtaposition. The control, the danger. The fact that though she achieved a certain level of mastery with each horse she worked with, they could still decide they weren't going to behave on a given day.

She had never felt much of that in the rest of her life. Often she felt like she was fighting against so much. Having something like this, something that made her feel both small and powerful had been essential to her well-being. Especially during all that crap that had happened ten years ago. She had been thinking more about it lately. Honestly, it had all started because of Christopher, because she had been considering breaking her celibacy. And it had only gotten worse after she actually had. After Sam.

Mostly because she couldn't stop thinking about him. Mostly because she felt like one weekend could never be enough. And she needed it to be. She badly needed it to be. She needed to be able to have sex with a guy without having lingering feelings for him. David had really done a number on her, and she did not want another number done on her.

It was for the best if she never saw Sam again. She knew that was unlikely, but it would be better. She let out a deep breath, walking into the barn, her riding boots making a strident sound on the hardpacked dirt as she walked in. Then she saw movement toward the end of the barn, someone coming out of one of the stalls.

She froze. It wasn't uncommon for there to be other people around. Her family employed a full staff to keep the ranch running smoothly, but for some reason this felt different. And a couple of seconds later, as the person came into view, she realized why.

Black cowboy hat, broad shoulders, muscular forearms. That lean waist and hips. That built, muscular physique that she was intimately acquainted with.

Dear Lord. Sam McCormack was here.

She had known that there would be some compromise on the never-seeing-him-again thing; she had just hoped that it wouldn't be seeing him now.

"Sam," she said, because she would be damned if she

appeared like she had been caught unawares. "I didn't expect you to be here."

"Your father wanted to make sure that all of the horses were in good shape before the holidays, since it was going to delay my next visit."

Maddy gritted her teeth. Christmas was in a couple of weeks, which meant her family would be having their annual party. The festivities had started to become a bit threadbare and brittle in recent years. Now that everybody knew Nathan West had been forced to sell off all of his properties downtown. Now that everyone knew he had a bastard son, Jack Monaghan, whose existence Nathan had tried to deny for more than thirty years. Yes, now that everybody had seen the cracks in the gleaming West family foundation, it all seemed farcical to Maddy.

But then, seeing as she had been one of the first major cracks in the foundation, she supposed that she wasn't really entitled to be too judgmental about it. However, she was starting to feel a bit exhausted.

"Right," she returned, knowing that her voice sounded dull.

"Have you seen Christopher?"

His question caught her off guard, as did his tone, which sounded a bit hard and possessive. It was funny, because this taciturn man in front of her was more what she had considered Sam to be before they had spent those days in the cabin together. Those days—where they had mostly been naked—had been a lot easier. Quieter. He had smiled more. But then, she supposed that any man receiving an endless supply of orgasms was prone to smiling more. They had barely gotten out of bed.

They had both been more than a little bit insatiable, and Maddy hadn't minded that at all. But this was a harsh slap back to reality. To a time that could almost have been before their little rendezvous but clearly wasn't, because his line of questioning was tinged with jealousy.

"No. As you guessed, I lied to him and didn't call him."

"And he call you?"

Maddy lifted her fingernail and began to chew on it, grimacing when she realized she had just ruined her manicure. "He did call," she said, her face heating slightly. "And I changed his name in my phone book to Don't Answer."

"Why did you do that?"

"Obviously you can't delete somebody from your phone book when you don't want to talk to them, Sam. You have to make sure that you know who's calling. But I like the reminder that I'm not speaking to him. Because then my phone rings and the screen says Don't Answer, and then I go, 'Okay.'"

"I really do pity the man who ends up wanting to chase after you."

"Good thing you don't. Except, oh wait, you're here."

She regretted that as soon as she said it. His gaze darkened, his eyes sweeping over her figure. Why did she want to push him?

Why did she always want to push him?

"You know why I'm here."

"Yes, because my daddy pays you to be here." She didn't know why she said that. To reinforce the difference between them? To remind him she was Lady of the Manor, and that regardless of his bank balance he was socially beneath her? To make herself look like a stupid rich girl he wouldn't want to mess around with anyway. Honestly, these days it was difficult for her to guess at her own motives.

"Is this all part of your fantasy? You want to be… taken by the stable boy or something? I mean, it's a nice one, Maddy, and I didn't really mind acting it out with you last weekend, but we both know that I'm not exactly the stable boy and you're not exactly the breathless virgin."

Heat streaked through her face, rage pooling in her stomach. "Right. Because I'm not some pure, snow-white virgin, my fantasies are somehow wrong?" It was too close to that wound. The one she wished wasn't there. The one she couldn't ignore, no matter how much she tried.

"That wasn't the point I was making. And anyway, when your whole fantasy about a man centers around him being bad for you, I'm not exactly sure where you get off trying to take the moral-outrage route."

"I will be as morally outraged as I please," she snapped, turning to walk away from him.

He reached out, grabbing hold of her arm and turning her back to face him, taking hold of her other arm and pulling her forward. "Everything was supposed to stay back up at those cabins," he said, his voice rough.

"So why aren't you letting it?" she spat. Reckless. Shaky. She was a hypocrite. Because she wasn't letting it rest either.

"Because you walked in in those tight pants and it made it a lot harder for me to think."

"My breeches," she said, keeping the words sharp and crisp as a green apple, "are not typically the sort of garment that inspire men to fits of uncontrollable lust." Except *she* was drowning in a fit of uncontrollable lust.

His gaze was hot, his hands on her arms even hotter. She wanted to arch against him, to press her breasts against his chest as she had done more times than she could count when they had been together. She wanted... She wanted the impossible. She wanted more. More of him. More of everything they had shared together, even though they had agreed that would be a bad idea.

Even though she knew it was something she shouldn't even want.

"Your pretty little ass in anything would make a man lose his mind. Don't tell me those breeches put any man off, or I'm gonna have to call you a liar."

"It isn't my breeches that put them off. That's just my personality."

"If some man can't handle you being a little bit hard, then he's no kind of man. I can take you, baby. I can take all of you. And that's good, since we both know you can take all of me."

"Are you just going to be a tease, Sam?" she asked, echoing back a phrase that had been uttered to her by many men over the years. "Or is this leading somewhere?"

"You don't want it to lead anywhere, you said so yourself." He released his hold on her, taking a step back.

"You're contrary, Sam McCormack—do you know that?"

He laughed. "That's about the only thing anyone calls me. We both know what I am. The only thing that confuses me is exactly why you seem surprised by it now."

She was kind of stumped by that question. Because really, the only answer was sex. That she had imagined that the two of them being together, that the man he had been during that time, meant something.

Which proved that she really hadn't learned anything about sexual relationships, in spite of the fact that she had been so badly wounded by one in the past. She had always known that she had a hard head, but really, this was ridiculous.

But it wasn't just her head that was hard. She had hardened up a considerable amount in the years since her relationship with David. Because she'd had to. Because within the equestrian community, she had spent the years following that affair known as the skank who had seriously jeopardized the marriage of an upright member of the community. Never mind that she had been his student. Never mind that she had been seventeen years old, a virgin who had believed every word that had come out of the esteemed older man's mouth. Who had believed that his marriage really was over and that he wanted a life and a future with her.

It was laughable to her now. Any man nearing his forties who found himself able to relate to a seventeen-year-old on an emotional level was a little bit suspect. A married one, in a position of power, was even worse. She knew all of that. She knew it down to her bones. Believing it was another thing.

So sometimes her judgment was in doubt. Sometimes she felt like an idiot. But she was much more equipped to deal with difficult situations now. She was a lot pricklier. A lot more inured.

And that was what came to her defense now.

"Sam, if you still want me, all you have to do is say it. Don't you stand there growling because you're hard and sexually frustrated and we both agreed that it would only be that one weekend. Just be a man and admit it."

"Are you sure you should be talking to me like that here? Anyone can catch us. If I backed you up against that wall and kissed your smart mouth, then people would know. Doesn't it make you feel dirty? Doesn't it make you feel ashamed?" His words lashed at her, made her feel all of those things but also aroused her. She had no idea what was wrong with her. Except that maybe part of it was that she simply didn't know how to feel desire without feeling ashamed. Another gift from her one and only love affair.

"You're the one that's saying all of this. Not me," she said, keeping her voice steely. She lifted a shoulder. "If I didn't know better, I would say you have issues. I don't want to help you work those out." A sudden rush of heat took over, a reckless thought that she had no business having, that she really should work to get a handle on. But she didn't.

She took a deep breath. "I don't have any desire to help you with your issues, but if you're horny, I can help you with that."

"What the hell?"

"You heard me," she said, crossing her arms and giving him her toughest air. "If you want me, then have me."

Sam could hardly believe what he was hearing. Yet again, Madison West was propositioning him. And this time, he was pissed off. Because he wasn't a dog that she could bring to heel whenever she wanted to. He wasn't the kind of man who could be manipulated.

Even worse, he wanted her. He wanted to say yes.

And he wasn't sure he could spite his dick to soothe his pride.

"You can't just come in here and start playing games with me," he said. "I'm not a dog that you can call whenever you want me to come."

He let the double meaning of that statement sit between them. "That isn't what I'm doing," she said, her tone waspish.

"Then what are you doing, Madison? We agreed that it would be one weekend. And then you come in here sniping at me, and suddenly you're propositioning me. I gave in to all of this when you asked the first time, because I'm a man. And I'm not going to say no in a situation like the one we were in. But I'm also not the kind of man you can manipulate."

Color rose high in her cheeks. "I'm not trying to manipulate you. Why is it that men are always accusing me of that?"

"Because no man likes to be turned on and then left waiting," he returned.

The color in her cheeks darkened, and then she turned on one boot heel and walked quickly away from him.

He moved after her, reaching out and grabbing hold of her arm, stopping her. "What? Now you're going to go?"

"I can't do this. I can't do this if you're going to wrap all of it up in accusations and shame. I've been there. I've done it, Sam, and I'm not doing it again. Trust me. I've been accused of a lot of things. I've had my fill of it. So, great, you don't want to be manipulated. I don't want to be the one that has to leave this affair feeling guilty."

Sam frowned. "That's not what I meant."

She was the one who was being unreasonable, blowing hot and cold on him. How was it that he had been the one to be made to feel guilty? He didn't like that. He didn't like feeling anything but irritation and desire for her. He certainly didn't want to feel any guilt.

He didn't want to feel any damn thing.

"Well, what did you mean? Am I a tease, Sam? Is that what I am? And men like you just can't help themselves?"

He took a step back. "No," he said. "But you do have to make a decision. Either you want this, or you don't."

"Or?"

"Or nothing," he said, his tone hard. "If you don't want it, you don't want it. I'm not going to coerce you into anything. But I don't do the hot-and-cold thing."

Of course, he didn't really do any kind of thing anymore. But this, this back and forth, reminded him too much of his interaction with Elizabeth. Actually, all of it reminded him a little bit too much of Elizabeth. This seemingly soft, sweet woman with a bit of an edge. Someone who was high-class and a little bit luxurious. Who felt like a break from his life on the ranch. His life of rough work and solitude.

But after too much back and forth, it had ended. And he didn't speak to her for months. Until he had gotten a call that he needed to go to the hospital.

He gritted his teeth, looking at Madison. He couldn't imagine anything with Madison ending quite that way, not simply because he refused to ever lose his control the way he had done with Elizabeth, but also because he couldn't imagine Maddy slinking off in silence. She might go hot and cold, but she would never do it quietly.

"Twelve days. There are twelve days until Christmas. That's what I want. Twelve days to get myself on the naughty list. So to speak." She leveled her blue gaze with his. "If you don't want to oblige me, I'm sure Christopher will. But I would much rather it be you."

"Why?" He might want this, but he would be damned if he would make it easy for her. Mostly because he wanted to make it a little harder on himself.

"Because I planned to go up to that cabin and have sex with Christopher. I had to, like, come up with a plan. A series of tactical maneuvers that would help me make the decision to get it over with after all that time. You," she said, gesturing at him, "you, I didn't plan to have anything happen with. Ever. But I couldn't stop myself. I think at the end of the day it's much better to carry on a sex-only affair with a man that you can't control yourself with. Like right now. I was not going to proposition you today, Sam. I promise. Not today, not ever again. In fact, I'm mad at you, so it should be really easy for me to walk away. But I don't want to. I want you. I want you even if it's a terrible idea."

He looked around, then took her arm again, dragging her into one of the empty stalls, where they would be out of sight if anyone walked into the barn. Then he pressed her against the wall, gripping her chin and taking her mouth in a deep, searing kiss. She whimpered, arching against him, grabbing hold of his shoulders and widening her stance so that he could press his hardened length against where she was soft and sensitive, ready for him already.

He slid his hand down her back, not caring that the hard wall bit into his knuckles as he grabbed hold of her rear, barely covered by those riding pants, which ought to have been illegal.

She whimpered, wiggling against him, obviously trying to get some satisfaction for the ache inside her. He knew that she felt it, because he felt the same way. He wrenched his mouth away from hers. "Dammit," he said, "I have to get back to work."

"Do you really?" She looked up at him, her expression so desperate it was nearly comical. Except he felt too desperate to laugh.

"Yes," he said.

"Well, since my family owns the property, I feel like I can give you permission to—"

He held up a hand. "I'm going to stop you right there. Nobody gives me permission to do anything. If I didn't want to finish the day's work, I wouldn't. I don't need the money. That's not why I do this. It's my reputation. My pride. I'm contracted to do it, and I will do what I promised I would. But when the contract is up? I won't."

"Oh," she said. "I didn't realize that."

"Everything is going well with the art business." At least, it would if he could think of something else to do. He supposed he could always do more animals and cowboys. People never got tired of that. They had been his most popular art installations so far.

"Great. That's great. Maybe you could…not press yourself up against me? Because I'm going to do something really stupid in a minute."

He did not comply with her request; instead, he kept her there, held up against the wall. "What's that?"

She frowned. "Something I shouldn't do in a public place."

"You're not exactly enticing me to let you go." His body was so hard he was pretty sure he was going to turn to stone.

"I'll bite you."

"Still not enticed."

"Are you telling me that you want to get bitten?"

He rolled his hips forward, let her feel exactly what she was doing to him. "Biting can be all part of the fun."

"I have some things to learn," she said, her blue eyes widening.

"I'm happy to teach them to you," he said, wavering on whether or not he would finish what they'd started here. "Where should I meet you tonight?"

"Here," she said, the word rushed.

"Are you sure? I live on the same property as Chase, but in different houses. We are close, but not that close."

"No, I have my own place here too. And there's always a lot of cars. It won't look weird. I just don't want anyone to see me…" She looked away from him. "I don't want to advertise."

"That's fine." It suited him to keep everyone in the dark too. He didn't want the kind of attention that would come with being associated with Madison West. Already, the attention that he got for the various art projects he did, for the different displays around town, was a little much for him.

It was an impossible situation for him, as always. He wanted things that seemed destined to require more of himself than he wanted to give. Things that seemed to need him to reach deep, when it was better if he never did. Yet he seemed to choose them. Women like Madison. A career like art.

Someday he would examine that. Not today.

"Okay," she said, "come over after it's dark."

"This is like a covert operation."

"Is that a problem?"

It really wasn't. It was hypocritical of him to pretend otherwise. Hell, his last relationship—the one with Elizabeth—had been conducted almost entirely in secrecy because he had been going out of town to see her. That had been her choice, because she knew her association with him would be an issue for her family.

And, as he already established, he didn't really want anyone to know about this thing with Maddy either. Still, sneaking around felt contrary to his nature too. In general, he didn't really care what people thought about him. Or about his decisions.

You're a liar.

He gritted his teeth. Everything with Elizabeth was its own exception. There was no point talking to anyone about it. No point getting into that terrible thing he had been a part of. The terrible thing he had caused.

"Not a problem," he said. "I'll see you in a few hours."

"I can cook," she said as he turned to walk out of the stall.

"You don't have to. I can grab something on my way."

"No, I would rather we had dinner."

He frowned. "Maddy," he began, "this isn't going to be a relationship. It can't be."

"I know," she said, looking up and away from him, swallowing hard. "But I need for it to be something a little more than just sex too. I just… Look, obviously you know that somebody that hasn't had a sexual partner in the past ten years has some baggage. I do. Shocking, I know, because I seem like a bastion of mental health. But I just don't like the feeling. I really don't."

His chest tightened. Part of him was tempted to ask

her exactly what had happened. Why she had been celibate for so long. But then, if they began to trade stories about their pasts, she might want to know something about his. And he wasn't getting into that. Not now, not ever.

"Is there anything you don't like?"

"No," he said, "I'm easy. I thought you said you didn't cook?"

She shrugged a shoulder. "Okay, if I'm being completely honest, I have a set of frozen meals in my freezer that my parents' housekeeper makes for me. But I can heat up a double portion so we can eat together."

He shook his head. "Okay."

"I have pot roast, meat loaf and roast chicken."

"I'll tell you what. The only thing I want is to have your body for dessert. I'll let you go ahead and plan dinner."

"Pot roast it is," she said, her voice a borderline squeak.

He chuckled, turning and walking away from her, something shifting in his chest. He didn't know how she managed to do that. Make him feel heavier one moment, then lighter the next. It was dangerous. That's what it was. And if he had a brain in his head, he would walk away from her and never look back.

Sadly, his ability to think with his brain had long since ceased to function.

Even if it was a stupid idea, and he was fairly certain it was, he was going to come to Madison's house tonight, and he was going to have her in about every way he could think of.

He fixed his mouth into a grim line and set about finishing his work. But while he kept his face completely stoic, inside he felt anticipation for the first time in longer than he could remember.

Six

Maddy wondered if seductresses typically wore pearls. Probably pearls and nothing else. Maybe pearls and lace. Probably not high-waisted pencil skirts and cropped sweaters. But warming pot roast for Sam had put her in the mind-set of a 1950s housewife, and she had decided to go ahead and embrace the theme.

She caught a glimpse of her reflection in the mirror in the hall of her little house and she laughed at herself. She was wearing red lipstick, her blond hair pulled back into a bun. She rolled her eyes, then stuck out her tongue. Then continued on into the kitchen, her high heels clicking on the tile.

At least underneath the sweater, she had on a piece of pretty hot lingerie, if she said so herself. She knew Sam was big on the idea that seduction couldn't be planned, but Maddy did like to have a plan. It helped her feel more in control, and when it came to Sam, she had never felt more out of control.

She sighed, reaching up into the cupboard and taking out a bottle of wine that she had picked up at Grassroots Winery that afternoon. She might not be the best cook, or any kind of cook at all, but she knew how to pick a good wine. Everyone had their strengths.

The strange thing was she kind of enjoyed feeling out of control with Sam, but it also made her feel cautious. Protective. When she had met David, she had dived into the affair headlong. She hadn't thought at all. She had led entirely with her heart, and in the end, she had gotten her heart broken. More than that, the aftermath had shattered her entire world. She had lost friends; she had lost her standing within a community that had become dear to her… Everything.

"But you aren't seventeen. And Sam isn't a married douche bag." She spoke the words fiercely into the silence of the kitchen, buoyed by the reality of them.

She could lose a little bit of control with Sam. Even within that, there would be all of her years, her wisdom—such as it was—and her experience. She was never going to be the girl she had been. That was a good thing. She would never be able to be hurt like that, not again. She simply didn't possess the emotional capacity.

She had emerged Teflon coated. Everything slid off now.

There was a knock on her front door and she straightened, closing her eyes and taking a deep breath, trying to calm the fluttering in her stomach. That reminded her a bit too much of the past. Feeling all fluttery and breathless just because she was going to see the man she was fixated on. That felt a little too much like emotion.

No. It wasn't emotion. It was just anticipation. She was old enough now to tell the difference between the two things.

She went quickly to the door, suddenly feeling a little bit ridiculous as she pulled it open. When it was too late for her to do anything about it. Her feeling of ridiculousness only increased when she saw Sam standing there, wearing his typical black cowboy hat, tight T-shirt and well-fitted jeans. Of course, he didn't need to wear anything different to be hotter to her.

A cowboy hat would do it every time.

"Hi," she said, taking a step back and gesturing with her hand. "Come in."

He obliged, walking over the threshold and looking around the space. For some reason, she found herself looking at it through his eyes. Wondering what kinds of conclusions he would draw about the neat, spare environment.

She had lived out in the little guesthouse ever since she was nineteen. Needing a little bit of distance from her family but never exactly leaving. For the first time, that seemed a little bit weird to her. It had always just been her life. She worked on the ranch, so there didn't seem to be any point in leaving it.

Now she tried to imagine explaining it to someone else—to Sam—and she wondered if it was weird.

"My mother's interior decorator did the place," she said. "Except for the yellow and red." She had added little pops of color through throw pillows, vases and art on the wall. But otherwise the surroundings were predominantly white.

"Great," he said, clearly not interested at all.

It had felt weird, thinking about him judging her

based on the space, thinking about him judging her circumstances. But it was even weirder to see that he wasn't even curious.

She supposed that was de rigueur for physical affairs. And that was what this was.

"Dinner is almost ready," she said, reminding them both of the nonphysical part of the evening. Now she felt ridiculous for suggesting that too. But the idea of meeting him in secret had reminded her way too much of David. Somehow, adding pot roast had seemed to make the whole thing aboveboard.

Pot roast was an extremely nonsalacious food.

"Great," he said, looking very much like he didn't actually care that much.

"I just have to get it out of the microwave." She treated him to an exaggerated wink.

That earned her an uneasy laugh. "Great," he said.

"Come on," she said, gesturing for him to follow her. She moved into the kitchen, grabbed the pan that contained the meat and the vegetables out of the microwave and set it on the table, where the place settings were already laid out and the salad was already waiting.

"I promise I'm not trying to Stepford-wife you," she said as they both took their seats.

"I didn't think that," he said, but his blank expression betrayed the fact that he was lying.

"You did," she said. "You thought that I was trying to become your creepy robot wife."

"No, but I did wonder exactly why dinner was so important."

She looked down. It wasn't as if David were a secret. In fact, the affair was basically open information. "Do you really want to know?"

Judging by the expression on his face, he didn't. "There isn't really a good way to answer that question."

"True. Honesty is probably not the best policy. I'll think you're uninterested in me."

"On the contrary, I'm very interested in you."

"Being interested in my boobs is not the same thing."

He laughed, taking a portion of pot roast out of the dish in the center of the table. "I'm going to eat. If you want to tell me…well, go ahead. But I don't think you're trying to ensnare me."

"You don't?"

"Honestly, Maddy, nobody would want me for that long."

Those words were spoken with a bit of humor, but they made her sad. "I'm sure that's not true," she said, even though she wasn't sure of any such thing. He was grumpy. And he wasn't the most adept emotionally. Still, it didn't seem like a very kind thing for a person to think about themselves.

"It is," he said. "Chase is only with me because he's stuck with me. He feels some kind of loyalty to our parents."

"I thought your parents…"

"They're dead," he responded, his tone flat.

"I'm sorry," she said.

"Me too."

Silence fell between them after that, and she knew the only way to break it was to go ahead and get it out. "The first guy…the one ten years ago, we were having a physical-only affair. Except I didn't know it."

"Ouch," Sam said.

"Very. I mean, trust me, there were plenty of signs. And even though he was outright lying to me about his

intentions, if I had been a little bit older or more experienced, I would have known. It's a terrible thing to
find out you're a cliché. I imagine you wouldn't know
what that's like."

"No, not exactly. Artist-cowboy-blacksmith is not
really a well-worn template."

She laughed and took a sip of her wine. "No, I guess
not." Then she took another sip. She needed something
to fortify her. Anything.

"But other woman that actually believes he'll leave
his wife for you, that is." She swallowed hard, waiting for his face to change, waiting for him to call her a
name, to get disgusted and walk out.

It occurred to her just then that that was why she
was telling him all of this. Because she needed him to
know. She needed him to know, and she needed to see
what he would think. If he would still want her. Or if
he would think that she was guilty beyond forgiving.

There were a lot of people who did.

But he didn't say anything. And his face didn't
change. So they just sat in silence for a moment.

"When we got involved, he told me that he was done
with her. That their marriage was a mess and they were
already starting divorce proceedings. He said that he
just wore his wedding ring to avoid awkward questions
from their friends. The dressage community around
here is pretty small, and he said that he and his wife
were waiting until they could tell people themselves,
personally, so that there were no rumors flying around."
She laughed, almost because she was unable to help it.
It was so ridiculous. She wanted to go back and shake
seventeen-year-old her. For being such an idiot. For caring so much.

"Anyway," she continued, "he said he wanted to protect me. You know, because of how unkind people can be."

"He was married," Sam said.

She braced herself. "Yes," she returned, unflinching.

"How old were you?"

"Seventeen."

"How old was he?"

"Almost forty."

Sam cursed. "He should have been arrested."

"Maybe," she said, "except I did want him."

She had loved the attention he had given her. Had loved feeling special. It had been more than lust. It had been neediness. For all the approval she hadn't gotten in her life. Classic daddy issues, basically. But, as messed up as a man his age had to be for wanting to fool around with a teenager, the teenager had to be pretty screwed up too.

"How did you know him?"

"He was my... He was my trainer."

"Right, so some jackass in a position of power. Very surprising."

Warmth bloomed in her chest and spread outward, a strange, completely unfamiliar sensation. There were only a few people on earth who defended her when the subject came up. And mostly, they kept it from coming up. Sierra, her younger sister, knew about it only from the perspective of someone who had been younger at the time. Maddy had shared a little bit about it, about the breakup and how much it had messed with her, when Sierra was having difficulty in her own love life.

And then there were her brothers, Colton and Gage. Who would both have cheerfully killed David if they had ever been able to get their hands on him. But Sam was the first person she had ever told the whole story to. And he was the first person who wasn't one of her siblings who had jumped to her defense immediately.

There had been no interrogation about what kinds of clothes she'd worn to her lessons. About how she had behaved. Part of her wanted to revel in it. Another part of her wanted to push back at it.

"Well, I wore those breeches around him. I know they made you act a little bit crazy. Maybe it was my fault."

"Is this why you got mad about what I said earlier?"

She lifted a shoulder. "Well, that and it was mean."

"I didn't realize this had happened to you," he said, his voice not exactly tender but full of a whole lot more sympathy than she had ever imagined getting from him. "I'm sorry."

"The worst part was losing all my friends," she said, looking up at him. "Everybody really liked him. He was their favorite instructor. As far as dressage instructors go, he was young and cool, trust me."

"So you bore the brunt of it because he turned out to be human garbage and nobody wanted to face it?"

The way he phrased that, so matter-of-fact and real, made a bubble of humor well up inside her chest. "I guess so."

"That doesn't seem fair."

"It really doesn't."

"So that's why you had to feed me dinner, huh? So I didn't remind you of that guy?"

"Well, you're nothing like him. For starters, he was... much more diminutive."

Sam laughed. "You make it sound like you had an affair with a leprechaun."

"Jockeys aren't brawny, Sam."

He only laughed harder. "That's true. I suppose that causes trouble with wind resistance and things."

She rolled her eyes. "You are terrible. Obviously he had some appeal." Though, she had a feeling it wasn't entirely physical. Seeing as she had basically been seeking attention and approval and a thousand other things besides orgasms.

"Obviously. It was his breeches," Sam said.

"A good-looking man in breeches is a thing."

"I believe you."

"But a good-looking man in Wranglers is better." At least, that was her way of thinking right at the moment.

"Good to know."

"But you can see. Why I don't really want to advertise this. It has nothing to do with what you do or who you are or who I am. Well, I guess it is all to do with who I am. What people already think about me. I've been completely defined by a sex life I barely have. And that was... It was the smallest part of that betrayal. At least for me. I loved him. And he was just using me."

"I hope his life was hell after."

"No. His wife forgave him. He went on to compete in the Olympics. He won a silver medal."

"That's kind of a karmic letdown."

"You're telling me. Meanwhile, I've basically lived like a nun and continued giving riding lessons here on the family ranch. I didn't go on to do any of the competing that I wanted to, because I couldn't throw a rock without hitting a judge who was going to be angry with me for my involvement with David."

"In my opinion," Sam said, his expression turning dark, focused, "people are far too concerned with who women sleep with and not near enough as concerned as they should be about whether or not the man does it well. Was he good?"

She felt her face heat. "Not like you."

"I don't care who you had sex with, how many times or who he was. What I do care is that I am the best you've ever had. I'm going to aim to make sure that's the case."

He reached across the table, grabbing hold of her hand. "I'm ready for dessert," he said.

"Me too," she said, pushing her plate back and moving to her feet. "Upstairs?"

He nodded once, the slow burn in his dark eyes searing through her. "Upstairs."

Seven

"Well, it looks like everything is coming together for Dad's Christmas party," Sierra said brightly, looking down at the car seat next to her that contained a sleeping newborn. "Gage will be there, kind of a triumphant return, coming-out kind of thing."

Maddy's older brother shifted in his seat, his arms crossed over his broad chest. "You make me sound like a debutante having a coming-out ball."

"That would be a surprise," his girlfriend, Rebecca Bear, said, putting her hand over his.

"I didn't mean it that way," Sierra said, smiling, her slightly rounder post-childbirth cheeks making her look even younger than she usually did.

Maddy was having a difficult time concentrating. She had met her siblings early at The Grind, the most popular coffee shop in Copper Ridge, so that they could all get on the same page about the big West family soiree that would be thrown on Christmas Eve.

Maddy was ambivalent about it. Mostly she wanted to crawl back under the covers with Sam and burrow until winter passed. But they had agreed that it would go on only until Christmas. Which meant that not only was she dreading the party, it also marked the end of their blissful affair.

By the time Sam had left last night, it had been the next morning, just very early, the sun still inky black as he'd walked out of her house and to his truck.

She had wanted him to stay the entire night, and that was dangerous. She didn't need all that. Didn't need to be held by him, didn't need to wake up in his arms.

"Madison." The sound of her full name jerked her out of her fantasy. She looked up, to see that Colton had been addressing her.

"What?" she asked. "I zoned out for a minute. I haven't had all the caffeine I need yet." Mostly because she had barely slept. She had expected to go out like a light after Sam had left her, but that had not been the case. She had just sort of lay there feeling a little bit achy and lonely and wishing that she didn't.

"Just wondering how you were feeling about Jack coming. You know, now that the whole town knows that he's our half brother, it really is for the best if he comes. I've already talked to Dad about it, and he agrees."

"Great," she said, "and what about Mom?"

"I expect she'll go along with it. She always does. Anyway, Jack is a thirty-five-year-old sin. There's not much use holding it against him now."

"There never was," Maddy said, staring fixedly at her disposable coffee cup, allowing the warm liquid inside to heat her fingertips. She felt like a hypocrite saying that. Mostly because there was something about Jack that was difficult for her.

Well, she knew what it was. The fact that he was evidence of an affair her father had had. The fact that her father was the sort of man who cheated on his wife.

That her father was the sort of man more able to identify with the man who had broken Maddy's heart than he was able to identify with Maddy herself.

But Jack had nothing to do with that. Not really. She knew that logically. He was a good man, married to a great woman, with an adorable baby she really *did* want in her life. It was just that sometimes it needled at her. Got under her skin.

"True enough," Colton said. If he noticed her unease, he certainly didn't betray that he did.

The idea of trying to survive through another West family party just about made her jump up from the coffee shop, run down Main Street and scamper under a rock. She just didn't know if she could do it. Stand there in a pretty dress trying to pretend that she was something the entire town knew she wasn't. Trying to pretend that she was anything other than a disappointment. That her whole family was anything other than tarnished.

Sam didn't feel that way. Not about her. Suddenly, she thought about standing there with him. Sam in a tux, warm and solid next to her...

She blinked, cutting off that line of thinking. There was no reason to be having those fantasies. What she and Sam had was not that. Whatever it was, it wasn't that.

"Then it's settled," Maddy said, a little bit too brightly. "Jack and his family will come to the party."

That sentence made another strange, hollow sensation echo through her. Jack would be there with his family. Sierra and Ace would be there together with their baby. Colton would be there with his wife, Lydia, and while they hadn't made it official yet, Gage and Rebecca were rarely anywhere without each other, and it was plain to anyone who had eyes that Rebecca had changed Gage in a profound way. That she was his support and he was hers.

It was just another way in which Maddy stood alone.

Wow, what a whiny, tragic thought. It wasn't like she wanted her siblings to have nothing. It wasn't like she wanted them to spend their lives alone. Of course she wanted them to have significant others. Maybe she would get around to having one too, eventually.

But it wouldn't be Sam. So she needed to stop having fantasies about him in that role. Naked fantasies. That was all she was allowed.

"Great," Sierra said, lifting up her coffee cup. "I'm going to go order a coffee for Ace and head back home. He's probably just now getting up. He worked closing at the bar last night and then got up to feed the baby. I owe him caffeine and my eternal devotion. But he will want me to lead with the caffeine." She waved and picked up the bucket seat, heading toward the counter.

"I have to go too," Colton said, leaning forward and kissing Maddy on the cheek. "See you later."

Gage nodded slowly, his dark gaze on Rebecca. She nodded, almost imperceptibly, and stood up. "I'm going to grab a refill," she said, making her way to the counter.

As soon as she was out of earshot, Gage turned his focus to her, and Maddy knew that the refill was only a decoy.

"Are you okay?"

This question, coming from the brother she knew the least, the brother who had been out of her life for seventeen years before coming back into town almost two months ago, was strange. And yet in some ways it wasn't. She had felt, from the moment he had returned, that there was something similar in the two of them.

Something broken and strong that maybe the rest of them couldn't understand.

Since then, she had learned more about the circumstances behind his leaving. The accident that he had been involved in that had left Rebecca Bear scarred as a child. Much to Maddy's surprise, they now seemed to be in love.

Which, while she was happy for him, was also a little annoying. Rebecca was the woman he had damaged—however accidentally—and she could love him, while Maddy seemed to be some kind of remote island no one wanted to connect with.

If she took the Gage approach, she could throw hot coffee on the nearest handsome guy, wait a decade and a half and see if his feelings changed for her over time. However, she imagined that was somewhat unrealistic.

"I'm fine," she said brightly. "Always fine."

"Right. Except I'm used to you sounding dry with notes of sarcasm and today you've been overly peppy and sparkly like a Christmas angel, and I think we both know that isn't real."

"Well, the alternative is me complaining about how this time of year gets me a little bit down, and given the general mood around the table, that didn't seem to be the best idea."

"Right. Why don't you like this time of year?"

"I don't know, Gage. Think back to all the years you spent in solitude on the road. Then tell me how you felt about Christmas."

"At best, it didn't seem to matter much. At worst, it reminded me of when I was happy. When I was home with all of you. And when home felt like a happy place. That was the hardest part, Maddy. Being away and longing for a home I couldn't go back to. Because it didn't exist. Not really. After everything I found out about Dad, I knew it wouldn't ever feel the same."

Her throat tightened, emotion swamping her. She had always known that Gage was the one who would understand her. She had been right. Because no one had ever said quite so perfectly exactly what she felt inside, what she had felt ever since news of her dalliance with her dressage trainer had made its way back to Nathan West's ears.

"It's so strange that you put it that way," she said, "because that is exactly how it feels. I live at home. I never left. And I... I ache for something I can never have again. Even if it's just to see my parents in the way that I used to."

"You saw how it was with all of us sitting here," Gage said. "It's something that I never thought I would have. The fact that you've all been willing to forgive me, to let me back into your lives after I was gone for so long, changes the shape of things. We are the ones that can make it different. We can fix what happened with Jack—or move forward into fixing it. There's no reason you and I can't be fixed too, Maddy."

She nodded, her throat so tight she couldn't speak. She stood, holding her coffee cup against her chest. "I am looking forward to seeing you at the Christmas party." Then she forced a smile and walked out of The Grind.

She took a deep breath of the freezing air, hoping that it might wash some of the stale feelings of sadness and grief right out of her body. Then she looked down Main Street, at all of the Christmas lights gilding the edges of the brick buildings like glimmering precious metal.

Christmas wreaths hung from every surface that would take them, velvet bows a crimson beacon against the intense green.

Copper Ridge at Christmas was beautiful, but walking around, she still felt a bit like a stranger, separate and somehow not a part of it all. Everyone here was so good. People like her and Gage had to leave when they got too bad. Except she hadn't left. She just hovered around the edges like a ghost, making inappropriate and sarcastic comments on demand so that no one would ever look at her too closely and see just what a mess she was.

She lowered her head, the wind whipping through her hair, over her cheeks, as she made her way down the street—the opposite direction of her car. She wasn't really sure what she was doing, only that she couldn't face heading back to the ranch right now. Not when she felt nostalgic for something that didn't exist anymore. When she felt raw from the conversation with Gage.

She kept going down Main, pausing at the front door of the Mercantile when she saw a display of Christmas candy sitting in the window. It made her smile to see it there, a sugary reminder of some old memory that wasn't tainted by reality.

She closed her eyes tight, and she remembered what it was. Walking down the street with her father, who was always treated like he was a king then. She had been small, and it had been before Gage had left. Before she had ever disappointed anyone.

It was Christmastime, and carolers were milling around, and she had looked up and seen sugarplums and candy canes, little peppermint chocolates and other sweets in the window. He had taken her inside and allowed her to choose whatever she wanted.

A simple memory. A reminder of a time when things hadn't been quite so hard, or quite so real, between herself and Nathan West.

She found herself heading inside, in spite of the fact that the entire point of this walk had been to avoid memories. But then, she really wanted to avoid the memories that were at the ranch. This was different.

She opened the door, taking a deep breath of gingerbread and cloves upon entry. The narrow little store with exposed brick walls was packed with goodies. Cakes, cheeses and breads, imported and made locally.

Lane Jensen, the owner of the Mercantile, was standing toward the back of the store talking to somebody. Maddy didn't see another person right away, and then, when the broad figure came into view, her heart slammed against her breastbone.

When she realized it was Sam, she had to ask herself if she had been drawn down this way because of a sense of nostalgia or because something in her head sensed that he was around. That was silly. Of course she didn't *sense* his presence.

Though, given pheromones and all of that, maybe it wasn't too ridiculous. It certainly wasn't some kind of emotional crap. Not her heart recognizing where his was beating or some such nonsense.

For a split second she considered running the other direction. Before he saw her, before it got weird. But she hesitated, just for the space of a breath, and that was long enough for Sam to look past Lane, his eyes locking with hers.

She stood, frozen to the spot. "Hi," she said, knowing that she sounded awkward, knowing that she looked awkward.

She was unaccustomed to that. At least, these days. She had grown a tough outer shell, trained herself to never feel ashamed, to never feel embarrassed—not in a way that people would be able to see.

Because after her little scandal, she had always imagined that it was the only thing people thought about when they looked at her. Walking around, feeling like that, feeling like you had a scarlet *A* burned into your skin, it forced you to figure out a way to exist.

In her case it had meant cultivating a kind of brash persona. So, being caught like this, looking like a deer in the headlights—which was what she imagined she looked like right now, wide-eyed and trembling—it all felt a bit disorienting.

"Maddy," Sam said, "I wasn't expecting to see you here."

"That's because we didn't make any plans to meet here," she said. "I promise I didn't follow you." She looked over at Lane, who was studying them with great interest. "Not that I would. Because there's no reason for me to do that. Because you're the farrier for my horses. And that's it." She felt distinctly detached and light-headed, as though she might drift away on a cloud of embarrassment at a moment's notice.

"Right," he said. "Thank you, Lane," he said, turning his attention back to the other woman. "I can bring the installation down tomorrow." He tipped his hat, then moved away from Lane, making his way toward her.

"Hi, Lane," she said. Sam grabbed hold of her elbow and began to propel her out of the store. "Bye, Lane."

As soon as they were back out on the street, she rounded on him. "What was that? I thought we were trying to be discreet."

"Lane Jensen isn't a gossip. Anyway, you standing there turning the color of a beet wasn't exactly subtle."

"I am not a beet," she protested, stamping.

"A tiny tomato."

"Stop comparing me to vegetables."

"A tomato isn't a vegetable."

She let out a growl and began to walk away from him, heading back up Main Street and toward her car. "Wait," he said, his voice possessing some kind of unknowable power to actually make her obey.

She stopped, rooted to the cement. "What?"

"We live in the same town. We're going to have to figure out how to interact with each other."

"Or," she said, "we continue on with this very special brand of awkwardness."

"Would it be the worst thing in the world if people knew?"

"You know my past, and you can ask me that?" She looked around the street, trying to see if anybody was watching their little play. "I'm not going to talk to you about this on the town stage."

He closed the distance between them. "Fine. We don't have to have the discussion. And it doesn't matter to me either way. But you really think you should spend the rest of your life punishing yourself for a mistake that happened when you were seventeen? He took advantage of you—it isn't your fault. And apart from any of that, you don't deserve to be labeled by a bunch of people that don't even know you."

That wasn't even it. And as she stood there, staring him down, she realized that fully. It had nothing to do with what the town thought. Nothing to do with whether or not the town thought she was a scarlet woman, or if people still thought about her indiscretion, or if people blamed her or David. None of that mattered.

She realized that in a flash of blinding brilliance that shone brighter than the Christmas lights all around her. And that realization made her knees buckle, because it made her remember the conversation that had happened in her father's office. The conversation that had occurred right after one of David's students had discovered the affair between the two of them and begun spreading rumors.

Rumors that were true, regrettably.

Rumors that had made their way all the way back to Nathan West's home office.

"I can't talk about this right now," she said, brushing past him and striding down the sidewalk.

"You don't have to talk about it with me, not ever. But what's going to happen when this is over? You're going to go another ten years between lovers? Just break down and hold your breath and do it again when you can't take the celibacy anymore?"

"Stop it," she said, walking faster.

"Like I said, it doesn't matter to me…"

She whirled around. "You keep saying it doesn't matter to you, and then you keep pushing the issue. So I would say that it does matter to you. Whatever complex you have about not being good enough, this is digging at that. But it isn't my problem. Because it isn't about you. Nobody would care if they knew that we were sleeping together. I mean, they would talk about it, but they wouldn't care. But it makes it something more. And I just… I can't have more. Not more than this."

He shifted uncomfortably. "Well, neither can I. That was hardly an invitation for something deeper."

"Good. Because I don't have anything deeper to give."

The very idea made her feel like she was going into a free fall. The idea of trusting somebody again…

The betrayals she had dealt with back when she was seventeen had made it so that trusting another human being was almost unfathomable. When she had told Sam that the sex was the least of it, she had been telling the truth.

It had very little to do with her body, and everything to do with the battering her soul had taken.

"Neither do I."

"Then why are you… Why are you pushing me like this?"

He looked stunned by the question, his face frozen. "I just… I don't want to leave you broken."

Something inside her softened, cracked a little bit. "I'm not sure that you have a choice. It kind of is what it is, you know?"

"Maybe it doesn't have to be."

"Did you think you were going to fix me, Sam?"

"No," he said, his voice rough.

But she knew he was lying. "Don't put that on yourself. Two broken people can't fix each other."

She was certain in that moment that he was broken too, even though she wasn't quite sure how.

"We only have twelve days. Any kind of fixing was a bit ambitious anyway," he said.

"Eleven days," she reminded him. "I'll see you tonight?"

"Yeah. See you then."

And then she turned and walked away from Sam McCormack for all the town to see, as if he were just a casual acquaintance and nothing more. And she tried to ignore the ache in the center of her chest that didn't seem to go away, even after she got in the car and drove home.

Eight

Seven days after beginning the affair with Maddy, she called and asked him if he could come down and check the shoes on one of the horses. It was the middle of the afternoon, so if it was her version of a booty call, he thought it was kind of an odd time. And since their entire relationship was a series of those, he didn't exactly see why she wouldn't be up front about it.

But when he showed up, she was waiting for him outside the stall.

"What are you up to?"

She lifted her shoulder. "I just wanted you to come and check on the horse."

"Something you couldn't check yourself?"

She looked slightly rueful. "Okay, maybe I could have checked it myself. But she really is walking a little bit funny, and I'm wondering if something is off."

She opened the stall door, clipped a lead rope to the horse's harness and brought her out into the main part of the barn.

He looked at her, then pushed up the sleeves on his thermal shirt and knelt down in front of the large animal, drawing his hand slowly down her leg and lifting it gently. Then he did the same to the next before moving to her hindquarters and repeating the motion again.

He stole a glance up at Maddy, who was staring at him with rapt attention.

"What?"

"I like watching you work," she said. "I've always liked watching you work. That's why I used to come down here and give orders. Okay, honestly? I wanted to give myself permission to watch you and enjoy it." She swallowed hard. "You're right. I've been punishing myself. So, I thought I might indulge myself."

"I'm going to have to charge your dad for this visit," he said.

"He won't notice," she said. "Trust me."

"I don't believe that. Your father is a pretty well-known businessman." He straightened, putting the horse on its haunches. "Everything looks fine."

Maddy looked sheepish. "Great."

"Why don't you think your dad would notice?"

"A lot of stuff has come out over the past few months. You know he had a stroke three months ago or so, and while he's recovered pretty well since then, it changed things. I mean, it didn't change *him*. It's not like he miraculously became some soft, easy man. Though, I think he's maybe a little bit more in touch with his mortality. Not happily, mind you. I think he always saw himself as something of a god."

"Well," Sam said, "what man doesn't?" At least, until he was set firmly back down to earth and reminded of just how badly he could mess things up. How badly things could hurt.

"Yet another difference between men and women," Maddy said drily. "But after he had his stroke, the control of the finances went to my brother Gage. That was why he came back to town initially. He discovered that there was a lot of debt. I mean, I know you've heard about how many properties we've had to sell downtown."

Sam stuffed his hands in his pockets, lifting his shoulders. "Not really. But then, I don't exactly keep up on that kind of stuff. That's Chase's arena. Businesses and the real estate market. That's not me. I just screw around with metal."

"You downplay what you do," she returned. "From the art to the physical labor. I've watched you do it. I don't know why you do it, only that you do. You're always acting like your brother is smarter than you, but he can't do what you do either."

"Art was never particularly useful as far as my father was concerned," Sam said. "I imagine he would be pretty damned upset to see that it's the art that keeps the ranch afloat so nicely. He would have wanted us to do it the way our ancestors did. Making leatherwork and pounding nails. Of course, it was always hard for him to understand that mass production was inevitably going to win out against more expensive handmade things. Unless we targeted our products and people who could afford what we did. Which is what we did. What we've been successful with far beyond what we even imagined."

"Dads," she said, her voice soft. "They do get in your head, don't they?"

"I mean, my father didn't have gambling debts and a secret child, but he was kind of a difficult bastard. I still wish he wasn't dead." He laughed. "It would kind of be nice to have him wandering around the place shaking his head disapprovingly as I loaded up that art installation to take down to the Mercantile."

"I don't know, having your dad hanging around disapproving is kind of overrated." Suddenly, her face contorted with horror. "I'm sorry—I had no business saying something like that. It isn't fair. I shouldn't make light of your loss."

"It was a long time ago. And anyway, I do it all the time. I think it's the way the emotionally crippled deal with things." Anger. Laughter. It was all better than hurt.

"Yeah," she said, laughing uneasily. "That sounds about right."

"What exactly does your dad disapprove of, Madison?" he asked, reverting back to her full name. He kind of liked it, because nobody else called her that. And she had gone from looking like she wanted to claw his eyes out when he used it to responding. There was something that felt deep about that. Connected. He shouldn't care. If anything, it should entice him not to do it. But it didn't.

"Isn't it obvious?"

"No," he returned. "I've done a lot of work on this ranch over the years. You're always busy. You have students scheduled all day every day—except today, apparently—and it is a major part of both the reputation and the income of this facility. You've poured everything you have into reinforcing his legacy while letting your own take a backseat."

"Well, when you put it like that," she said, the smile on her lips obviously forced, "I am kind of amazing."

"What exactly does he disapprove of?"

"What do you think?"

"Does it all come back to that? Something you did when you were seventeen?" The hypocrisy of the outrage in his tone wasn't lost on him.

"I'm not sure," she said, the words biting. "I'm really not." She grabbed hold of the horse's lead rope, taking her back into the stall before clipping the rope and coming back out, shutting the door firmly.

"What do you mean by that?"

She growled, making her way out of the barn and walking down the paved path that led toward one of the covered arenas. "I don't know. Feel free to choose your own adventure with that one."

"Come on, Maddy," he said, closing the distance between them and lowering his voice. "I've tasted parts of you that most other people have never seen. A little bit of honesty isn't going to hurt you."

She whipped around, her eyes bright. "Maybe it isn't him. Maybe it's me. Maybe I'm the one that can't look at him the same way."

Maddy felt rage simmering over her skin like heat waves. She had not intended to have this conversation—not with Sam, not with anyone.

But now she had started, she didn't know if she could stop. "The night that he found out about my affair with David was the night I found out about Jack."

"So, it isn't a recent revelation to all of you?"

"No," she said. "Colton and Sierra didn't know. I'm sure of that. But I found out that Gage did. I didn't know who it was, I should clarify. I just found out that he had another child." She looked away from Sam, trying to ignore the burning sensation in her stomach. Like there was molten lava rolling around in there. She associated that feeling with being called into her father's home office.

It had always given her anxiety, even before everything had happened with David. Even before she had ever seriously disappointed him.

Nathan West was exacting, and Maddy had wanted nothing more than to please him. That desire took up much more of her life than she had ever wanted it to. But then, she knew that was true in some way or another for all of her siblings. It was why Sierra had gone to school for business. Why Colton had taken over the construction company. It was even what had driven Gage to leave.

It was the reason Maddy had poured all of her focus into dressage. Because she had anticipated becoming great. Going to the Olympics. And she knew her father had anticipated that. Then she had ruined all of it.

But not as badly as he had ruined the relationship between the two of them.

"Like I told you, one of David's other students caught us together. Down at the barn where he gave his lessons. We were just kissing, but it was definitely enough. That girl told her father, who in turn went to mine as a courtesy."

Sam laughed, a hard, bitter sound. "A courtesy to who?"

"Not to me," Maddy said. "Or maybe it was. I don't

know. It was so awful. The whole situation. I wish there had been a less painful way for it to end. But it had to end, whether it ended that way or some other way, so... so I guess that worked as well as anything."

"Except you had to deal with your father. And then rumors were spread anyway."

She looked away from Sam. "Well, the rumors I kind of blame on David. Because once his wife knew, there was really no reason for the whole world not to know. And I think it suited him to paint me in an unflattering light. He took a gamble. A gamble that the man in the situation would come out of it all just fine. It was not a bad gamble, it turned out."

"I guess not."

"Full house. Douche bag takes the pot."

She was avoiding the point of this conversation. Avoiding the truth of it. She didn't even know why she should tell him. She didn't know why anything. Except that she had never confided any of this to anyone before. She was close to her sister, and Sierra had shared almost everything about her relationship with Ace with Maddy, and here Maddy was keeping more secrets from her.

She had kept David from her. She had kept Sam from her too. And she had kept this all to herself, as well.

She knew why. In a blinding flash she knew why. She couldn't stand being rejected, not again. She had been rejected by her first love; she had been rejected by an entire community. She had been rejected by her father with a few cold dismissive words in his beautifully appointed office in her childhood home.

But maybe, just maybe, that was why she should confide in Sam. Because at the end of their affair it wouldn't matter. Because then they would go back to sniping at each other or not talking to each other at all.

Because he hadn't rejected her yet.

"When he called me into his office, I knew I was in trouble," she said, rubbing her hand over her forehead. "He never did that for good things. Ever. If there was something good to discuss, we would talk about it around the dinner table. Only bad things were ever talked about in his office with the door firmly closed. He talked to Gage like that. Right before he left town. So, I always knew it had to be bad."

She cleared her throat, looking out across the arena, through the gap in the trees and at the distant view of the misty waves beyond. It was so very gray, the clouds hanging low in the sky, touching the top of the angry, steel-colored sea.

"Anyway, I *knew*. As soon as I walked in, I knew. He looked grim. Like I've never seen him before. And he asked me what was going on with myself and David Smithson. Well, I knew there was no point in denying it. So I told him. He didn't yell. I wish he had. He said… He said the worst thing you could ever do was get caught. That a man like David spent years building up his reputation, not to have it undone by the temptation of some young girl." She blinked furiously. "He said that if a woman was going to present more temptation than a man could handle, the least she could do was keep it discreet."

"How could he say that to you? To his daughter? Look, my dad was a difficult son of a bitch, but if he'd had a daughter and some man had hurt her, he'd have ridden out on his meanest stallion with a pair of pliers to dole out the world's least sterile castration."

Maddy choked out a laugh that was mixed with a sob. "That's what I thought. It really was. I thought… I thought he would be angry, but one of the things that scared me most, at least initially, was the idea that he would take it out on David. And I still loved David then. But no. He was angry at me."

"I don't understand how that's possible."

"That was when he told me," she choked out. "Told me that he had mistresses, that it was just something men did, but that the world didn't run if the mistress didn't know her place, and if I was intent on lowering myself to be that sort of woman when I could have easily been a wife, that was none of his business. He told me a woman had had his child and never betrayed him." Her throat tightened, almost painfully, a tear sliding down her cheek. "Even he saw me as the villain. If my own father couldn't stand up for me, if even he thought it was my fault somehow, how was I ever supposed to stand up for myself when other people accused me of being a whore?"

"Maddy…"

"That's why," she said, the words thin, barely making their way through her constricted throat. "That's why it hurts so much. And that's why I'm not over it. There were two men involved in that who said they loved me. There was David, the man I had given my heart to, the man I had given my body to, who had lied to me from the very beginning, who threw me under the bus the moment he got the opportunity. And then there was my own father. My own father, who should have been on my side simply because I was born his. I loved them both. And they both let me down." She blinked, a mist rolling over her insides, matching the setting all around them. "How do you ever trust anyone after that? If it had only been David, I think I would have been over it a long time ago."

Sam was looking at her, regarding her with dark, intense eyes. He looked like he was about to say something, his chest shifting as he took in a breath that seemed to contain purpose. But then he said nothing. He simply closed the distance between them, tugging her into his arms, holding her against his chest, his large, warm hand moving between her shoulder blades in a soothing rhythm.

She hadn't rested on anyone in longer than she could remember. Hadn't been held like this in years. Her mother was too brittle to lean on. She would break beneath the weight of somebody else's sorrow. Her father had never offered a word of comfort to anyone. And she had gotten in the habit of pretending she was tough so that Colton and Sierra wouldn't worry about her. So that they wouldn't look too deeply at how damaged she was still from the events of the past.

So she put all her weight on him and total peace washed over her. She shouldn't indulge in this. She shouldn't allow herself this. It was dangerous. But she couldn't stop. And she didn't want to.

She squeezed her eyes shut, a few more tears falling down her cheeks, soaking into his shirt. If anybody knew that Madison West had wept all over a man in the broad light of day, they wouldn't believe it. But she didn't care. This wasn't about anyone else. It was just about her. About purging her soul of some of the poison that had taken up residence there ten years ago and never quite left.

About dealing with some of the heavy longing that

existed inside her for a time and a place she could never return to. For a Christmas when she had walked down Main Street with her father and seen him as a hero.

But of course, when she was through crying, she felt exposed. Horribly. Hideously, and she knew this was why she didn't make a habit out of confiding in people. Because now Sam McCormack knew too much about her. Knew more about her than maybe anybody else on earth. At least, he knew about parts of her that no one else did.

The tenderness. The insecurity. The parts that were on the verge of cracking open, crumbling the foundation of her and leaving nothing more than a dusty pile of Maddy behind.

She took a deep breath, hoping that the pressure would squeeze some of those shattering pieces of herself back together with the sheer force of it. Too bad it just made her aware of more places down deep that were compromised.

Still, she wiggled out of his grasp, needing a moment to get ahold of herself. Needing very much to not get caught being held by a strange man down at the arena by any of the staff or anyone in her family.

"Thank you," she said, her voice shaking. "I just… I didn't know how much I needed that."

"I didn't do anything."

"You listened. You didn't try to give me advice or tell me I was wrong. That's actually doing a lot. A lot more than most people are willing to do."

"So, do you want me to come back here tonight?"

"Actually," she said, grabbing hold of her hands, twisting them, trying to deal with the nervous energy that was rioting through her, "I was thinking maybe I could come out a little bit early. And I could see where you work."

She didn't know why she was doing this. She didn't know where she imagined it could possibly end or how it would be helpful to her in any way. To add more pieces of him to her heart, to her mind.

That's what it felt like she was trying to do. Like collecting shells on the seashore. Picking up all the shimmering pieces of Sam she possibly could and sticking them in her little pail, hoarding them. Making a collection.

For what? Maybe for when it was over.

Maybe that wasn't so bad.

She had pieces of David, whether she wanted them or not. And she'd entertained the idea that maybe she could sleep with someone and not do that. Not carry them forward with her.

But the reality of it was that she wasn't going to walk away from this affair and never think of Sam again. He was never going to be the farrier again. He would always be Sam. Why not leave herself with beautiful memories instead of terrible ones? Maybe this was what she needed to do.

"You want to see the forge?" he asked.

"Sure. That would be interesting. But also your studio. I'm curious about your art, and I realize that I don't really know anything about it. Seeing you in the Mercantile the other day talking to Lane…" She didn't know how to phrase what she was thinking without sounding a little bit crazy. Without sounding overly attached. So she just let the sentence trail off.

But she was curious. She was curious about him. About who he was when he wasn't here. About who he was as a whole person, without the blinders around him that she had put there. She had very purposefully gone out of her way to know nothing about him. And so he had always been Sam McCormack, grumpy guy who worked at her family ranch on occasion and who she often bantered with in the sharpest of senses.

But there was more to him. So much more. This man who had held her, this man who had listened, this man who seemed to know everyone in town and have decent relationships with them. Who created beautiful things that started in his mind and were then formed with his hands. She wanted to know him.

Yeah, she wouldn't be telling him any of that.

"Were you jealous? Because there is nothing between myself and Lane Jensen. First of all, anyone who wants anything to do with her has to go through Finn Donnelly, and I have no desire to step in the middle of *that* weird dynamic and his older-brother complex."

It struck her then that jealousy hadn't even been a component to what she had felt the other day. How strange. Considering everything she had been through with men, it seemed like maybe trust should be the issue here. But it wasn't. It never had been.

It had just been this moment of catching sight of him at a different angle. Like a different side to a prism that cast a different color on the wall and made her want to investigate further. To see how one person could contain so many different things.

A person who was so desperate to hide anything beyond that single dimension he seemed comfortable with.

Another thing she would definitely not say to him. She couldn't imagine the twenty shades of rainbow horror that would cross Sam's face if she compared him to a prism out loud.

"I was not," she said. "But it made me aware of the fact that you're kind of a big deal. And I haven't fully appreciated that."

"Of course you haven't," he said, his tone dry. "It interferes with your stable-boy fantasy."

She made a scoffing sound. "I do not have a stable-boy fantasy."

"Yes, you do. You like slumming it."

Those words called up heated memories out of the depths of her mind. Him whispering things in her ear. His rough hands skimming over her skin. She bit her lip. "I like nothing of the kind, Sam McCormack. Not with you, not with any man. Are you going to show me your pretty art or not?"

"Not if you call it pretty."

"You'll have to take your chances. I'm not putting a cap on my vocabulary for your comfort. Anyway, if you haven't noticed, unnerving people with what I may or may not say next is kind of my thing."

"I've noticed."

"You do it too," she said.

His lips tipped upward into a small smile. "Do I?"

She rolled her eyes. "Oh, don't pretend you don't know. You're way too smart for that. And you act like the word *smart* is possibly the world's most vile swear when it's applied to you. But you are. You can throw around accusations of slumming it all you want, but if we didn't connect mentally, and if I didn't respect you in some way, this wouldn't work."

"Our brains have nothing to do with this."

She lifted a finger. "A woman's largest sexual organ is her brain."

He chuckled, wrapping his arm around her waist and drawing her close. "Sure, Maddy. But we both know what the most important one is." He leaned in, whispering dirty things in her ear, and she laughed, pushing against his chest. "Okay," he said, finally. "I will let you come see my studio."

She fought against the trickle of warmth that ran through her, that rested deep in her stomach and spread out from there, making her feel a kind of languid satisfaction that she had no business feeling over something like this. "Then I guess I'll see you for the art show."

Nine

Sam had no idea what in hell had possessed him to let Maddy come out to his property tonight. Chase and Anna were not going to let this go ignored. In fact, Anna was already starting to make comments about the fact that he hadn't been around for dinner recently. Which was why he was there tonight, eating as quickly as possible so he could get back out to his place on the property before Maddy arrived. He had given her directions to go on the road that would allow her to bypass the main house, which Chase and Anna inhabited.

"Sam." His sister-in-law's voice cut into his thoughts. "I thought you were going to join us for dinner tonight?"

"I'm here," he said.

"Your body is. Your brain isn't. And Chase worked very hard on this meal," Anna said.

Anna was a tractor mechanic, and formerly Chase's

best friend in a platonic sense. All of that had come to an end a few months ago when they had realized there was a lot more between them than friendship.

Still, the marriage had not transformed Anna into a domestic goddess. Instead, it had forced Chase to figure out how to share a household with somebody. They were never going to have a traditional relationship, but it seemed to suit Chase just fine.

"It's very good, Chase," Sam said, keeping his tone dry.

"Thanks," Chase said, "I opened the jar of pasta sauce myself."

"Sadly, no one in this house is ever going to win a cooking competition," Anna said.

"You keep *me* from starving," Sam pointed out.

Though, in all honesty, he was a better cook than either of them. Still, it was an excuse to get together with his brother. And sometimes it felt like he needed excuses. So that he didn't have to think deeply about a feeling that was more driving than hunger pangs.

"Not recently," Chase remarked. "You haven't been around."

Sam let out a heavy sigh. "Yes, sometimes a man assumes that newlyweds want time alone without their crabby brother around."

"We always want you around," Anna said. Then she screwed up her face. "Okay, we don't *always* want you around. But for dinner, when we invite you, it's fine."

"Just no unexpected visits to the house," Chase said. "In the evening. Or anytime. And maybe also don't walk into Anna's shop without knocking after hours."

Sam grimaced. "I get the point. Anyway, I've just been busy. And I'm about to be busy again." He stood up, anticipation shooting through him. He had gone a long time without sex, and now sex with Maddy was about all he could think about. Five years of celibacy would do that to a man.

Made a man do stupid things, like invite the woman he was currently sleeping with to come to his place and to come see his art. Whatever the hell she thought that would entail. He was inclined to figure it out. Just so she would feel happy, so he could see her smile again.

So she would be in the mood to put out. And nothing more. Certainly no emotional reasoning behind that.

He couldn't do that. Not ever again.

"Okay," Anna said, "you're always cagey, Sam, I'll give you that. But you have to give me a hint about what's going on."

"No," Sam said, turning to go. "I really don't."

"Sculpture? A woman?"

Well, sadly, Anna was mostly on point with both. "Not your business."

"That's hilarious," Chase said, "coming from the man who meddled in our relationship."

"You jackasses needed meddling," Sam said. "You were going to let her go." Of the two of them, Chase was undoubtedly the better man. And Anna was one of the best, man or woman. When Sam had realized his brother was about to let Anna get away because of baggage from his past, Sam had had no choice but to play the older-brother card and give advice that he himself would never have taken.

But it was different for Chase. Sam wanted it to be different for Chase. He didn't want his younger brother living the same stripped-down existence he did.

"Well, maybe you need meddling too, jackass," Anna said.

Sam ignored his sister-in-law and continued on out of the house, taking the steps on the porch two at a time, the frosted ground crunching beneath his boots as he walked across the field, taking the short route between the two houses.

He shoved his hands in his pockets, looking up, watching his breath float up into the dense sky, joining the mist there. It was already getting dark, the twilight hanging low around him, a deep blue ink spill that bled down over everything.

It reminded him of grief. A darkness that descended without warning, covering everything around it, changing it. Taking things that were familiar and twisting them into foreign objects and strangers.

That thought nibbled at the back of his mind. He couldn't let it go. It just hovered there as he made his way back to his place, trying to push its way to the front of his mind and form the obvious conclusion.

He resisted it. The way that he always did. Anytime he got inspiration that seemed related to these kinds of feelings. And then he would go out to his shop and start working on another Texas longhorn sculpture. Because that didn't mean anything and people would want to buy it.

Just as he approached his house, so did Maddy's car. She parked right next to his truck, and a strange feeling of domesticity overtook him. Two cars in the driveway. His and hers.

He pushed that aside too.

He watched her open the car door, her blond hair even paler in the advancing moonlight. She was wearing a hat, the shimmering curls spilling out from underneath it. She also had on a scarf and gloves. And there was something about her, looking soft and bundled up, and very much not like prickly, brittle Maddy, that made him want to pull her back into his arms like he had done earlier that day and hold her up against his chest.

Hold her until she quit shaking. Or until she started shaking for a different reason entirely.

"You made it," he said.

"You say that like you had some doubt that I would."

"Well, at the very least I thought you might change your mind."

"No such luck for you. I'm curious. And once my curiosity is piqued, I will have it satisfied."

"You're like a particularly meddlesome cat," he said.

"You're going to have to make up your mind, Sam," Maddy said, smiling broadly.

"About what?"

"Am I vegetable or mammal? You have now compared me to both."

"A tomato is a fruit."

"Whatever," she said, waving a gloved hand.

"Do you want to come out and see the sculptures or do you want to stand here arguing about whether or not you're animal, vegetable or mineral?"

Her smile only broadened. "Sculptures, please."

"Well, follow me. And it's a good thing you bundled up."

"This is how much I had to bundle to get in the car and drive over here. My heater is *not* broken. I didn't know that I was going to be wandering around out in the dark, in the cold."

He snorted. "You run cold?"

"I do."

"I hadn't noticed."

She lifted a shoulder, taking two steps to his every one, doing her best to keep up with him as he led them both across the expanse of frozen field. "Well, I'm usually very hot when you're around. Anyway, the combination of you and blankets is very warming."

"What happens when I leave?"

"I get cold," she returned.

Something about those words felt like a knife in the center of his chest. Damned if he knew why. At least, damned if he wanted to know why.

What he wanted was to figure out how to make it go away.

They continued on the rest of the walk in silence, and he increased his pace when the shop came into view. "Over here is where Chase and I work," he said, gesturing to the first building. "Anna's is on a different section of the property, one closer to the road so that it's easier for her customers to get in there, since they usually have heavy equipment being towed by heavier equipment. And this one is mine." He pointed to another outbuilding, one that had once been a separate machine shed.

"We remodeled it this past year. Expanded and made room for the new equipment. I have a feeling my dad would piss himself if he knew what this was being used for now," he continued, not quite able to keep the thought in his mind.

Maddy came up beside him, looping her arm through his. "Maybe. But I want to see it. And I promise you I won't…do *that*."

"Appreciated," he said, allowing her to keep hold of him while they walked inside.

He realized then that nobody other than Chase and Anna had ever been in here. And he had never grandly showed it to either of them. They just popped in on occasion to let him know that lunch or dinner was ready or to ask if he was ever going to resurface.

He had never invited anyone here. Though, he supposed that Maddy had invited herself here. Either way, this was strange. It was exposing in a way he hadn't anticipated it being. Mostly because that required he admit that there was something of himself in his work. And he resisted that. Resisted it hard.

It had always been an uncomfortable fit for him. That he had this ability, this compulsion to create things, that could come only from inside him. Which was a little bit like opening up his chest and showing bits of it to the world. Which was the last thing on earth he ever wanted to do. He didn't like sharing himself with other people. Not at all.

Maddy turned a slow circle, her soft, pink mouth falling open. "Wow," she said. "Is this all of them?"

"No," he said, following her line of sight, looking at the various iron sculptures all around them. Most of them were to scale with whatever they were representing. Giant two-ton metal cows and horses, one with a cowboy upon its back, took up most of the space in the room.

Pieces that came from what he saw. From a place he loved. But not from inside him.

"What are these?"

"Works in progress, mostly. Almost all of them are close to being done. Which was why I was up at the cabin, remember? I'm trying to figure out what I'm going to do next. But I can always make more things like this. They sell. I can put them in places around town and tourists will always come in and buy them. People pay obscene amounts of money for stuff like this." He let out a long, slow breath. "I'm kind of mystified by it."

"You shouldn't be. It's amazing." She moved around the space, reaching out and brushing her fingertips over the back of one of the cows. "We have to get some for the ranch. They're perfect."

Something shifted in his chest, a question hovering on the tip of his tongue. But he held it back. He had been about to ask her if he should do something different. If he should follow that compulsion that had hit him on the walk back. Those ideas about grief. About loss.

Who the hell wanted to look at something like that? Anyway, he didn't want to show anyone that part of himself. And he sure as hell didn't deserve to profit off any of his losses.

He gritted his teeth. "Great."

"You sound like you think it's great," she said, her tone deeply insincere.

"I wasn't aware my enthusiasm was going to be graded."

She looked around, the shop light making her hair look even deeper gold than it normally did. She reached up, grabbing the knit hat on her head and flinging it onto the ground. He knew what she was doing. He wanted to stop her. Because this was his shop. His studio. It was personal in a way that nothing else was. She could sleep in his bed. She could go to his house, stay there all night, and it would never be the same as her getting naked here.

He was going to stop her.

But then she grabbed the zipper tab on her jacket and shrugged it off before taking hold of the hem of her top, yanking it over her head and sending it the same way as her outerwear.

Then Maddy was standing there, wearing nothing but a flimsy lace bra, the pale curve of her breasts rising and falling with every breath she took.

"Since it's clear how talented your hands are, particularly here…" she said, looking all wide-eyed and innocent. He loved that. The way she could look like this, then spew profanities with the best of them. The way she could make her eyes all dewy, then do something that would make even the most hardened cowboy blush. "I thought I might see if I could take advantage of the inspirational quality of the place."

Immediately, his blood ran hotter, faster, desire roaring in him like a beast. He wanted her. He wanted this. There was nowhere soft to take her, not here. Not in this place full of nails and iron, in this place that was hard and jagged just like his soul, that was more evidence of what he contained than anyone would ever know.

"The rest," he said, his voice as uncompromising as the sculpture all around them. "Take off the rest, Madison."

Her lashes fluttered as she looked down, undoing the snap on her jeans, then the zipper, maddeningly slowly. And of course, she did her best to look like she had no idea what she was doing to him.

She pushed her jeans down her hips, and all that was left covering her was those few pale scraps of lace. She was so soft. And everything around her was so hard.

It should make him want to protect her. Should make him want to get her out of here. Away from this place. Away from him. But it didn't. He was that much of a bastard.

He didn't take off any of his own clothes, because there was something about the contrast that turned him on even more. Instead, he moved toward her, slowly, not bothering to hide his open appreciation for her curves.

He closed the distance between them, wrapping his hand around the back of her head, sifting his fingers through her hair before tightening his hold on her, tugging gently. She gasped, following his lead, tilting her face upward.

He leaned in, and he could tell that she was expecting a kiss. By the way her lips softened, by the way her eyes fluttered closed. Instead, he angled his head, pressing his lips to that tender skin on her neck. She shivered, the contact clearly an unexpected surprise. But not an unwelcome one.

He kept his fingers buried firmly in her hair, holding her steady as he shifted again, brushing his mouth over the line of her collarbone, following it all the way toward the center of her chest and down to the plush curves of her breasts.

He traced that feathery line there where lace met skin with the tip of his tongue, daring to delve briefly beneath the fabric, relishing the hitch in her breathing when he came close to her sensitized nipples.

He slid his hands up her arms, grabbed hold of the delicate bra straps and tugged them down, moving slowly, ever so slowly, bringing the cups down just beneath her breasts, exposing those dusky nipples to him.

"Beautiful," he said. "Prettier than anything in here."

"I didn't think you wanted the word *pretty* uttered in here," she said, breathless.

"About my work. About you... That's an entirely different situation. You are pretty. These are pretty."

He leaned in, brushing his lips lightly over one tightened bud, relishing the sweet sound of pleasure that
she made.

"Now who's a tease?" she asked, her voice labored.

"I haven't even started to tease you yet."

He slid his hands around her back, pressing his palms
hard between her shoulder blades, lowering his head so
that he could draw the center of her breast deep into his
mouth. He sucked hard until she whimpered, until she
squirmed against him, clearly looking for some kind
of relief for the intense arousal that he was building
inside her.

He looked up, really looked at her face, a deep, primitive sense of pleasure washing through him. That he
was touching such a soft, beautiful woman. That he
was allowing himself such an indulgence. That he was
doing this to her.

He had forgotten. He had forgotten what it was like
to really relish the fact that he possessed the power to
make a woman feel good. Because he had reduced his
hands to something else entirely. Hands that had failed
him, that had failed Elizabeth.

Hands that could form iron into impossible shapes
but couldn't be allowed to handle something this fragile.

But here he was with Madison. She was soft, and he
wasn't breaking her. She was beautiful, and she was his.

Not yours. Never yours.

He tightened his hold on her, battling the unwelcome thoughts that were trying to crowd in, trying to
take over this experience, this moment. When Madison
was gone, he would go back to the austere existence
he'd been living for the past five years. But right now,

he had her, and he wasn't going to let anything damage that. Not now.

Instead of thinking, which was never a good thing, not for him, he continued his exploration of her body. Lowering himself down to his knees in front of her, kissing her just beneath her breasts, and down lower, tracing a line across her soft stomach.

She was everything a woman should be. He was confident of that. Because she was the only woman he could remember. Right now, she was everything.

He moved his hands down her thighs, then back up again, pushing his fingertips beneath the waistband of her panties as he gripped her hips and leaned in, kissing her just beneath her belly button. She shook beneath him, a sweet little trembling that betrayed just how much she wanted him.

She wouldn't, if she knew. If she knew, she wouldn't want him. But she didn't know. And she never had to. There were only five days left. They would never have to talk about it. Ever. They would only ever have this. That was important. Because if they ever tried to have more, there would be nothing. She would run so far the other direction he would never see her again.

Or maybe she wouldn't. Maybe she would stick around. But that was even worse. Because of what he would have to do.

He flexed his fingers, the blunt tips digging into that soft skin at her hips. He growled, moving them around to cup her ass beneath the thin lace fabric on her panties. He squeezed her there too and she moaned, her obvious enjoyment of his hands all over her body sending a surge of pleasure through him.

He shifted, delving between her thighs, sliding his

fingers through her slick folds, moving his fingers over her clit before drawing them back, pushing one finger inside her.

She gasped, grabbing his shoulders, pitching forward. He could feel her thigh muscles shaking as he pleasured her slowly, drawing his finger in and out of her body before adding a second. Her nails dug into his skin, clinging to him harder and harder as he continued tormenting her.

He looked up at her and allowed himself to get lost in this. In the feeling of her slick arousal beneath his hands, in the completely overwhelmed, helpless expression on her beautiful face. Her eyes were shut tight, and she was biting her lip, probably to keep herself from screaming. He decided he had a new goal.

He lowered his head, pressing his lips right to the center of her body, her lace panties holding the warmth of his breath as he slowly lapped at her through the thin fabric.

She swore, a short, harsh sound that verged on being a scream. But it wasn't enough. He teased her that way, his fingers deep inside her, his mouth on her, for as long as he could stand it.

Then he took his other hand, swept the panties aside and pushed his fingers in deep while he lapped at her bare skin, dragging his tongue through her folds, over that sensitized bundle of nerves.

And then she screamed.

Her internal muscles pulsed around him, her pleasure ramping his up two impossible degrees.

"I hope like *hell* you brought a condom," he said, his voice ragged, rough.

"I think I did," she said, her tone wavering. "Yes, I did. It's in my purse. Hurry."

"You want me to dig through your purse."

"I can't breathe. I can't move. If I do anything, I'm going to fall down. So I suggest you get the condom so that I don't permanently wound myself attempting to procure it."

"Your tongue seems fine," he said, moving away from her and going to grab the purse that she had discarded along with the rest of her clothes.

"So does yours," she muttered.

And he knew that what she was referring to had nothing to do with talking.

He found the condom easily enough, since it was obviously the last thing she had thrown into her bag. Then he stood, stripping his shirt off and his pants, adding to the pile of clothing that Maddy had already left on the studio floor.

Then he tore open the packet and took care of the protection. He looked around the room, searching for some surface that he could use. That they could use.

There was no way to lay her down, which he kind of regretted. Mostly because he always felt like she deserved a little bit more than the rough stuff that he doled out to her. Except she seemed to like it. So if it was what she wanted, she was about to get the full experience tonight.

He wrapped his arm around her waist, pulling her up against him, pressing their bodies together, her bare breasts pressing hard against his chest. He was so turned on, his arousal felt like a crowbar between them.

She didn't seem to mind.

He took hold of her chin, tilting her face up so she

had to look at him. And then he leaned in, kissing her lightly, gently. It would be the last gentle thing he did all night.

He slid his hands along her body, moving them to grip her hips. Then he turned her so that she was facing away from him. She gasped but followed the momentum as he propelled her forward, toward one of the iron figures—a horse—and placed his hand between her shoulder blades.

"Hold on to the horse, cowgirl," he said, his voice so rough it sounded like a stranger's.

"What?"

He pushed more firmly against her back, bending her forward slightly, and she lifted her hands, placing them over the back of the statue. "Just like that," he said.

Her back arched slightly, and he drew his fingertips down the line of her spine, all the way down to her butt. He squeezed her there, then slipped his hand to her hip.

"Spread your legs," he instructed.

She did, widening her stance, allowing him a good view and all access. He moved his hand back there, just for a second, testing her readiness. Then he positioned his arousal at the entrance to her body. He pushed into her, hard and deep, and she let out a low, slow sound of approval.

He braced himself, putting one hand on her shoulder, his thumb pressed firmly against the back of her neck, the other holding her hip as he began to move inside her.

He lost himself. In her, in the moment. In this soft, beautiful woman, all curves and round shapes in the middle of this hard, angular garden of iron.

The horse was hard in front of her; he was hard behind her. Only Maddy was soft.

Her voice was soft—the little gasps of pleasure that escaped her lips like balm for his soul. Her body was soft, her curves giving against him every time he thrust home.

When she began to rock back against him, her desperation clearly increasing along with his, he moved his hand from her hip to between her thighs. He stroked her in time with his thrusts, bringing her along with him, higher and higher until he thought they would both shatter. Until he thought they might shatter everything in this room. All of these unbreakable, unbending things.

She lowered her head, her body going stiff as her release broke over her, her body spasming around his, that evidence of her own loss of control stealing every ounce of his own.

He gave himself up to this. Up to her. And when his climax hit him, it was with the realization that it was somehow hers. That she owned this. Owned this moment. Owned his body.

That realization only made it more intense. Only made it more arousing.

His muscles shook as he poured himself into her. As he gave himself up to it totally, completely, in a way he had given himself up to nothing and no one for more than five years. Maybe ever.

In this moment, surrounded by all of these creations that had come out of him, he was exposed, undone. As though he had ripped his chest open completely and exposed his every secret to her, as though she could see everything, not just these creations, but the ugly, secret things that he kept contained inside his soul.

It was enough to make his knees buckle, and he had to reach out, pressing his palm against the rough surface of the iron horse to keep himself from falling to the ground and dragging Maddy with him.

The only sound in the room was their broken breathing, fractured and unsteady. He gathered her up against his body, one hand against her stomach, the other still on the back of the horse, keeping them upright.

He angled his head, buried his face in her neck, kissed her.

"Well," Maddy said, her voice unsteady, "that was amazing."

He couldn't respond. Because he couldn't say anything. His tongue wasn't working; his brain wasn't working. His voice had dried up like a desert. Instead, he released his grip on the horse, turned her to face him and claimed her mouth in a deep, hard kiss.

Ten

Maybe it wasn't the best thing to make assumptions, but when they got back to Sam's house, that was exactly what Maddy did. She simply assumed that she would be invited inside because he wanted her to stay.

If her assumption was wrong, he didn't correct her.

She soaked in the details of his home, the simple, completely spare surroundings, and how it seemed to clash with his newfound wealth.

Except, in many ways it didn't, she supposed. Sam just didn't seem the type to go out and spend large. He was too…well, Sam.

The cabin was neat, well kept and small. Rustic and void of any kind of frills. Honestly, it was more rustic than the cabins they had stayed in up in the mountain.

It was just another piece that she could add to the Sam puzzle. He was such a strange man. So difficult to find the center of. To find the key to. He was one giant sheet of code and she was missing some essential bit that might help her make heads or tails of him.

He was rough; he was distant. He was caring and kinder in many ways than almost anyone else she had ever known. Certainly, he had listened to her in a way that no one else ever had before. Offering nothing and simply taking everything onto his shoulders, letting her feel whatever she did without telling her it was wrong.

That was valuable in a way that she hadn't realized it would be.

She wished that she could do the same for him. That she could figure out what the thing was that made Sam… Sam. That made him distant and difficult and a lot like a brick wall. But she knew there was more behind his aloofness. A potential for feeling, for emotion, that surpassed what he showed the world.

She didn't even bother to ask herself why she cared. She suspected she already knew.

Sam busied himself making a fire in the simple, old-fashioned fireplace in the living room. It was nothing like the massive, modern adorned piece that was in the West family living room. One with fake logs and a switch that turned it on. One with a mantel that boasted the various awards won by Nathan West's superior horses.

There was something about this that she liked. The lack of pretension. Though, she wondered if it reflected Sam any more honestly than her own home—decorated by her mother's interior designer—did her. She could see it, in a way. The fact that he was no-nonsense and a little bit spare.

And yet in other ways she couldn't.

His art pieces looked like they were ready to take a breath and come to life any moment. The fact that such beautiful things came out of him made her think there had to be beautiful things in him. An appreciation for aesthetics. And yet none of that was in evidence here. Of course, it would be an appreciation for a hard aesthetic, since there was nothing soft about what he did.

Still, he wasn't quite this cold and empty either.

Neither of them spoke while he stoked the fire, and pretty soon the small space began to warm. Her whole body was still buzzing with the aftereffects of what had happened in his studio. But still, she wanted more.

She hadn't intended to seduce him in his studio; it had just happened. But she didn't regret it. She had brought a condom, just in case, so she supposed she couldn't claim total innocence. But still.

It had been a little bit reckless. The kind of thing a person could get caught doing. It was definitely not as discreet as she should have been. The thought made her smile. Made her feel like Sam was washing away some of the wounds of her past. That he was healing her in a way she hadn't imagined she could be.

She walked over to where he was, still kneeling down in front of the fireplace, and she placed her hands on his shoulders. She felt his muscles tighten beneath her touch. All of the tension that he carried in his shoulders. Why? Because he wanted her again and that bothered him? It wasn't because he didn't want her, she was convinced of that. There was no faking what was between them.

She let her fingertips drift down lower. Then she leaned in, pressing a kiss to his neck, as he was so fond of doing to her. As she was so fond of him doing.

"What are you doing?" he asked, his voice rumbling inside him.

"Honestly, if you have to ask, I'm not doing a very good job of it."

"Aren't you exhausted?"

"The way I see it, I have five days left with you. I could go five days without sleep if I needed to."

He reached up, grabbing hold of her wrist and turning, then pulling her down onto the floor, onto his lap. "Is that a challenge? Because I'm more than up to meeting that."

"If you want to take it as one, I suppose that's up to you."

She put her hands on his face, sliding her thumbs alongside the grooves next to his mouth. He wasn't that old. In his early to midthirties, she guessed. But he wore some serious cares on that handsome face of his, etched into his skin. She wondered what they were. It was easy to assume it was the death of his parents, and perhaps that was part of it. But there was more.

She'd had the impression earlier today that she'd only ever glimpsed a small part of him. That there were deep pieces of himself that he kept concealed from the world. And she had a feeling this was one of them. That he was a man who presented himself as simple, who lived in these simple surroundings, hard and spare, while he contained multitudes of feeling and complexity.

She also had a feeling he would rather die than admit that.

"All right," he said, "if you insist."

He leaned in, kissing her. It was slower and more luxurious than any of the kisses they had shared back in the studio. A little bit less frantic. A little bit less desperate. Less driven toward its ultimate conclusion, much more about the journey.

She found herself being disrobed again, for the second time that day, and she really couldn't complain. Especially not when Sam joined her in a state of undress.

She pressed her hand against his chest, tracing the strongly delineated muscles, her eyes following the movement.

"I'm going to miss this," she said, not quite sure what possessed her to speak the words out loud. Because they went so much deeper than just appreciation for his body. So much deeper than just missing his beautiful chest or his perfect abs.

She wished that they didn't, but they did. She wished she were a little more confused by the things she did and said with him, like she had been earlier today. But somehow, between her pouring her heart out to him at the ranch today and making love with him in the studio, a few things had become a lot clearer.

His lips twitched, like he was considering making light of the statement. Saying something to defuse the tension between them. Instead, he wrapped his fingers around her wrist, holding her tight, pressing her palms flat against him so that she could feel his heart beating. Then he kissed her. Long, powerful. A claiming, a complete and total invasion of her soul.

She didn't even care.

Or maybe, more accurately, she did care. She cared all the way down, and what she couldn't bother with anymore was all the pretending that she didn't. That she cared about nothing and no one, that she existed on the Isle of Maddy. Where she was wholly self-sufficient.

She was pretty sure, in this moment, that she might

need him. That she might need him in ways she hadn't needed another person in a very long time, if ever. When she had met David, she had been a teenager. She hadn't had any baggage; she hadn't run into any kind of resistance in the world. She was young, and she didn't know what giving her heart away might cost.

She knew now. She knew so much more. She had been hurt; she had been broken. And when she allowed herself to see that she needed someone, she could see too just how badly it could go.

When they parted, they were both breathing hard, and his dark eyes were watchful on hers. She felt like she could see further than she normally could. Past all of that strength that he wore with ease, down to the parts of him that were scarred, that had been wounded.

That were vulnerable.

Even Sam McCormack was vulnerable. What a revelation. Perhaps if he was, everyone was.

He lifted his hand, brushing up against her cheek, down to her chin, and then he pushed her hair back off her face, slowly letting his fingers sift through the strands. And he watched them slide through his fingers, just as she had watched her own hand as she'd touched his chest. She wondered what he was thinking. If he was thinking what she'd been. If he was attached to her in spite of himself.

Part of her hoped so. Part of her hoped not.

He leaned down, kissing her on the shoulder, the seemingly nonsexual contact affecting her intensely. Making her skin feel like it was on fire, making her heart feel like it might burst right out of her chest.

She found herself being propelled backward, but it

felt like slow motion, as he lowered her down onto the floor. Onto the carpet there in front of the fireplace.

She had the thought that this was definitely a perfect component for a winter affair. But then the thought made her sad. Because she wanted so much more than a winter affair with him. So much more than this desperate grab in front of the fire, knowing that they had only five days left with each other.

But then he was kissing her and she couldn't think anymore. She couldn't regret. She could only kiss him back.

His hands skimmed over her curves, her breasts, her waist, her hips, all the way down to her thighs, where he squeezed her tight, held on to her as though she were his lifeline. As though he were trying to memorize every curve, every dip and swell.

She closed her eyes, gave herself over to it, to the sensation of being known by Sam. The thought filled her, made her chest feel like it was expanding. He knew her. He really knew her. And he was still here. Still with her. He didn't judge her; he didn't find her disgusting.

He didn't treat her like she was breakable. He could still bend her over a horse statue in his studio, then be like this with her in front of the fire. Tender. Sweet.

Because she was a woman who wanted both things. And he seemed to know it.

He also seemed to be a man who might need both too.

Or maybe everybody did. But you didn't see it until you were with the person you wanted to be both of those things with.

"Hang on just a second," he said, suddenly, breaking into her sensual reverie. She had lost track of time.

Lost track of everything except the feel of his hands on her skin.

He moved away from her, the loss of his body leaving her cold. But he returned a moment later, settling himself in between her thighs. "Condom," he said by way of explanation.

At least one of them had been thinking. She certainly hadn't been.

He joined their bodies together, entering her slowly, the sensation of fullness, of being joined to him, suddenly so profound that she wanted to weep with it. It always felt good. From the first time with him it had felt good. But this was different.

It was like whatever veil had been between them, whatever stack of issues had existed, had been driving them, was suddenly dropped. And there was nothing between them. When he looked at her, poised over her, deep inside her, she felt like he could see all the way down.

When he moved, she moved with him, meeting him thrust for thrust, pushing them both to the brink. And when she came, he came along with her, his rough gasp of pleasure in her ears ramping up her own release.

In the aftermath, skin to skin, she couldn't deny anymore what all these feelings were. She couldn't pretend that she didn't know.

She'd signed herself up for a twelve-day fling with a man she didn't even like, and only one week in she had gone and fallen in love with Sam McCormack.

"Sam." Maddy's voice broke into his sensual haze. He was lying on his back in front of the fireplace, feeling drained and like he had just had some kind of out-of-body experience. Except he had been firmly in his body and feeling everything, everything and then some.

"What?" he asked, his voice rusty.

"Why do you make farm animals?"

"What the hell kind of question is that?" he asked.

"A valid one," she said, moving nearer to him, putting her hand on his chest, tracing shapes there. "I mean, not that they aren't good."

"The horse seemed good enough for you a couple hours ago."

"It's good," she said, her tone irritated, because she obviously thought he was misunderstanding her on purpose.

Which she wasn't wrong about.

"Okay, but you don't think I should be making farm animals."

"No, I think it's fine that you make farm animals. I just think it's not actually you."

He shifted underneath her, trying to decide whether or not he should say anything. Or if he should sidestep the question. If it were anyone else, he would laugh. Play it off. Pretend like there was no answer. That there was nothing deeper in him than simply re-creating what he literally saw out in the fields in front of him.

And a lot of people would have bought that. His own brother probably would have, or at the very least, he wouldn't have pushed. But this was Maddy. Maddy, who had come apart in his arms in more than one way over the past week. Maddy, who perhaps saw deeper inside him than anyone else ever had.

Why not tell her? Why not? Because he could sense her getting closer to him. Could sense it like an invisible cord winding itself around the two of them, no matter that he was going to have to cut it in the end. Maybe it would be best to do it now.

"If I don't make what I see, I'll have to make what I feel," he said. "Nobody wants that."

"Why not?"

"Because the art has to sell," he said, his voice flat. Although, that was somewhat disingenuous. It wasn't that he didn't think he could sell darker pieces. In fact, he was sure that he could. "I don't do it for myself. I do it for Chase. I was perfectly content to keep it some kind of weird hobby that I messed around with after hours. Chase was the one who thought that I needed to pursue it full-time. Chase was the one who thought it was the way to save our business. And it started out doing kind of custom artistry for big houses. Gates and the detail work on stairs and decks and things. But then I started making bigger pieces and we started selling them. I say *we* because without Chase they would just sit in the shop."

"So you're just making what sells. That's the beginning and end of the story." Her blue eyes were too sharp, too insightful and far too close to the firelight for him to try to play at any games.

"I make what I want to let people see."

"What happened, Sam? And don't tell me nothing. You're talking to somebody who clung to one event in the past for as long as humanly possible. Who let it dictate her entire life. You're talking to the queen of residual issues here. Don't try to pretend that you don't have any. I know what it looks like." She took a deep breath. "I know what it looks like when somebody uses anger, spite and a whole bunch of unfriendliness to keep the world at a safe distance. I know, because I've spent the past ten years doing it. Nobody gets too close to the girl who says unpredictable things. The one who might come out and tell you that your dress does make you look fat and then turn around and say something crude about male anatomy. It's how you give yourself power in social situations. Act like you don't care about the rules that everyone else is a slave to." She laughed. "And why not? I already broke the rules. That's me. It's been me for a long time. And it isn't because I didn't know better. It's because I absolutely knew better. You're smart, Sam. The way that you walk around, the way you present yourself, even here, it's calculated."

Sam didn't think anyone had ever accused him of being calculated before. But it was true. Truer than most things that had been leveled at him. That he was grumpy, that he was antisocial. He was those things. But for a very specific reason.

And of course Madison would know. Of course she would see.

"I've never been comfortable sharing my life," Sam said. "I suppose that comes from having a father who was less than thrilled to have a son who was interested in art. In fact, I think my father considered it a moral failing of his. To have a son who wanted to use materials to create frivolous things. Things that had no use. To have a son who was more interested in that than honest labor. I learned to keep things to myself a long time ago. Which all sounds a whole lot like a sad, cliché story. Except it's not. It worked. I would have made a relationship with my dad work. But he died. So then it didn't matter anymore. But still, I just never... I never wanted to keep people up on what was happening with my life. I was kind of trained that way."

Hell, a lot of guys were that way, anyway. A lot of men didn't want to talk about what was happening in their day-to-day existence. Though most of them wouldn't have gone to the lengths that Sam did to keep everything separate.

"Most especially when Chase and I were neck-deep in trying to keep the business afloat, I didn't like him seeing that I was working on anything else. Anything at all." Sam took a deep breath. "That included any kind of relationships I might have. I didn't have a lot. But you know Chase never had a problem with people in town knowing that he was spreading it around. He never had a problem sleeping with the women here."

"No, he did not," Maddy said. "Never with me, to be clear."

"Considering I'm your first in a decade, I wasn't exactly that worried about it."

"Just making sure."

"I didn't like that. I didn't want my life to be part of this real-time small-town TV program. I preferred to find women out of town. When I was making deliveries, going to bigger ranches down the coast, that was when I would…"

"When you would find yourself a buckle bunny for the evening?"

"Yes," he said. "Except I met a woman I liked a lot. She was the daughter of one of the big ranchers down near Coos County. And I tried to keep things business oriented. We were actually doing business with her family. But I… I saw her out at a bar one night, and even though I knew she was too young, too nice of a girl for a guy like me… I slept with her. And a few times after. I was pretty obsessed with her, actually."

He was downplaying it. But what was the point of doing anything else? Of admitting that for just a little while he'd thought he'd found something. Someone who wanted him. All of him. Someone who knew him.

The possibility of a future. Like the first hint of spring in the air after a long winter.

Maddy moved closer to him, looking up at him, and he decided to take a moment to enjoy that for a second. Because after this, she would probably never want to touch him again.

"Without warning, she cut me off. Completely. Didn't want to see me anymore. And since she was a few hours down the highway, that really meant not seeing her. I'd had to make an effort to work her into my life. Cutting her out of it was actually a lot easier."

"Sure," Maddy said, obviously not convinced.

"I got a phone call one night. Late. From the hospital. They told me to come down because Elizabeth was asking for me. They said it wasn't good."

"Oh, Sam," Maddy said, her tone tinged with sympathy.

He brush right past that. Continued on. "I white-knuckled it down there. Went as fast as I could. I didn't tell anyone I was going. When I got there, they wouldn't let me in. Because I wasn't family."

"But she wanted them to call you."

"It didn't matter." It was difficult for him to talk about that day. In fact, he never had. He could see it all playing out in his mind as he spoke the words. Could see the image of her father walking out of the double doors, looking harried, older than Sam had ever seen him look during any of their business dealings.

"I never got to see her," Sam said. "She died a few minutes after I got there."

"Sam, I'm so sorry…"

"No, don't misunderstand me. This isn't a story about me being angry because I lost a woman that I loved. I *didn't* love her. That's the worst part." He swallowed hard, trying to diffuse the pressure in his throat crushing down, making it hard to breathe. "I mean, maybe I could have. But that's not the same. You know who loved her? Her family. Her family loved her. I have never seen a man look so destroyed as I did that day. Looking at her father, who clearly wondered why in hell I was sitting down there in the emergency room. Why I had been called to come down. He didn't have to wonder long. Not when they told him exactly how his daughter died." Sam took a deep breath. "Elizabeth died of internal bleeding. Complications from an ectopic pregnancy."

Maddy's face paled, her lips looking waxen. "Did you…? You didn't know she was pregnant."

"No. Neither did anyone in her family. But I know it was mine. I know it was mine, and she didn't want me to know. And that was probably why she didn't tell me, why she broke things off with me. Nobody knew because she was ashamed. Because it was my baby. Because it was a man that she knew she couldn't have a future with. Nobody knew, so when she felt tired and lay down for a nap because she was bleeding and feeling discomfort, no one was there."

Silence settled around them, the house creaking beneath the weight of it.

"Did you ever find out why…why she called you then?"

"I don't know. Maybe she wanted me there to blame

me. Maybe she just needed me. I'll never know. She was gone before I ever got to see her."

"That must have been…" Maddy let that sentence trail off. "That's horrible."

"It's nothing but horrible. It's everything horrible. I know why she got pregnant, Maddy. It's because… I was so careless with her. I had sex with her once without a condom. And I thought that it would be fine. Hell, I figured if something did happen, I'd be willing to marry her. All of that happened because I didn't think. Because I lost control. I don't deserve…"

"You can't blame yourself for a death that was some kind of freak medical event."

"Tell me you wouldn't blame yourself, Maddy. Tell me you wouldn't." He sat up, and Maddy sat up too. Then he gripped her shoulders, holding her steady, forcing her to meet his gaze. "You, who blame yourself for the affair with your dressage teacher even though you were an underage girl. You could tell me you don't. You could tell me that you were just hurt by the way everybody treated you, but I know it's more than that. You blame yourself. So don't you dare look at me with those wide blue eyes and tell me that I have no business blaming myself."

She blinked. "I… I don't blame myself. I don't. I mean, I'm not proud of what I did, but I'm not going to take all of the blame. Not for something I couldn't control. He lied to me. I was dumb, yes. I was naive. But dammit, Sam, my father should have had my back. My friends should have had my back. And my teacher should never have taken advantage of me."

He moved away from her then, pushing himself into a standing position and forking his fingers through his hair. She wasn't blaming him. It was supposed to push her away. She certainly wasn't supposed to look at him with sympathy. She was supposed to be appalled. Appalled that he had taken the chances he had with Elizabeth's body. Appalled at his lack of control.

It was the object lesson. The one that proved that he wasn't good enough for a woman like her. That he wasn't good enough for anyone.

"You don't blame yourself at all?"

"I don't know," she said. "It's kind of a loaded question. I could have made another decision. And because of that, I guess I share blame. But I'm not going to sit around feeling endless guilt. I'm hurt. I'm wounded. But that's not the same thing. Like I told you, the sex was the least of it. If it was all guilt, I would have found somebody a long time ago. I would have dealt with it. But it's more than that. I think it's more than that with you. Because you're not an idiot. You know full well that it isn't like you're the first man to have unprotected sex with a woman. You know full well you weren't in control of where an embryo implanted inside a woman. You couldn't have taken her to the hospital, because you didn't know she was pregnant. You didn't know she needed you. She sent you away. She made some choices here, and I don't really think it's her fault either, because how could she have known? But still. It isn't your fault."

He drew back, anger roaring through him. "I'm the one…"

"You're very dedicated to this. But that doesn't make it true."

"Her father thought it was my fault," he said. "That

matters. I had to look at a man who was going to have to bury his daughter because of me."

"Maybe he felt that way," Maddy said. "I can understand that. People want to blame. I know. Because I've been put in that position. Where I was the one that people wanted to blame. Because I wasn't as well liked. Because I wasn't as important. I know that David's wife certainly wanted to blame me, because she wanted to make her marriage work, and if she blamed David, how would she do that? And without blame, your anger is aimless."

Those words hit hard, settled somewhere down deep inside him. And he knew that no matter what, no matter that he didn't want to think about them, no matter that he didn't want to believe them, they were going to stay with him. Truth had a funny way of doing that.

"I'm not looking for absolution, Maddy." He shook his head. "I was never looking for it."

"What are you looking for, then?"

He shrugged. "Nothing. I'm not looking for anything. I'm not looking for you to forgive me. I'm not looking to forgive myself."

"No," she said, "you're just looking to keep punishing yourself. To hold everything inside and keep it buried down deep. I don't think it's the rest of the world you're hiding yourself from. I think you're hiding from yourself."

"You think that you are qualified to talk about my issues? You. The woman who didn't have a lover for ten years because she's so mired in the past?"

"Do you think that's going to hurt my feelings? I know I'm messed up. I'm well aware. In fact, I would argue that it takes somebody as profoundly screwed up as I am to look at another person and see it. Maybe other people would look at you and see a man who is strong. A man who has it all laid out. A man who has iron control. But I see you for what you are. You're completely and totally bound up inside. And you're ready to crack apart. You can't go on like this."

"Watch me," he said.

"How long has it been?" she asked, her tone soft.

"Five years," he ground out.

"Well, it's only half the time I've been punishing myself, but it's pretty good. Where do you see it ending, Sam?"

"Well, you were part of it for me too."

He gritted his teeth, regretting introducing that revelation into the conversation.

"What do you mean?"

"I haven't been with a woman in five years. So I guess you could say you are part of me dealing with some of my issues."

Maddy looked like she'd been slapped. She did not, in any way, look complimented. "What does that mean? What does that mean?" She repeated the phrase twice, sounding more horrified, more frantic each time.

"It had to end at some point. The celibacy, I mean. And when you offered yourself, I wasn't in a position to say no."

"After all of your righteous indignation—the accusation that I was using you for sexual healing—it turns out you were using me for the same thing?" she asked.

"Why does that upset you so much?"

"Because…because you're still so completely wrapped up in it. Because you obviously don't have any intention to really be healed."

Unease settled in his chest. "What's me being healed to you, Maddy? What does that mean? I changed something, didn't I? Same as you."

"But…" Her tone became frantic. "I just… You aren't planning on letting it change you."

"What change are you talking about?" he pressed.

"I don't know," she said, her throat sounding constricted.

"Like hell, Madison. Don't give me that. If you've changed the rules in your head, that's hardly my fault."

She whirled around, lowering her head, burying her face in her hands. "You're so infuriating." She turned back to him, her cheeks crimson. "I don't know what either of us was thinking. That we were going to go into this and come out the other side without changing anything? We are idiots. We are idiots who didn't let another human being touch us for years. And somehow we thought we could come together and nothing would change? I mean, it was one thing when it was just me. I assumed that you went around having sex with women you didn't like all the time."

"Why would you think that?"

"Because you don't like anyone. So, that stands to reason. That you would sleep with women you don't like. I certainly didn't figure you didn't sleep with women at all. That's ridiculous. You're… *Look* at you. Of course you have sex. Who would assume that you didn't? Not me. That's who."

He gritted his teeth, wanting desperately to redirect the conversation. Because it was going into territory that would end badly for both of them. He wanted to leave the core of the energy arcing between them unspoken. He wanted to make sure that neither of them acknowledged it. He wanted to pretend he had no idea what she was thinking. No idea what she was about to say.

The problem was, he knew her. Better than he knew anyone else, maybe. And it had all happened in a week. A week of talking, of being skin to skin. Of being real.

No wonder he had spent so many years avoiding exactly this. No wonder he had spent so long hiding everything that he was, everything that he wanted. Because the alternative was letting it hang out there, exposed and acting as some kind of all-access pass to anyone who bothered to take a look.

"Well, you assumed wrong. But it doesn't have to change anything. We have five more days, Maddy. Why does it have to be like this?"

"Honest?"

"Why do we have to fight with each other? We shouldn't. We don't have to. We don't have to continue this discussion. We are not going to come to any kind of understanding, whatever you might think. Whatever you think you're pushing for here...just don't."

"Are you going to walk away from this and just not change? Are you going to find another woman? Is that all this was? A chance for you to get your sexual mojo back? To prove that you could use a condom every time? Did you want me to sew you a little sexual merit badge for your new Boy Scout vest?" She let out a frustrated growl. "I don't want you to be a Boy Scout, Sam. I want you to be you."

Sam growled, advancing on her. She backed away from him until her shoulder blades hit the wall. Then he pressed his palms to the flat surface on either side of her face. "You don't want me to be me. Trust me. I don't know how to give the kinds of things you want."

"You don't want to," she said, the words soft, penetrating deeper than a shout ever could have.

"No, you don't want me to."

"Why is that so desperately important for you to make yourself believe?"

"Because it's true."

She let silence hang between them for a moment. "Why won't you let yourself feel this?"

"What?"

"*This* is why you do farm animals. That's what you said. And you said it was because nobody would want to see this. But that isn't true. Everybody feels grief, Sam. Everybody has lost. Plenty of people would want to see what you would make from this. Why is it that you can't do it?"

"You want me to go ahead and make a profit off my sins? Out of the way I hurt other people? You want me to make some kind of artistic homage to a father who never wanted me to do art in the first place? You want me to do a tribute to a woman whose death I contributed to."

"Yes. Because it's not about how anyone else feels. It's about how you feel."

He didn't know why this reached in and cut him so deeply. He didn't know why it bothered him so much. Mostly he didn't know why he was having this conversation with her at all. It didn't change anything. It didn't change him.

"No," she said, "that isn't what I think you should do. It's not about profiting off sins—real or perceived.

It's about you dealing with all of these things. It's about you acknowledging that you have feelings."

He snorted. "I'm entitled to more grief than Elizabeth's parents? To any?"

"You lost somebody that you cared about. That matters. Of course it matters. You lost... I don't know. She was pregnant. It was your baby. Of course that matters. Of course you think about it."

"No," he said, the words as flat as everything inside him. "I don't. I don't think about that. Ever. I don't talk about it. I don't do anything with it."

"Except make sure you never make a piece of art that means anything to you. Except not sleep with anyone. Except punish yourself. Which you had such a clear vision of when you felt like I was doing it to myself but you seem to be completely blind to when it comes to you."

"All right. Let's examine your mistake, then, Maddy. Since you're so determined to draw a comparison between the two of us. Who's dead? Come on. Who died as a result of your youthful mistakes? No one. Until you make a mistake like that, something that's that irreversible, don't pretend you have any idea what I've been through. Don't pretend you have any idea of what I should feel."

He despised himself for even saying that. For saying he had been through something. He didn't deserve to walk around claiming that baggage. It was why he didn't like talking about it. It was why he didn't like thinking about it. Because Elizabeth's family members were the ones who had been left with a giant hole in their lives. Not him. Because they were the ones who had to deal with her loss around the dinner table, with thinking about her on her birthday and all of the holidays they didn't have her.

He didn't even know when her birthday was.

"Well, I care about you," Maddy said, her voice small. "Doesn't that count for anything?"

"No," he said, his voice rough. "Five more days, Maddy. That's it. That's all it can ever be."

He should end it now. He knew that. Beyond anything else, he knew that he should end it now. But if Maddy West had taught him anything, it was that he wasn't nearly as controlled as he wanted to be. At least, not where she was concerned. He could stand around and shout about it, self-flagellate all he wanted, but when push came to shove, he was going to make the selfish decision.

"Either you come to bed with me and we spend the rest of the night not talking, or you go home and we can forget the rest of this."

Maddy nodded mutely. He expected her to turn and walk out the door. Maybe not even pausing to collect her clothes, in spite of the cold weather. Instead, she surprised him. Instead, she took his hand, even knowing the kind of devastation it had caused, and she turned and led him up the stairs.

Eleven

Maddy hadn't slept at all. It wasn't typical for her and Sam to share a bed the entire night. But they had last night. After all that shouting and screaming and love-making, it hadn't seemed right to leave. And he hadn't asked her to.

She knew more about him now than she had before. In fact, she had a suspicion that she knew everything about him. Even if it wasn't all put together into a complete picture. It was there. And now, with the pale morning light filtering through the window, she was staring at him as though she could make it all form a cohesive image.

As if she could will herself to somehow understand what all of those little pieces meant. As if she could make herself see the big picture.

Sam couldn't even see it, of that she was certain. So

she had no idea how she could expect herself to see it. Except that she wanted to. Except that she needed to. She didn't want to leave him alone with all of that. It was too much. It was too much for any one man. He felt responsible for the death of that woman. Or at least, he was letting himself think he did.

Protecting himself. Protecting himself with pain.

It made a strange kind of sense to her, only because she was a professional at protecting herself. At insulating herself from whatever else might come her way. Yes, it was a solitary existence. Yes, it was lonely. But there was control within that. She had a feeling that Sam operated in much the same way.

She shifted, brushing his hair out of his face. He had meant to frighten her off. He had given her an out. And she knew that somehow he had imagined she would take it. She knew that he believed he was some kind of monster. At least, part of him believed it.

Because she could also tell that he had been genuinely surprised that she hadn't turned tail and run.

But she hadn't. And she wouldn't. Mostly because she was just too stubborn. She had spent the past ten years being stubborn. Burying who she was underneath a whole bunch of bad attitude and sharp words. Not letting anyone get close, even though she had a bunch of people around her who cared. She had chosen to focus on the people who didn't. The people who didn't care enough. While simultaneously deciding that the people who did care enough, who cared more than enough, somehow weren't as important.

Well, she was done with that. There were people in her life who loved her. Who loved her no matter what. And she had a feeling that Sam had the ability to be one of those people. She didn't want to abandon him to this. Not when he had—whether he would admit it or not—been instrumental in digging her out of her self-imposed emotional prison.

"Good morning," she whispered, pressing her lips to his cheek.

As soon as she did that, a strange sense of foreboding stole over her. As though she knew that the next few moments were going to go badly. But maybe that was just her natural pessimism. The little beast she had built up to be the strongest and best-developed piece of her. Another defense.

Sam's eyes opened, and the shock that she glimpsed there absolutely did not bode well for the next few moments. She knew that. "I stayed the night," she said, in response to the unasked question she could see lurking on his face.

"I guess I fell asleep," he said, his voice husky.

"Clearly." She took a deep breath. Oh well. If it was all going to hell, it might as well go in style. "I want you to come to the family Christmas party with me."

It took only a few moments for her to decide that she was going to say those words. And that she was going to follow them up with everything that was brimming inside her. Feelings that she didn't feel like keeping hidden. Not anymore. Maybe it was selfish. But she didn't really care. She knew his stuff. He knew hers. The only excuse she had for not telling him how she felt was self-protection.

She knew where self-protection got her. Absolutely nowhere. Treading water in a stagnant pool of her own failings, never advancing any further on in her life. In her existence. It left her lonely. It left her without any real, true friends. She didn't want that. Not anymore. And if she had to allow herself to be wounded in the name of authenticity, in the name of trying again, then she would.

An easy decision to make before the injury occurred. But it was made nonetheless.

"Why?" Sam asked, rolling away from her, getting up out of bed.

She took that opportunity to drink in every detail of his perfect body. His powerful chest, his muscular thighs. Memorizing every little piece of him. More Sam for her collection. She had a feeling that eventually she would walk away from him with nothing but that collection. A little pail full of the shadows of what she used to have.

"Because I would like to have a date." She was stalling now.

"You want to make your dad mad? Is that what we're doing? A little bit of revenge for everything he put you through?"

"I would never use you that way, Sam. I hope you know me better than that."

"We don't know each other, Maddy. We don't. We've had a few conversations, and we've had some sex. But that doesn't mean knowing somebody. Not really."

"That just isn't true. Nobody else knows how I feel about what happened to me. Nobody. Nobody else knows about the conversation I had with my dad. And I would imagine that nobody knows about Elizabeth. Not the way that I do."

"We used each other as a confessional. That isn't the same."

"The funny thing is it did start that way. At least

for me. Because what did it matter what you knew. We weren't going to have a relationship after. So I didn't have to worry about you judging me. I didn't have to worry about anything."

"And?"

"That was just what I told myself. It was what made it feel okay to do what I wanted to do. We lie to ourselves. We get really deep in it when we feel like we need protection. That was what I was doing. But the simple truth is I felt a connection with you from the beginning. It was why I was so terrible to you. Because it scared me."

"You should have kept on letting it scare you, baby girl."

Those words acted like a shot of rage that went straight to her stomach, then fired onto her head. "Why? Because it's the thing that allows you to maintain your cranky-loner mystique? That isn't you. I thought maybe you didn't feel anything. But now I think you feel everything. And it scares you. I'm the same way."

"I see where this is going, Maddy. Don't do it. Don't. I can tell you right now it isn't going to go the way you think it will."

"Oh, go ahead, Sam. Tell me what I think. Please. I'm dying to hear it."

"You think that because you've had some kind of transformation, some kind of deep realization, that I'm headed for the same. But it's bullshit. I'm sorry to be the one to tell you. Wishful thinking on a level I never wanted you to start thinking on. You knew the rules. You knew them from the beginning."

"Don't," she said, her throat tightening, her chest constricting. "Don't do this to us. Don't pretend it can stay the same thing it started out as. Because it isn't. And you know it."

"You're composing a really compelling story, Madison." The reversion back to her full name felt significant. "And we both know that's something you do. Make more out of sex than it was supposed to be."

She gritted her teeth, battling through. Because he wanted her to stop. He wanted this to intimidate, to hurt. He wanted it to stop her. But she wasn't going to let him win. Not at this. Not at his own self-destruction. "Jackass 101. Using somebody's deep pain against them. I thought you were above that, Sam."

"It turns out I'm not. You might want to pay attention to that."

"I'm paying attention. I want you to come with me to the Christmas party, Sam. Because I want it to be the beginning. I don't want it to be the end."

"Don't do this."

He bent down, beginning to collect his clothes, his focus on anything in the room but her. She took a deep breath, knowing that what happened next was going to shatter all of this.

"I need more. I need more than twelve days of Christmas. I want it every day. I want to wake up with you every morning and go to bed with you every night. I want to fight with you. I want to make love with you. I want to tell you my secrets. To show you every dark, hidden thing in me. The serious things and the silly things. Because I love you. It's that complicated and that simple. I love you and that means I'm willing to do this, no matter how it ends."

Sam tugged his pants on, did them up, then pulled his shirt over his head. "I told you not to do this, Maddy.

But you're doing it anyway. And you know what that makes it? A suicide mission. You stand there, thinking you're being brave because you're telling the truth. But you know how it's going to end. You know that after you make this confession, you're not actually going to have to deal with the relationship with me, because I already told you it isn't happening. I wonder if you would have been so brave if you knew I might turn around and offer you forever."

His words hit her with the force of bullets. But for some reason, they didn't hurt. Not really. She could remember distinctly when David had broken things off with her. Saying that she had never been anything serious. That she had been only a little bit of tail on the side and he was of course going to have to stay with his wife. Because she was the center of his life. Of his career. Because she mattered, and Maddy didn't. That had hurt. It had hurt because it had been true.

Because David hadn't loved her. And it had been easy for him to break up with her because he had never intended on having more with her, and not a single part of him wanted more.

This was different. It was different because Sam was trying to hurt her out of desperation. Because Sam was lying. Or at the very least, was sidestepping. Because he didn't want to have the conversation.

Because he would have to lie to protect himself. Because he couldn't look her in the eye and tell her that he didn't love her, that she didn't matter.

But she wasn't certain he would let himself feel it. That was the gamble. She knew he felt it. She knew it. That deep down, Sam cared. She wasn't sure if he knew it. If he had allowed himself access to those feelings.

Feelings that Sam seemed to think were a luxury, or a danger. Grief. Desire. Love.

"Go ahead and offer it. You won't. You won't, because you know I would actually say yes. You can try to make this about how damaged I am, but all of this is because of you."

"You have to be damaged to want somebody like me. You know what's in my past."

"Grief. Grief that you won't let yourself feel. Sadness you don't feel like you're allowed to have. That's what's in your past. Along with lost hope. Let's not pretend you blame yourself. You felt so comfortable calling me out, telling me that I was playing games. Well, guess what. That's what you're doing. You think if you don't want anything, if you don't need anything, you won't be hurt again. But you're just living in hurt and that isn't better."

"You have all this clarity about your own emotional situation, and you think that gives you a right to talk about mine?"

She threw the blankets off her and got out of bed. "Why not?" she asked, throwing her arms wide. She didn't care that she was naked. In fact, in many ways it seemed appropriate. That Sam had put clothes on, that he had felt the need to cover himself, and that she didn't even care anymore. She had no pride left. But this wasn't about pride.

"You think you have the right to talk about mine," she continued. "You think you're going to twist everything that I'm saying and eventually you'll find some little doubt inside me that will make me believe you're telling the truth. I've had enough of that. I've had enough of men telling me what I feel. Of them telling me what I should do. I'm not going to let you do it. You're better than that. At least, I thought you were."

"Maybe I'm not."

"Right now? I think you don't want to be. But I would love you through this too, Sam. You need to know that. You need to know that whatever you say right now, in this room, it's not going to change the way that I feel about you. You don't have that kind of power."

"That's pathetic. There's nothing I can say to make you not love me? Why don't you love yourself a little bit more than that, Madison," he said, his tone hard.

And regardless of what she had just said, that did hit something in her. Something vulnerable and scared. Something that was afraid she really hadn't learned how to be anything more than a pathetic creature, desperate for a man to show her affection.

"I love myself just enough to put myself out there and demand this," she said finally, her voice vibrating with conviction. "I love myself too much to slink off silently. I love myself too much not to fight for what I know we could have. If I didn't do this, if I didn't say this, it would only be for my pride. It would be so I could score points and feel like maybe I won. But in the end, if I walk away without having fought for you with everything I have in me, we will have both lost. I think you're worth that. I know you are. Why don't you think so?"

"Why do you?" he asked, his voice thin, brittle. "I don't think I've shown you any particular kindness or tenderness."

"Don't. Don't erase everything that's happened between us. Everything I told you. Everything you gave me."

"Keeping my mouth shut while I held a beautiful woman and let her talk? That's easy."

"I love you, Sam. That's all. I'm not going to stand here and have an argument. I'm not going to let you get in endless barbs while you try to make those words something less than true. I love you. I would really like it if you could tell me you loved me too."

"I don't." His words were flat in the room. And she knew they were all she would get from him. Right now, it was all he could say. And he believed it. He believed it down to his bones. That he didn't love her. That everything that had taken place between them over the past week meant nothing. Because he had to. Because behind that certainty, that flat, horrifying expression in his eyes, was fear.

Strong, beautiful Sam, who could bend iron to his will, couldn't overpower the fear that lived inside him. And she would never be able to do it for him.

"Okay," she said softly, beginning to gather her clothes. She didn't know how to do this. She didn't know what to do now. How to make a triumphant exit. So she decided she wouldn't. She decided to let the tears fall down her cheeks; she decided not to make a joke. She decided not to say anything flippant or amusing.

Because that was what the old Maddy would have done. She would have played it off. She would have tried to laugh. She wouldn't have let herself feel this, not all the way down. She wouldn't have let her heart feel bruised or tender. Wouldn't have let a wave of pain roll over her. Wouldn't have let herself feel it, not really.

And when she walked out of his house, sniffling, her shoulders shaking, and could no longer hold back the sob that was building in her chest by the time she reached her car, she didn't care. She didn't feel ashamed.

There was no shame in loving someone.

She opened the driver-side door and sat down. And then the dam burst. She had loved so many people who had never loved her in return. Not the way she loved them. She had made herself hard because of it. She had put the shame on her own shoulders.

That somehow a seventeen-year-old girl should have known that her teacher was lying to her. That somehow a daughter whose father had walked her down Main Street and bought her sweets in a little shop should have known that her father's affection had its limits.

That a woman who had met a man who had finally reached deep inside her and moved all those defenses she had erected around her heart should have known that in the end he would break it.

No. It wasn't her. It wasn't the love that was bad. It was the pride. The shame. The fear. Those were the things that needed to be gotten rid of.

She took a deep, shaking breath. She blinked hard, forcing the rest of her tears to fall, and then she started the car.

She would be okay. Because she had found herself again. Had learned how to love again. Had found a deep certainty and confidence in herself that had been missing for so long.

But as she drove away, she still felt torn in two. Because while she had been made whole, she knew that she was leaving Sam behind, still as broken as she had found him.

Twelve

Sam thought he might be dying. But then, that could easily be alcohol poisoning. He had been drinking and going from his house into his studio for the past two days. And that was it. He hadn't talked to anyone. He had nothing to say. He had sent Maddy away, and while he was firmly convinced it was the only thing he could have done, it hurt like a son of a bitch.

It shouldn't. It had been necessary. He couldn't love her the way that she wanted him to. He couldn't. There was no way in hell. Not a man like him.

Her words started to crowd in on him unbidden, the exact opposite thing that he wanted to remember right now. About how there was no point blaming himself. About how that wasn't the real issue. He growled, grabbing hold of the hammer he'd been using and flinging it across the room. It landed in a pile of scrap metal, the sound satisfying, the lack of damage unsatisfying.

He had a fire burning hot, and the room was stifling. He stripped his shirt off, feeling like he couldn't catch his breath. He felt like he was losing his mind. But then, he wasn't a stranger to it. He had felt this way after his parents had died. Again after Elizabeth. There was so much inside him, and there was nowhere for it to go.

And just like those other times, he didn't deserve this pain. Not at all. He was the one who had hurt her. He was the one who couldn't stand up to that declaration of love. He didn't deserve this pain.

But no matter how deep he tried to push it down, no matter how he tried to pound it out with a hammer, it still remained. And his brain was blank. He couldn't even figure out how the hell he might fashion some of this material into another cow.

It was like the thing inside him that told him how to create things had left along with Maddy.

He looked over at the bottle of Jack Daniel's that was sitting on his workbench. And cursed when he saw that it was empty. He was going to have to get more. But he wasn't sure he had more in the house. Which meant leaving the house. Maybe going to Chase's place and seeing if there was anything to take. Between that and sobriety it was a difficult choice.

He looked around, looked at the horse that he had bent Maddy over just three days ago. Everything seemed dead now. Cold. Dark. Usually he felt the life in the things that he made. Something he would never tell anyone, because it sounded stupid. Because it exposed him.

But it was like Maddy had come in here and changed things. Taken everything with her when she left.

He walked over to the horse, braced his hands on the

back of it and leaned forward, giving into the wave of pain that crashed over him suddenly, uncontrollably.

"I thought I might find you in here."

Sam lifted his head at the sound of his brother's voice. "I'm busy."

"Right. Which is why there is nothing new in here, but it smells flammable."

"I had a drink."

"Or twelve," Chase said, sounding surprisingly sympathetic. "If you get too close to that forge, you're going to burst into flame."

"That might not be so bad."

"What's going on? You're always a grumpy bastard, but this is different. You don't usually disappear for days at a time. Actually, I can pick up a couple of times that you've done that in the past. You usually reemerge worse and even more impossible than you were before. So if that is what's happening here, I would appreciate a heads-up."

"It's nothing. Artistic temper tantrum."

"I don't believe that." Chase crossed his arms and leaned against the back wall of the studio, making it very clear that he intended to stay until Sam told him something.

Fine. The bastard could hang out all day for all he cared. It didn't mean he had to talk.

"Believe whatever you want," Sam said. "But it's not going to make hanging out here any more interesting. I can't figure out what to make next. Are you happy? I have no idea. I have no inspiration." Suddenly, everything in him boiled over. "And I hate that. I hate that it matters. I should just be able to think of something to do. Or not care if I don't want to do it. But somehow,

I can't make it work if I don't care at least a little bit. I hate caring, Chase. I *hate* it."

He hated it for every damn thing. Every damn, fragile thing.

"I know," Chase said. "And I blame Dad for that. He didn't understand. That isn't your fault. And it's not your flaw that you care. Think about the way he was about ranching. It was ridiculous. Weather that didn't go his way would send him into some kind of emotional tailspin for weeks. And he felt the same way about iron that you do. It's just that he felt compelled to shape it into things that had a function. But he took pride in his work. And he was an artist with it—you know he was. If anything, I think he was shocked by what you could do. Maybe even a little bit jealous. And he didn't know what to do with it."

Sam resisted those words. And the truth in them. "It doesn't matter."

"It does. Because it's why you can't talk about what you do. It's why you don't take pride in it the way that you should. It's why you're sitting here downplaying the fact you're having some kind of art block when it's been pretty clear for a few months that you have been."

"It shouldn't be a thing."

Chase shrugged. "Maybe not. But the very thing that makes your work valuable is also what makes it difficult. You're not a machine."

Sam wished he was. More than anything, he wished that he was. So that he wouldn't care about a damn thing. So that he wouldn't care about Maddy.

Softness, curves, floated to the forefront of his mind. Darkness and grief. All the inspiration he could ever want. Except that he couldn't take it. It wasn't his. He didn't own it. None of it.

He was still trying to pull things out of his own soul, and all he got was dry, hard work that looked downright ugly to him.

"I should be," he said, stubborn.

"This isn't about Dad, though. I don't even think it's about the art, though I think it's related. There was a woman, wasn't there?"

Sam snorted. "When?"

"Recently. Like the past week. Mostly I think so because I recognize that all-consuming obsession. Because I recognize this. Because you came and kicked my ass when I was in a very similar position just a year ago. And you know what you told me? With great authority, you told me that iron had to get hot to get shaped into something. You told me that I was in my fire, and I had to let it shape me into the man Anna needed me to be."

"Yeah, I guess I did tell you that," Sam said.

"Obviously I'm not privy to all the details of your personal life, Sam, which is your prerogative. But you're in here actively attempting to drink yourself to death. You say that you can't find any inspiration for your art. I would say that you're in a pretty damn bad situation. And maybe you need to pull yourself out of it. If that means grabbing hold of her—whoever she is— then do it."

Sam felt like the frustration inside him was about to overflow. "I can't. There's too much… There's too much. If you knew, Chase. If you knew everything about me, you wouldn't think I deserved it."

"Who deserves it?" Chase asked. "Does anybody?

Do you honestly think I deserve Anna? I don't. But I love her. And I work every day to deserve her. It's a work in progress, let me tell you. But that's love. You just kind of keep working for it."

"There are too many other things in the way," Sam said, because he didn't know how else to articulate it. Without having a confessional, here in his studio, he didn't know how else to have this conversation.

"What things? What are you afraid of, Sam? Having a feeling? Is that what all this is about? The fact you want to protect yourself? The fact that it matters more to you that you get to keep your stoic expression and your who-gives-a-damn attitude intact?"

"It isn't that. It's never been that. But how—" He started again. "How was I supposed to grieve for Dad when you lost your mentor? How was I supposed to grieve for Mom when you were so young? It wasn't fair." And how the hell was he supposed to grieve for Elizabeth, for the child he didn't even know she had been carrying, when her own family was left with nothing.

"Of course you could grieve for them. They were your parents."

"Somebody has to be strong, Chase."

"And you thought I was weak? You think somehow grieving for my parents was weak?"

"Of course not. But… I was never the man that Dad wanted me to be. Now when he was alive. I didn't do what he wanted me to do. I didn't want the things that he wanted."

"Neither did I. And we both just about killed ourselves working this place the way that he wanted us to while it slowly sank into the ground. Then we had to do things on our terms. Because actually, we did know what we were talking about. And who we are, the gifts that we have, those mattered. If it wasn't for the fact that I have a business mind, if it wasn't for the fact that you could do the artwork, the ranch wouldn't be here. McCormack Ironworks wouldn't exist. And if Dad had lived, he would be proud of us. Because in the end we saved this place."

"I just don't… I had a girlfriend who died." He didn't know why he had spoken the words. He hadn't intended to. "She wasn't my girlfriend when she died. But she bled to death. At the hospital. She had been pregnant. And it was mine."

Chase cursed and fell back against the wall, bracing himself. "Seriously?"

"Yes. And I want… I want to do something with that feeling. But her family is devastated, Chase. They lost so much more than I did. And I don't know how… I don't know what to do with all of this. I don't know what to do with all of these feelings. I don't feel like I deserve them. I don't feel like I deserve the pain. Not in the way that I deserve to walk away from it unscathed. But I feel like it isn't mine. Like I'm taking something from them, or making something about me that just shouldn't be. But it's there all the same. And it follows me around. And Maddy loves me. She said she loves me. And I don't know how to take that either."

"Bullshit," Chase said, his voice rough. "That's not it."

"Don't tell me how it is, Chase, not when you don't know."

"Of course I know, Sam. Loss is hell. And I didn't lose half of what you did."

"It was just the possibility of something. Elizabeth. It wasn't… It was just…"

"Sam. You lost your parents. And a woman you were involved with who was carrying your baby. Of course you're screwed up. But walking around pretending you're just grumpy, pretending you don't want anything, that you don't care about anything, doesn't protect you from pain. It's just letting fear poison you from the inside."

Sam felt like he was staring down into an abyss that had no end. A yawning, bottomless cavern that was just full of need. All the need he had ever felt his entire life. The words ricocheted back at him, hit him like shrapnel, damaging, wounding. They were the truth. That it was what drove him, that it was what stopped him.

Fear.

That it was why he had spent so many years hiding.

And as blindingly clear as it was, it was also clear that Maddy was right about him. More right about him than he'd ever been about himself.

That confession made him think of Maddy too. Of the situation she was in with her father. Of those broken words she had spoken to him about how if her own father didn't think she was worth defending, who would? And he had sent her away, like he didn't think she was worth it either. Like he didn't think she was worth the pain or the risk.

Except he did. He thought she was worth defending. That she was worth loving. That she was worth everything.

Sam felt… Well, nothing on this earth had ever made him feel small before. But this did it. He felt scared. He felt weak. Mostly he felt a kind of overwhelming sadness for everything he'd lost. For all the words that were left unsaid. The years of grief that had built up.

It had never been about control. It had never been based in reality. Or about whether or not he deserved something. Not really. He was afraid of feeling. Of loss. More loss after years and years of it.

But his father had died without knowing. Without knowing that even though things weren't always the best between them, Sam had loved him. Elizabeth had died without knowing Sam had cared.

Protecting himself meant hurting other people. And it damn well hurt him.

Maddy had been brave enough to show him. And he had rejected it. Utterly. Completely. She had been so brave, and he had remained shut down as he'd been for years.

She had removed any risk of rejection and still he had been afraid. He had been willing to lose her this time.

"Do you know why the art is hard?" he asked.

"Why?"

"Because. If I make what I really want to, then I actually have to feel it."

He hated saying it. Hated admitting it. But he knew, somehow, that this was essential to his soul. That if he was ever going to move on from this place, from this dry, drunken place that produced nothing but anguish, he had to start saying these things. He had to start committing to these things.

"I had a lot behind this idea that I wasn't good enough. That I didn't deserve to feel. Because…the alternative is feeling it. It's caring when it's easier to be mad at everything. Hoping for things when so much is already dead."

"What's the alternative?" Chase asked.

He looked around his studio. At all the lifeless things. Hard and sharp. Just like he was. The alternative was living without hope. The alternative was acting like he was dead too.

"This," he said finally. "And life without Maddy. I'd rather risk everything than live without her."

Thirteen

Madison looked around the beautifully appointed room. The grand party facility at the ranch was decorated in evergreen boughs and white Christmas lights, the trays of glittering champagne moving by somehow adding to the motif. Sparkling. Pristine.

Maddy herself was dressed in a gown that could be described in much the same manner. A pale yellow that caught the lights and glimmered like sun on new-fallen snow.

However, it was a prime example of how appearances can be deceiving. She felt horrible. Much more like snow that had been mixed up with gravel. Gritty. Gray.

Hopefully no one was any the wiser. She was good at putting on a brave face. Good at pretending everything was fine. Something she had perfected over the years. Not just at these kinds of public events but at family events too.

Self-protection was her favorite accessory. It went with everything.

She looked outside, at the terrace, which was lit by a thatch of Christmas lights, heated by a few freestanding heaters. However, no one was out there. She took a deep breath, seeing her opportunity for escape. And she took it. She just needed a few minutes. A few minutes to feel a little bit less like her face would crack beneath the weight of her fake smile.

A few minutes to take a deep breath and not worry so much that it would turn into a sob.

She grabbed hold of a glass of champagne, then moved quickly to the door, slipping out into the chilly night air. She went over near one of the heaters, wrapping her arms around herself and simply standing for a moment, looking out into the inky blackness, looking at nothing. It felt good. It was a relief to her burning eyes. A relief to her scorched soul.

All of this feelings business was rough. She wasn't entirely certain she could recommend it.

"What's going on, Maddy?"

She turned around, trying to force a smile when she saw her brother Gage standing there.

"I just needed a little bit of quiet," she said, lifting her glass of champagne.

"Sure." He stuffed his hands in his pockets. "I'm not used to this kind of thing. I spent a lot of time on the road. In crappy hotels. Not a lot of time at these sorts of get-togethers."

"Regretting the whole return-of-the-prodigal-son thing? Because it's too late to unkill that fatted calf, young man. You're stuck."

He laughed. "No. I'm glad that I'm back. Because of you. Because of Colton, Sierra. Even Jack."

"Rebecca?"

"Of course." He took a deep breath, closing the distance between them. "So what's going on with you?"

"Nothing," she said, smiling.

"I have a feeling that everybody else usually buys that. Which is why you do it. But I don't. Is it Jack? Is it having him here?"

She thought about that. Seriously thought about it. "No," she said, truthful. "I'm glad. I'm so glad that we're starting to fix some of this. I spent a long time holding on to my anger. My anger at Dad. At the past. All of my pain. And Jack got caught up in that. Because of the circumstances. We are all very different people. And getting to this point… I feel like we took five different paths. But here we are. And it isn't for Dad. It's for us. I think that's good. I spent a lot of time doing things in response to him. In response to the pain that he caused me. I don't want to do that anymore. I don't want to act from a place of pain and fear anymore."

"That's quite a different stance. I mean, since last we talked at The Grind."

She tried to smile again, wandering over to one of the wooden pillars. "I guess some things happened." She pressed her palm against the cold surface, then her forehead. She took a deep breath. In and out, slowly, evenly.

"Are you okay?"

She shook her head. "Not really. But I will be."

"I know I missed your first big heartbreak. And I feel like I would have done that bastard some bodily harm. I have quite a bit of internalized rage built up. If you need me to hurt anyone… I will. Gladly."

She laughed. "I appreciate that. Really, I do. It's just that…it's a good thing this is happening. It's making me realize a lot of things. It's making me change a lot of things. I just wish it didn't hurt."

"You know…when Rebecca told me that she loved me, it scared the hell out of me. And I said some things that I shouldn't have said. That no one should ever say to anyone. I regretted it. But I was running scared, and I wanted to make sure she didn't come after me. I'm so glad that she forgave me when I realized what an idiot I was."

She lifted her head, turning to face him. "That sounds a lot like brotherly advice."

"It is. And maybe it's not relevant to your situation. I don't know. But what I do know is that we both have a tendency to hold on to pain. On to anger. If you get a chance to fix this, I hope you forgive the bastard. As long as he's worthy."

"How will I know he's worthy?" she asked, a bit of humor lacing her voice.

"Well, I'll have to vet him. At some point."

"Assuming he ever speaks to me again, I would be happy to arrange that."

Gage nodded. "If he's half as miserable as you are, trust me, he'll be coming after you pretty quick."

"And you think I should forgive him?"

"I think that men are a bunch of hardheaded dumb-asses. And some of us need more chances than others. And I thank God every day I got mine. With this family. With Rebecca. So it would be mean-spirited of me not to advocate for the same for another of my species."

"I'll keep that under advisement."

Gage turned to go. "Do that. But if he keeps being

a dumbass, let me know. Because I'll get together a posse or something."

"Thank you," she said. "Hopefully the posse won't be necessary."

He shrugged, then walked back into the party. She felt fortified then. Because she knew she had people on her side. No matter what. She wasn't alone. And that felt good. Even when most everything felt bad.

She let out a long, slow breath and rested her forearms on the railing, leaning forward, staring out across the darkened field. If she closed her eyes, she could almost imagine that she could see straight out to the ocean in spite of the fact that it was dark.

She was starting to get cold, even with the artificial heat. But it was entirely possible the chill was coming from inside her. Side effects of heartbreak and all of that.

"Merry Christmas Eve."

She straightened, blinking, looking out into the darkness. Afraid to turn around. That voice was familiar. And it didn't belong to anyone in her family.

She turned slowly, her heart stalling when she saw Sam standing there. He was wearing a white shirt unbuttoned at the collar, a black jacket and a pair of black slacks. His hair was disheveled, and she was pretty sure she could see a bit of soot on his chest where the open shirt exposed his skin.

"What are you doing here?"

"I had to see you." He took a step closer to her. "Bad enough that I put this on."

"Where did you get it?"

"The secondhand store on Main."

"Wow." No matter what he had to say, the fact that

Sam McCormack had shown up in a suit said a whole lot without him ever opening his mouth.

"It doesn't really fit. And I couldn't figure out how to tie the tie." And of course, he hadn't asked anyone for help. Sam never would. It just wasn't him.

"Well, then going without was definitely the right method."

"I have my moments of brilliance." He shook his head. "But the other day wasn't one of them."

Her heart felt as if it were in a free fall, her stomach clenching tight. "Really?"

"Yeah."

"I agree. I mean, unreservedly. But I am open to hearing about your version of why you didn't think you were brilliant. Just in case we have differing opinions on the event."

He cursed. "I'm not good at this." He took two steps toward her, then reached out, gripping her chin between his thumb and forefinger. "I hate this, in fact. I'm not good at talking about feelings. And I've spent a lot of years trying to bury them down deep. I would like to do it now. But I know there's no good ending to that. I know that I owe you more."

"Go on," she said, keeping her eyes on his, her voice trembling, betraying the depth of emotion she felt.

She had never seen Sam quite like this, on edge, like he might shatter completely at any moment. "I told you I thought I didn't deserve these feelings. And I believed it."

"I know you did," she said, the words broken. "I know that you never lied on purpose, Sam. I know."

"I don't deserve that. That certainty. I didn't do anything to earn it."

She shook her head. "Stop. We're not going to talk like that. About what we deserve. I don't know what I deserve. But I know what I want. I want you. And I don't care if I'm jumping the gun. I don't care if I didn't make you grovel enough. It's true. I do."

"Maddy…"

"This all comes because we tried to protect ourselves for too long. Because we buried everything down deep. I don't have any defenses anymore. I can't do it anymore. I couldn't even if I wanted to. Which you can see, because I'm basically throwing myself at you again."

"I've always been afraid there was something wrong with me." His dark eyes were intense, and she could tell that he was wishing he could turn to stone rather than finish what he was saying. But that he was determined. That he had put his foot on the path and he wasn't going to deviate from it. "Something wrong with what I felt. And I pushed it all down. I always have. I've been through stuff that would make a lot of people crazy. But if you keep shoving it on down, it never gets any better." He shook his head. "I've been holding on to grief. Holding on to anger. I didn't know what else to do with it. My feelings about my parents, my feelings about Elizabeth, the baby. It's complicated. It's a lot. And I think more than anything I just didn't want to deal with it. I had a lot of excuses, and they felt real. They even felt maybe a little bit noble?"

"I can see that. I can see it being preferable to grief."

"Just like you said, Maddy. You put all those defenses in front of it, and then nothing can hurt you, right?"

She nodded. "At least, that's been the way I've handled it for a long time."

"You run out. Of whatever it is you need to be a

person. Whatever it is you need to contribute, to create. That's why I haven't been able to do anything new with my artwork." He rolled his eyes, shaking his head slightly. "It's hard for me to…"

"I know. You would rather die than talk about feelings. And talk about this. But I think you need to."

"I told myself it was wrong to make something for my dad. My mom. Because they didn't support my work. I told myself I didn't deserve to profit off Elizabeth's death in any way. But that was never the real issue. The real issue was not wanting to feel those things at all. I was walking across the field the other night, and I thought about grief. The way that it covers things, twists the world around you into something unrecognizable." He shook his head. "When you're in the thick of it, it's like walking in the dark. Even if you're in a place you've seen a thousand times by day, it all changes. And suddenly what seemed safe is now full of danger."

He took a sharp breath and continued. "You can't trust anymore. You can't trust everything will be okay, because you've seen that sometimes it isn't. That's what it's like to have lost people like I have. And I can think about a thousand pieces that I could create that would express that. But it would mean that I had to feel it. And it would mean I would have to show other people what I felt. I wanted… From the moment I laid my hands on you, Maddy, I wanted to turn you into something. A sculpture. A painting. But that would mean looking at how I felt about you too. And I didn't want to do that either."

Maddy lifted her hand, cupping Sam's cheek. "I understand why you work with iron, Sam. Because it's just like you. You're so strong. And you really don't want to bend. But if you would just bend…just a little bit, I think you could be something even more beautiful than you already are."

"I'll do more than bend. If I have to, to have you, I'll break first. But I've decided… I don't care about protecting myself. From loss, from pain…doesn't matter. I just care about you. And I know that I have to fix myself if I'm going to become the kind of man you deserve. I know I have to reach inside and figure all that emotional crap out. I can't just decide that I love you and never look at the rest of it. I have to do all of it. To love you the way that you deserve, I know I have to deal with all of it."

"Do you love me?"

He nodded slowly. "I do." He reached into his jacket pocket and took out a notebook. "I've been working on a new collection. Just sketches right now. Just plans." He handed her the notebook. "I want you to see it. I know you'll understand."

She took it from him, opening it with shaking hands, her heart thundering hard in her throat. She looked at the first page, at the dark twisted mass he had sketched there. Maybe it was a beast, or maybe it was just menacing angles—it was hard to tell. She imagined that was the point.

There was more. Broken figures, twisted metal. Until the very last page. Where the lines smoothed out into rounded curves, until the mood shifted dramatically and everything looked a whole lot more like hope.

"It's hard to get a sense of scale and everything in the drawings. This is just me kind of blocking it out."

"I understand," she whispered. "I understand perfectly." It started with grief, and it ended with love. Unimaginable pain that was transformed.

"I lost a lot of things, Maddy. I would hate for you to be one of them. Especially because you're the one thing I chose to lose. And I have regretted it every moment since. But this is me." He put his fingertip on the notebook. "That's me. I'm not the nicest guy. I'm not what anybody would call cheerful. Frankly, I'm a grumpy son of a bitch. It's hard for me to talk about what I'm feeling. Harder for me to show it, and I'm in the world's worst line of work for that. But if you'll let me, I'll be your grumpy son of a bitch. And I'll try. I'll try for you."

"Sam," she said, "I love you. I love you, and I don't need you to be anything more than you. I'm willing to accept the fact that getting to your feelings may always be a little bit of an excavation. But if you promise to work on it, I'll promise not to be too sensitive about it. And maybe we can meet somewhere in the middle. One person doesn't have to do all the changing. And I don't want you to anyway." She smiled, and this time it wasn't forced. "You had me at 'You're at the wrong door.'"

He chuckled. "I think you had me a lot sooner than that. I just didn't know it."

"So," she said, looking up at him, feeling like the sun was shining inside her, in spite of the chill outside, "you want to go play Yahtzee?"

"Only if you mean it euphemistically."

"Absolutely not. I expect you to take the time to woo me, Sam McCormack. And if that includes board games, that's just a burden you'll have to bear."

Sam smiled. A real smile. One that showed his heart, his soul, and held nothing back. "I would gladly spend the rest of my life bearing your burdens, Madison West."

"On second thought," she said, "board games not required."

"Oh yeah? What do you need, then?"

"Nothing much at all. Just hold me, cowboy. That's enough for me."

* * * * *

Meet all the cowboys in Copper Ridge!

Shoulda Been a Cowboy *(prequel novella)*
Part Time Cowboy
Brokedown Cowboy
Bad News Cowboy
A Copper Ridge Christmas *(novella)*
Hometown Heartbreaker *(novella)*
Take Me, Cowboy
One Night Charmer
Tough Luck Hero
Last Chance Rebel
Hold Me, Cowboy

If you can't get enough Maisey Yates,
try her bestselling books
from Harlequin Presents!

Don't miss
The Prince's Pregnant Mistress
Second in her fabulous
Heirs Before Vows series.

WE HOPE YOU
ENJOYED THIS BOOK!

SPECIAL EXCERPT FROM

Cowboy Caleb Dalton has loved single mom Ellie Bell for years, but as his best friend's widow, she's strictly off-limits. Until Caleb discovers that a kiss under the mistletoe is on Ellie's Christmas wish list!

Read on for a sneak preview of
Cowboy Christmas Redemption *by* New York Times *and* USA TODAY *bestselling author Maisey Yates.*

Caleb took a step forward, and he wrapped his arms around her waist, his blood roaring hot through his veins, his heart thundering hard. And he couldn't believe that he was doing it. That he was holding her in his arms.

This was no lapse of control on his part. His control was made of iron. And he had proved it more times than she would ever know. So many times that the moments faded into memory, had become nothing more than a dull pain, a downpour beating against the tin roof. Dull, continuous. And he had learned to let it wash away into the background.

Not now.

Now it was sharp. Hard.

It wouldn't be denied and neither would he.

It wasn't for her. Not anymore. All that mental dancing he'd done a moment before was a lie. This was for him.

Because he'd damn well earned it.

He was going to kiss Ellie Bell.

And he wouldn't be rushed.

Her eyes were wide, her lips parted slightly, and she was looking at him like he was a stranger. But maybe that was for the best.

She was soft. Even now with his hand resting on the small of her back, he could tell that. He raised his hand and cupped her face; the lightning that conducted between that space where his palm met her cheek immobilized him for a moment.

Then he let his thumb drift over her skin there, looked at the faint freckles that scattered across her nose. And he let his eyes drop to her lips. Pale pink and full, turning down slightly at the ends like a little pout that he'd always found unbearably sexy. He had the shape of her mouth memorized, and he'd never touched it. Never pressed his lips to it, no matter how much he wanted to.

The need to do it now was like a prowling, insistent beast. Clawing at its cage. Demanding to be let out.

· So he did.

He leaned in, closed the distance between them.

And his world became fire. Nothing could have prepared him for this. Not a decade of anticipation, not charts and graphs, nothing.

Because this went beyond a kiss, deeper than how she tasted, more than how soft her skin was against his, more than the sigh that she made when he parted those lips with his own and slid his tongue against hers.

His knees nearly buckled. It was more than the blood roaring through his veins like a lion, more than the instantaneous hardening of his body. It was something beneath his skin, something in his bones. In his veins.

In him.

In the way that he breathed. The way that he was knit together. From the beginning of time, maybe. As if he had been created for the purpose of kissing Ellie.

And she kissed him back.

Don't miss
Cowboy Christmas Redemption *by Maisey Yates,*
available October 2019 wherever
Harlequin® books and ebooks are sold.

www.Harlequin.com

*Becoming guardian of his young niece is tough
for Westmoreland neighbor Pete Higgins.
But Myra Hollister, the irresistible new nanny with a
dangerous past, pushes him to the brink. Will desire for
the nanny distract him from duty to his niece?*

Read on for a sneak peek at
Duty or Desire
by New York Times *bestselling author Brenda Jackson!*

"That's it, Peterson Higgins, no more. You've had three servings already," Myra said, laughing, as she guarded the pan of peach cobbler on the counter.

He stood in front of her, grinning from ear to ear. "You should not have baked it so well. It was delicious."

"Thanks, but flattery won't get you any more peach cobbler tonight. You've had your limit."

He crossed his arms over his chest. "I could have you arrested, you know."

Crossing her arms over her own chest, she tilted her chin and couldn't stop grinning. "On what charge?"

The charge that immediately came to Pete's mind was that she was so darn beautiful. Irresistible. But he figured that was something he could not say.

She snapped her fingers in front of his face to reclaim his attention. "If you have to think that hard about a charge, then that means there isn't one."

"Oh, you'll be surprised what all I can do, Myra."

She tilted her head to the side as if to look at him better. "Do tell, Pete."

Her words—those three little words—made a full-blown attack on his senses. He drew in a shaky breath, then touched her chin. She blinked, as if startled by his touch. "How about 'do show,' Myra?"

Pete watched the way the lump formed in her throat and detected her shift in breathing. He could even hear the pounding of her heart. Damn, she smelled good, and she looked good, too. Always did.

"I'm not sure what 'do show' means," she said in a voice that was as shaky as his had been.

He tilted her chin up to gaze into her eyes, as well as to study the shape of her exquisite lips. "Then let me demonstrate, Ms. Hollister," he said, lowering his mouth to hers.

The moment he swept his tongue inside her mouth and tasted her, he was a goner. It took every ounce of strength he had to keep the kiss gentle when he wanted to devour her mouth with a hunger he felt all the way in his bones. A part of him wanted to take the kiss deeper, but then another part wanted to savor her taste. Honestly, either worked for him as long as she felt the passion between them.

He had wanted her from the moment he'd set eyes on her, but he'd fought the desire. He could no longer do that. He was a man known to forego his own needs and desires, but tonight he couldn't.

Whispering close to her ear, he said, "Peach cobbler isn't the only thing I could become addicted to, Myra."

Will their first kiss distract him from his duty?

Find out in
Duty or Desire
by New York Times *bestselling author Brenda Jackson.*

Available December 2019 wherever
Harlequin® Desire books and ebooks are sold.

Harlequin.com

HARLEQUIN Desire

**Sensual dramas starring powerful heroes,
scandalous secrets…and burning desires.**

Save **$1.00**

on the purchase of ANY
Harlequin® Desire book.

Available wherever books are sold,
including most bookstores, supermarkets,
drugstores and discount stores.

Save **$1.00**

on the purchase of any Harlequin® Desire book.

Coupon valid until January 31, 2020.
Redeemable at participating outlets in the U.S. and Canada only.
Not redeemable at Barnes & Noble stores. Limit one coupon per customer.

52616538

5 65373 00076 2 (8100)0 12440

® and ™ are trademarks owned and used by the trademark owner and/or its licensee.

© 2019 Harlequin Enterprises Limited

HDCOUP1119